O9-AIF-036

RESCUER'S KISS

"Thank you, Captain," Alisha said. Her head reeled from the wine.

"Call me Justin, Alisha," he replied. "I have hopes that we can become friends. After all, we shall be sharing this cabin for the next few days while you're aboard the *Vixen*."

Justin stepped from behind the desk and bent to move her chair up to the table. She felt his warm breath on the side of her face as he bent over her. Then he moved around to the other side and sat opposite her. "Shall we dine now?" he asked softly. "Are you not hungry, Alisha?" The husky tremor of his voice seemed to wrap about her and set her pulses racing.

She shook her head.

"Perhaps we should make ourselves comfortable then," Justin said. He circled the table, took her hand, and led her to the large, silk-draped bed.

She opened her mouth to protest, but could only sigh.

"What was it you wished to say, lovely Alisha?" he whispered. He reached out and caressed the creamy flesh of her cheek, his hand brushing the fine strands of hair that lay over her shoulder.

Alisha could neither move nor speak as his lips descended upon hers. Slowly, his kiss grew more intense as he pressed his body fully against hers.

"Alisha!" The name caressed her in a breathless spiral of passion . . .

HEART STOPPING ROMANCE BY ZEBRA BOOKS

MIDNIGHT BRIDE   (3265, $4.50)
by Kathleen Drymon

With her youth, beauty, and sizable dowry, Kellie McBride had her share of ardent suitors, but the headstrong miss was bewitched by the mysterious man called The Falcon, a dashing highwayman who risked life and limb for the American Colonies. Twice the Falcon had saved her from the hands of the British, then set her blood afire with a moonlit kiss.

No one knew the dangerous life The Falcon led—or of his secret identity as a British lord with a vengeful score to settle with the Crown. There was no way Kellie would discover his deception, so he would woo her by day as the foppish Lord Blakely Savage . . . and ravish her by night as The Falcon! But each kiss made him want more, until he vowed to make her his *Midnight Bride*.

SOUTHERN SEDUCTION   (3266, $4.50)
by Thea Devine

Cassandra knew her husband's will required her to hire a man to run her Georgia plantation, but the beautiful redhead was determined to handle her own affairs. To satisfy her lawyers, she invented Trane Taggart, her imaginary step-son. But her plans go awry when a handsome adventurer shows up and claims to *be* Trane Taggart!

After twenty years of roaming free, Trane was ready to come home and face the father who always treated him with such contempt. Instead he found a black wreath and a bewitching, sharp-tongued temptress trying to cheat him out of his inheritance. But he had no qualms about kissing that silken body into languid submission to get what he wanted. But he never dreamed that *he* would be the one to succumb to *her* charms.

SWEET OBSESSION   (3233, $4.50)
by Kathy Jones

From the moment rancher Jack Corbett kept her from capturing the wild white stallion, Kayley Ryan detested the man. That animal had almost killed her father, and since the accident Kayley had been in charge of the ranch. But with the tall, lean Corbett, it seemed she was *never* the boss. He made her blood run cold with rage one minute, and hot with desire the next.

Jack Corbett had only one thing on his mind: revenge against the man who had stolen his freedom, his ranch, and almost his very life. And what better way to get revenge than to ruin his mortal enemy's fiery red-haired daughter. He never expected to be captured by her charms, to long for her silken caresses and to thirst for her never-ending kisses.

Available wherever paperbacks are sold, or order direct from the Publisher. Send cover price plus 50¢ per copy for mailing and handling to Zebra Books, Dept. 3569, 475 Park Avenue South, New York, N.Y. 10016. Residents of New York, New Jersey and Pennsylvania must include sales tax. DO NOT SEND CASH.

KATHLEEN DRYMON
CASTAWAY ANGEL

From the Personal
Library of
Amy L. Reese

ZEBRA BOOKS
KENSINGTON PUBLISHING CORP.

To my sister Jo-ann
with all my love,
Kathleen

ZEBRA BOOKS

are published by

Kensington Publishing Corp.
475 Park Avenue South
New York, NY 10016

First printing: November, 1991

Printed in the United States of America

Chapter One

1781 Yorktown, Virginia:

The solid thudding of boot-heels on a wood plank sidewalk and the brushing of sheathed bayonets against the pant legs of the red-coated soldiers broke the quiet of the late night hour as the British troops made their way down the deserted main street.

Lieutenant Jefferson's orders had been explicitly laid out for him earlier in the evening, and as his destination came into view, light spilled out onto the street from the small building that was the newspaper office. He had been advised that the old man known as Charles Whitlaw, who ran the newspaper office, kept late hours and this was the reason that he and his detail were afield at this hour of the night.

He had also been warned to have no witness to the destruction he was about to inflict. The clank of a musket hitting the side gear of one of his men drew Lieutenant Jefferson's attention, and with a glare he warned them to have a care. He did not wish the traitor to be aware of their approach and have time to flee out the back door.

Lieutenant Jefferson put a hand up and halted his men several paces from the building which boasted a square-cut glass pane with the words *The Yorktown Press.* To be sure he made no mistakes, Lieutenant Jefferson peered through the glass and saw an elderly gray-haired man sitting behind a small desk, his head bent over a display of papers spread before him.

Nodding toward the officer directly behind him, Lieutenant Jefferson took hold of the outside knob and swung the door wide. Within seconds the small front office was filled with British soldiers.

Charles Whitlaw's gaze rose from his papers and he looked at the soldiers filling his office. "What is the meaning of this?" he asked, trying to hold his voice steady. Only the old man himself knew of the wild beating of his heart.

With slow, deliberate movements Lieutenant Jefferson pulled a piece of crisp paper from his jacket. His expression was firm as his cool blue eyes stared unrelentingly at the older man. "I hold here a warrant by the Crown for your arrest." His tone was as cold and impersonal as his appearance.

"And what is the charge?" Charles Whitlaw's only visible reaction to the Lieutenant's words was a small pulsing of a muscle beneath his right cheekbone. Though he had dreaded this moment, he had known it was inevitable. In fact, the real surprise was that it had not come sooner. Over the past months he had wondered why the British hesitated to put a stop to the newspaper. All of Virginia knew of his daily outcry as he urged the colonists to rise up against the

6

tyranny that had swept over the South, brought by men such as Cornwallis, Tarleton and Benedict Arnold. The atrocities committed against the colonists were without precedent and Charles Whitlaw was a man who had given most of his life to bring the truth, no matter how unpleasant, to his fellow countrymen. Without regard for himself he felt honor-bound to print the facts about the British and encourage everyone to stand firm against the injustices.

"Your charge is treason against the Crown!" The Lieutenant spoke with contempt and turned to one of his junior officers. "Sergeant Mullens, see to it that no other traitors will be able to use this office or any of its contents to produce heretical propaganda against the Crown."

"Hop to it, men," ordered Sergeant Mullens as he and his soldiers began to destroy the newspaper office. They scattered papers, turned over filing cabinets, and splattered ink over the wood floor.

Seeing his life's work being destroyed, Charles Whitlaw at last reacted. "Stop this savagery at once!" he shouted, and hurrying around his desk he grabbed a soldier's arm as the young man was about to smash a small table against the printing press. "I'll go with you without argument, whatever you wish, only do not destroy all that I have worked for!" At this moment it did not occur to Charles Whitlaw that it mattered little what happened to his printing office. His chances of reclaiming his possessions were slim. He had been charged with treason against the Crown!

The soldier shrugged off the offending arm and

Charles stumbled backwards, his tall, frail frame no contest for the young soldier's strength.

It was Lieutenant Jefferson who grabbed Charles Whitlaw before he fell. "Do you think we would leave everything here so another rebel could step in and take your place?" The Lieutenant's features were a mask of anger and as he held the older man by the upper arm all of his loyalist beliefs rose to the surface. "By God, this night's work will teach all traitors that would listen to your slander that the Crown will demand its due respect!"

Charles Whitlaw had never been a violent man. His ideas and beliefs had always been revealed through his pen and printing press, but at this moment all of his pent-up fury over the outrageous dictates of an unjust and demanding King came rushing to mind. "You and your soldiers are the rebels in this land that belongs to American colonists! You and your kind hold the yoke of tyranny about our necks and crush our rights beneath your heels!" So saying Charles turned and with a powerful swing, struck the Lieutenant full upon the jaw—feeling in connection with bone and flesh a relief that he had not known since the beginning of this war.

Lieutenant Jefferson's hand slipped from his prisoner's arm as he stumbled back in surprise. Quickly he steadied himself and drew his sword from the scabbard at his side. With a glimmering light glowing deep in the blue of his eyes, he lunged at the aged gentleman. A thin smile played about his full lips as the gush of red spread across Charles Whitlaw's white shirt front. "Hold this thought in your heart as you reach your rebel heaven, traitor. There will be many more following you soon!" Pulling his sword slowly from the body of his victim, Lieutenant Jefferson watched the old man crumple to the floor at his feet, a froth of blood coming out of his mouth. This traitor would no longer be a threat.

The soldiers had stopped their destruction of the office as they watched the Lieutenant put an end to any further objections on the part of the old man.

"That's enough. Leave everything like it is." Lieutenant Jefferson looked about him at the disheveled office and then his pale eyes lowered to the man lying upon the floor. "Our job is finished here." He turned about with a swagger and his men followed him from the cluttered room. The General would be pleased with his report. The old man had made it easier than expected, Lieutenant Jefferson thought. His orders had been clear: Charles Whitlaw was not to be brought back to the guardhouse alive!

As Amos McKenzie made his way toward the newspaper office with a canister of piping hot coffee to be shared with his employer, he saw the British soldiers making their way up the dark Yorktown street. He wondered what they were about, then hurried on his way.

Even before entering the newspaper office, Amos felt his insides begin to churn. The door was standing wide. Having shut it tight earlier that evening and knowing that Charles would never have left it ajar, his steps faltered as an unknown dread swept over him.

The canister slipped from his fingers, the contents spilling and blending with the other debris in the room. "Charles!" The cry was torn from his throat as Amos fell to his knees at his life-long friend's side. "What have they done?" Tears fell from his dark brown eyes and dampened his thick, gray beard as Amos cradled Charles Whitlaw's head against his chest.

There was no answer, no explanation for such savagery against such a kind and gentle man. There was only the quiet emptiness of lifeless eyes that stared into his friend's grief-stricken face.

"I warned you, my friend," Amos murmured softly. Charles had stood for what he believed in and had paid the ultimate price. There had never been a little right or a little wrong in Charles Whitlaw's mind. Daily he voiced his beliefs for all to read and though he and Amos had known that the British would one day put a halt to the Yorktown Press, never could they have imagined this wanton display of destruction and murder.

There was a dull ache in his chest as Amos rose to his feet with Charles still cradled in his arms. Amos was not an overly large man and his aging body felt the strain of Charles Whitlaw's frail weight. But he would do this one last thing for his friend, he told himself. He would take the body home and prepare it for burial and then see that Charles was laid to rest next to his dear Linette.

As he reached the door he gave one last look at the malicious violence that had taken place in the small room. With a sigh, he shut the door and turned the key in the outside lock.

He would have to send word to Charles's daughter, Amos thought as he made his way to the Whitlaw house. Alisha Whitlaw had been a lovely young girl at the start of this war with England when Charles had sent her to her mother's family in France.

Amos remembered how tragic the loss of Linette had been for Alisha and Charles. He could only imagine how she would handle the death of her father whom she had not seen in years.

He knew the letter would have to be sent to the Island of Martinique where Alisha had been living with relatives for the past two years. Perhaps he could get John Walker to help him get the letter to its destination, Amos thought. The man was trusted by the patriots and perhaps he knew of a ship that was bound for the Island.

He would see to this the first thing in the morning. For now his duty was to care for his dear friend.

Chapter Two

Bright morning sunlight stole into the bedchamber as the heavy, velvet draperies were pulled back to reveal an artfully created display of flowered leaded glass windows. The pleasant voice of a young woman singing softly as she arranged roses in a crystal vase brought about the desired effect of rousing the young woman who lay asleep upon the carved French bed.

A slim form slowly began to move beneath the cream and peach satin coverlet. A head full of glistening, russet curls emerged followed by one slim arm and then the other.

"I was beginning to wonder if you were going to sleep the whole day through." The singing stopped as the young woman turned from the flowers and smiled warmly.

"As though you would allow such a pleasant thing, Estelle?" The copper-haired beauty sat up straighter against the goose-down pillows and yawned.

"I should say not. You're much too young to waste away in your bedchamber. Why, already this morning you have had a gentleman caller, who was turned away heart-stricken because he could not catch a single glimpse of you." Estelle Glanville enjoyed bantering lightly with her cousin.

The young man was probably Dory Rollins, thought the woman upon the bed. She had met him last night at the Governor's Ball and had been hard pressed to fight off his attentions. "Did he leave the roses?" she asked, her thickly lashed, gray-blue eyes moving to the arrangement.

"No, they were delivered after the young man left." Estelle gathered the shimmering, emerald-ice gown that her cousin had worn the night before from the back of the chair where it had been carelessly thrown and proceeded to hang it in the wardrobe.

"You shouldn't be doing that, Estelle. Where is Marion?"

"I sent her for your breakfast tray. And please try and refrain from sounding like my husband. Cordell anxiously waits for me to make a mistake so he can scold me."

The young woman upon the bed smiled generously at her cousin. "It's because Cordell and I both love you that we wish you to have a care for your condition."

"The fact that I'm with child does not mean I should sit upon a pillow with my feet propped up and be waited upon."

"No, I could never imagine that." The other laughed aloud, knowing that her cousin was much too active to allow anyone to wait on her.

14

"Come now, Alisha, let me help you dress while we wait for Marion. It's a beautiful day. I thought we could take a walk down near the ocean. If you want you can even sunbathe. I would join you, but I fear my misshapen condition will not permit such pleasure." She patted her protruding abdomen.

Alisha threw back the coverlet and revealed long, slim legs beneath the scanty silk nightgown which she had insisted her seamstress shorten because of the warm, tropical nights on the island. "The prospect of a leisurely swim does sound inviting."

Estelle held forth a pastel yellow dress. As the younger girl pulled the nightgown over her head, Estelle felt a sharp stab of jealousy. Alisha's golden skin and shapely curves were fully displayed as she shook out her mass of fiery curls to rid them of their tangles. Yes indeed, Alisha Whitlaw was the most beautiful woman on the Island of Martinique, Estelle Glanville thought to herself; but even with such a thought and with her own figure so ungainly, Estelle forbade such jealousy to persist. She loved her cousin dearly from their first meeting in her mother's small villa in the South of France. And Estelle admitted willingly that even without the babe beneath her breasts, she had not been blessed with the rare beauty that Alisha had.

"Is something amiss?" Alisha's face showed her concern at the thoughtful look on her cousin's face.

"Whatever could be wrong?" Estelle's lips curled up into a smile as she forced such thoughts from her mind. "I was only wondering if you need more sun? Your skin is so tanned now, I fear it is not quite proper."

"Come now, Estelle, your own coloring was of the same shade before you became pregnant and thought it best to stop lying about nude beneath the sun's rays. I'm sure with your dark hair and violet eyes Cordell could not resist you." Alisha laughed aloud as she pulled the gown over her head.

Estelle blushed lightly and made no more mention of Alisha's sunbathing, for she was right. Her husband had loved his wife's bronzed skin, complimenting her frequently about her healthy glow compared to the pasty, pale features of the other women on the island.

"Are you not even slightly interested in who sent you the roses? There was a card," said Estelle as the cousins walked barefoot on the cool sand at the water's edge.

"Are you going to tell me or should I guess?" Alisha hiked her skirts above her shapely knees and waded a bit deeper into the rushing, blue-green water.

"I will tell you then." Estelle pouted a little from her cousin's lack of interest. "The note claimed undying love from the Governor's son, Jeffery SaintClair."

Alisha's comely features twisted into a grimace. "Let's hurry to the cove, Estelle. The water feels wonderful." She was not in the mood to listen to her cousin sing the praises of Jeffery SaintClair.

Estelle held her tongue until they reached the small, private alcove at the back of her husband's property. Finding a comfortable spot beneath a shaded palm tree, she spread out a quilt and then slowly eased herself down. "I think you should give

Jeffery some consideration, Alisha. He would make a perfect husband. He's handsome in a devilish sort of way and very charming and besides all of this, it's obvious to everyone that he's infatuated with you.''

"Jeffery is a nice man,'' Alisha allowed. ''But I do not wish to find a husband. You know that I'll return to Virginia as soon as the war is finished. Would Jeffery wish to leave his tropical paradise here on Martinique and settle in Yorktown? No, I think not.''

"But you don't have to leave Martinique either. You could wed Jeffery and stay here near me and Cordell and visit your father from time to time.'' Estelle used this same argument each time this subject came up.

Feeling no need for modesty in the presence of her cousin, for they had become closer than sisters over the past two years, Alisha pulled off her gown and stretched her young, lithe body. ''But I would not be happy here forever. I must return to Virginia. Perhaps I shall even help my father with his newspaper business.'' She turned and started toward the water. ''Besides, why should I ever marry? If the right man comes into my life, I'll need no vows to know what is right and what is wrong.''

Estelle could only shake her curly head. She was no longer shocked by anything Alisha said. She knew the girl made such declarations to surprise her. At first this had indeed been the way of things. Estelle had been trained by her mother to desire but two things in life: a good husband and a beautiful home. On the other hand, Alisha had been raised in the American colonies where people were more bold and willful. Her mother had died when Alisha had been but a child and her care had been handled by her father and another gentleman called Amos. It was no wonder she was so headstrong, having known little of the more womanly refinements.

But still Estelle hoped she would be able to change Alisha's mind about leaving Martinique. Perhaps this war with England and the colonists would last many more years and during this time the right man would come into Alisha's life. A small smile hovered about her lips with this thought. Then her life would really be complete. Her husband, child *and* her cousin—all her dear loved ones would fill her days with joy.

The rest of the morning was given over to relaxation and enjoyment. Alisha floated upon the surface of the water, delighting in the cool touch of the velvet liquid and welcoming the feel of the warm sun upon her body. Later the pair walked along the water's edge and gathered shells, shared confidences and spoke often of the baby's arrival.

It was with much gaiety that the two women entered the front door of the two-story, white sandstone house belonging to Estelle and her husband.

As they entered the black and white marble front foyer they were met by Cordell. The look on his usually pleasant face stilled their laughter.

"Is something wrong, Cordell?" Estelle was the first to ask. She had expected her husband to be busy all day seeing his crops aboard a ship bound for France.

"A letter arrived from Virginia today," he said softly.

His manner puzzled Alisha for Cordell always seemed very enthusiastic when he brought her a letter from her father. "A letter from my father?" She did not know what made her ask. Who else would be writing to her?

"No, Alisha, it's from Amos McKenzie." Cordell handed her the wrinkled envelope that had passed through many hands to find its way to her.

"From Amos?" Alisha did not wait for an answer but started to make her way to the small front parlor. Amos had never written to her. He always bade her well in her father's letters, but he had never written himself. She remembered his words when she left Yorktown so long ago: *"Now don't be looking for a letter from me, my girl, for I don't be taking well to pen and parchment. Just know I will always love you, lass."*

Not understanding the fear that gripped her as she stared at the envelope, Alisha sat on the edge of the ivory and gold settee.

Cordell took his wife's hand and the couple followed Alisha into the parlor. Somehow Cordell had sensed what was in the sealed envelope from the moment it was given into his care.

"I'm sure everything is fine. Amos probably decided it was time, for once, that he wrote to me." Alisha's words were barely audible as she tried to reassure herself. Slowly she broke the wax seal, her pearl-gray eyes quickly scanning the contents of the parchment within. A tear slowly rolled down her smooth cheek as the paper eased from her fingers and fell to her lap.

With a cry of distress, Estelle ran to the settee.

"What is it, dear? What has happened?"

As though in a trance, Alisha's gaze rose to Cordell. "I must obtain passage to Virginia at once."

Cordell Glanville nodded his head, trusting her judgment and offering her any assistance that was within his power.

"But why, why must you leave us?" Estelle asked anxiously. "What could be so important to make you leave now before the baby is born?"

"My father has been murdered!" She would not have spoken so bluntly to her cousin but she knew no way to soften her answer. Amos's message had been short and to the point, advising her that her father had been killed by the British. He told her no more, no reason or date.

Estelle gasped aloud, shaking her head in denial. "But how?" she said at last. "Who would do such a thing?"

"Amos says only that the British are responsible. I must return and find out what happened."

"Of course you must. Forgive me, Alisha, for my selfishness." Though Estelle hated to say these words, she knew she must. "You will return, though. After you find out everything, you will come back here to Martinique. We are your family." Tears glistened in her dark blue eyes for the pain she knew her cousin was feeling.

Alisha did not answer. The raw ache in her heart was beginning to penetrate every part of her body. Her father was dead! The fact kept repeating itself over and over as the loving image of his kind features filled her mind. He had loved her so well he had sent her away from the war and violence in her homeland

and now she found he had been slain by the same ugly forces from which he had tried so hard to protect her. "I wish to go to my room now." Her voice cracked as she hurried from the parlor and with tears blinding her, she made her way up the stairs and shut her chamber door. She collapsed upon the bed, the letter from Amos still clutched in her hand.

Chapter Three

Dark gray thunderclouds rolled over the Island of Martinique and stretched out across the sea. Caught up in a tropical breeze, a drizzling rain showered down upon the cool sand and wood plank sidewalks of Fort-de-France. The day was as dark and dismal as Alisha's feelings. From the carriage window she watched the near-deserted streets as she and her cousin's husband made their way toward the docks.

It had only been a week since Alisha had received the letter from Amos telling her of her father's death. A week, which to Alisha had seemed an eternity. A week to force herself to accept the fact that she would never again know her father's tender love. All that was left were her memories and need for justice. Whoever had killed her father would be forced to pay! Her anger and thoughts of revenge aided her in this time of grief and allowed her to keep going.

"This is the ship, Alisha." Cordell pointed out the window toward a trim looking vessel secured to the docks. The name *Velvet Venture* was painted on her side and a long gangplank was stretched from her deck to the wooden dock. "Captain Frazer should be waiting for us. The last of his cargo was loaded yesterday afternoon and since you are the only passenger, he informed me he would set sail as soon as you boarded this morning."

"I want to thank you again, Cordell, for everything you and Estelle have done for me. I don't know what I would have done without you at my side this past week."

Cordell reached over and picked up her hand and gave it a tender kiss. "There is no need to thank us, Alisha. You are our family—we could do no less than stand beside you in your time of need." He released her hand and then added, "I know Estelle wishes you to return to us, but I understand that you must set your mind to rest and find out the reason for your father's death."

"Thank you, Cordell." Alisha felt a stab of pain in her heart each time she heard mention of her father's death; but she appreciated Cordell's words, for Estelle had indeed let her know how lonely and disheartened she would be until she returned.

"Estelle thinks she is being deserted, but with the birth of our child she will find every minute occupied. She loves you well, Alisha, but deep inside she knows that you must find your own course in life."

Estelle was so lucky to have such a wise and loving husband, Alisha thought as she listened. One day she hoped she would be as fortunate as her cousin in her choice of a husband.

The carriage had drawn to a stop before the ship

and as Cordell opened the door, he cautioned Alisha to pull the hood of her cloak about her head. "This weather is too nasty and we would not wish you to take a drenching. I'm glad I refused to allow Estelle to come along even though I'll have to face her wrath when I return home."

Alisha smiled at the truth of his words. Her cousin had indeed been upset as she stood at the front door and tearfully waved them on their way. "Please tell her how much I love her and will miss her," Alisha said as Cordell hurried her across the dock and over the gangplank. With his head bent against the rain, the driver laboriously began to unstrap her trunks from atop the vehicle and carry them to the deck of the ship.

Having been told of his passenger's arrival, Captain Darrell Frazer hurriedly pulled on his jacket and cap and left the shelter of his cabin. He would have left the obligation of seeing his passenger to her cabin to his first mate, if not for the fact that Cordell Glanville had paid him so handsomely for the lady's passage to the colonies.

"Ah, Captain Frazer," Cordell called as he glimpsed the Captain walking briskly toward them. "I hope we haven't kept you waiting. This is my wife's cousin, Alisha Whitlaw." Cordell pulled the collar of his jacket up about his neck to stave off the dampness.

Captain Frazer quickly shook Cordell's outstretched hand and then looked to the young woman at his side. Surprise showed on Darrell Frazer's lean features. He had expected an older, more sedate woman to be boarding his ship. But the heart-shaped face and blue-gray, darkly lashed eyes that looked back at him from within the cover of her hooded cloak were anything but matronly. Breathtaking was the word that most suited this beauty, he thought to himself as he glimpsed a few stray titian-colored curls about her face. Slowly his neatly trimmed mustache pulled back as he smiled. "It's a pleasure, Mademoiselle," he said as he bent from the waist and fleetingly wondered what lay under the cover of the cloak.

The Captain must have been in his mid-thirties, Alisha thought, and he was rather handsome in a darkly intriguing sort of way. Perhaps he would be pleasant company during this voyage. Her bow-shaped lips turned up into a smile that showed white, straight teeth. "I do hope my presence aboard your ship will not be a bother, Captain. Cordell has told me you're taking a shipment of goods to the colonies and I'll be the only passenger."

Even the sound of her voice was a delight. How could one such as she ever be a bother? "Indeed no bother at all, Mademoiselle. Your presence shall be a welcome pleasure aboard this vessel."

Over the past two years Cordell had watched as more men than he could number had held this same look, a look of captivation in the presence of Alisha. The Captain would see to her safety, he felt assured, though the man may well know a heartache he would not easily forget when he delivered her to her destination.

Standing before Alisha Whitlaw's unusual beauty, it took Captain Frazer a moment to come to his senses. "Allow me to show you to your cabin before you take ill from this dampness." He caught himself just before making profound apologies for the foul weather, which he had no means to control. He held out his arm and the vision of loveliness still wearing that glorious smile graciously placed her hand upon his jacket and allowed him the privilege of escorting her across the deck and down the companionway to her cabin.

Cordell followed closely with a knowing grin. Alisha would be treated with every courtesy and attention while aboard the *Velvet Venture*.

After opening her cabin door, Captain Frazer made his excuses and left the pair to their farewells. Most of his men were in the galley drinking tea and coffee; they could now ready the ship for sailing.

Staying only long enough for his driver to bring her baggage into her cabin and allowing that the room seemed comfortable, Cordell placed a light kiss upon Alisha's cheek and bid her farewell. "Don't forget to send us word of your arrival in Yorktown, Alisha. Estelle will be in a state until she hears from you."

Alisha hugged Cordell tightly and promised to write as soon as possible. "Tell Estelle I will return when I am able." She felt a small tear slip from her eye.

Reaching up, Cordell brushed it away. "No more of these. Look at life as an adventure. You are young and as you pass over one hurdle in life there will always be another. Tears are wasted. You are far too beautiful to shed them."

With a weak smile, Alisha slowly nodded her head. Cordell was right, of course. She had shed so many tears over this past week, to no avail. Her father was still gone and she was on her own. At that moment she decided she would take his advice. She would be strong and harden herself so that nothing else would ever hurt her again. Straightening her backbone, she spoke softly but firmly. "I'll be fine, Cordell. You had best hurry home to Estelle."

With one last smile of affection, Cordell left the cabin and made his way back to the carriage; his thoughts turned to his wife and her need for comfort now that her cousin had left their home. For a moment he compared the two women in his mind. Estelle had always appeared to need much affection and attention, depending on others always to be near at hand for her happiness. Her cousin, on the other hand, was much the opposite. Alisha was headstrong and very independent, at times almost too much so for a woman, he reflected. But perhaps life had created her in this fashion for the ordeals she would go through. His Estelle would never have ventured off alone in search of her father's killers.

Pulling off the pale blue cloak, Alisha looked about the cabin. It was not very big and was sparsely furnished. A small, built-in bed was fashioned into one wall; against the other was a bureau and washstand. In one corner of the room was an overstuffed, flower-printed brocade chair near a hanging oil lantern. It would suit her needs, she thought, as she opened the small bag that held her toilet articles. She placed her hair brushes and perfume bottles on the bureau; her short, sheer nightgowns she placed in a drawer and reminded herself that she would need more sensible night clothes as soon as she arrived in Yorktown.

With little else to do and feeling the motion of the ship as it pulled away from the dock and started out to sea, she sat down in the comfortable chair. Once again she went over in her mind all that Cordell had told her after arranging her passage aboard the *Velvet Venture*. Captain Frazer would take her to a place above Yorktown near Richmond and see that she could make arrangements to reach her destination. The small purse of gold coins in her trunk would be used for the purchase or hiring of a carriage and driver to Yorktown; then Captain Frazer would continue on with his blockade running. The *Velvet Venture* carried much needed supplies to General Washington and his troops.

Alisha sighed deeply. She would soon be home, though she knew by the letters from her father over the years that much had changed in Yorktown. Five long years had passed since she had been sent to France to live with her Aunt Marcelle. It was strange, she thought, how often she had felt homesick for the American colonies which she could barely remember from her childhood.

A light knock upon the cabin door startled her from her thoughts. Expecting it to be the Captain returning to see about her comfort after they put to sea, Alisha opened the door and was surprised to find a boy of about thirteen standing in the hallway holding a covered tray.

"The Captain thought you may be wanting some tea, Miss," the shy youth stated. His bright green eyes and freckled face looked for a moment in awe at the woman standing before him and then he quickly lowered his bright, carrot-red head.

"Tea would be most pleasant." Alisha smiled and stepped away from the door to allow the boy into the cabin.

For a moment he stood in the center of the room holding the tray tightly in his hands, undecided as he looked around for a place to set it.

"Perhaps this end of the bureau will do," Alisha ventured as she saw the boy's confusion and hurriedly moved her brushes to the other end of the dresser.

With some haste the cabin boy did as she directed. His experience around beautiful women was limited, so he desired only to make his escape and perhaps think about her later.

"What is your name?" Alisha softly questioned as he turned to flee out the cabin door.

"Benny, Miss." The boy appeared to freeze in his tracks as he stammered out his answer.

"Well, Benny, the Captain is certainly lucky to have such a hard-working cabin boy on his ship." Alisha hoped to make friends with the youth and put him more at ease in her presence.

"Thank you, Miss." Benny glanced up at her with a wide grin.

"Thank you, Benny, for the tea." Alisha smiled back and watched as the boy bumped into her luggage and then turned and fled through the open doorway.

Alisha's soft laughter filled the cabin as she poured herself a cup of tea. What a delightful boy, she thought, as she sat down and began to drink the warm, honey-sweetened brew.

In only a few minutes, there was another knock upon the cabin door. Finding the cabin boy once again standing in the hallway, Alisha smiled. "Well, Benny, if you've come for the tray, I am not quite finished."

"No, Miss," he quickly assured. "The Captain sent me to ask if you would like to have dinner with him this evening." The freckled face looked at her with open admiration. Her friendliness had won him over and this time he was not as quick to hurry out.

"Tell Captain Frazer I would be delighted to have dinner with him," Alisha replied with little thought. What else was there for her to do, she asked herself. Captain Frazer had seemed charming enough, and if she did not accept his invitation, she would be forced to eat alone here in her cabin.

"The Captain will be pleased, Miss." Benny started to turn away from the door, but remembering the tray, he ventured. "I'll be back later for the tray, Miss. No need to hurry." Benny scampered off to take her answer to the Captain, knowing he would anxiously count the minutes until he could return to gather the tray and gaze upon her beauty once again.

The rest of the day Alisha stayed within the confines of the small cabin. Twice she tried to read a book she had brought along for the voyage, but could not concentrate. Her thoughts were consumed by the letter from Amos and what had been left unsaid about her father's death. Why had he been killed? Had it been a British loyalist or a British soldier that had done the deed? Had the murderer been charged with the crime? There were so many things she did not know and she could not free her mind from the horrible fact that her father was no longer alive. Each time she tried to force herself to put Amos's letter aside, the image of her father's kindly face would come to mind. Her only relief was to pace the interior of the small room she had been assigned aboard the *Velvet Venture* and hold her thoughts on revenge.

It was almost seven o'clock when Captain Frazer dressed in his finest Captain's jacket and, having shaved the stubble off his chin and groomed his dark hair, arrived at Alisha's cabin door and escorted her to his larger cabin to share the evening meal.

"This weather is still rather unfavorable. I apologize for your having to stay in your cabin all day," the Captain stated as they went through the companionway to his cabin. "I had hoped the rain would have cleared by this evening, but I fear it has increased somewhat throughout the afternoon."

"Perhaps tomorrow will see the sun shining brightly, Captain," Alisha offered, as he seemed a bit anxious about the weather.

As Captain Frazer opened his cabin door, he added almost as an afterthought, "I would have waited this storm out in Martinique if not for the fact that I am already behind schedule."

Entering the Captain's cabin, Alisha took in the large quarters furnished with dark, rich pieces of furniture. The Captain's bed was against the far wall, built into a small alcove with sheer draperies concealing it from the rest of the room. A large, elegantly carved oak desk took up much of one corner and a settee and two matching chairs were situated beneath a large, paned glass window.

It was toward the settee that Captain Frazer led Alisha. "Benny will bring our dinner shortly. Would you care for a glass of wine while we wait?" As she settled her skirts upon the settee, the Captain's dark eyes drank in her lush form from head to slippers. Never had he seen such a lovely creature, he told himself as his gaze devoured the gleaming, bronze tresses, golden creaminess of her smooth skin, and sparkling silver-blue eyes. Roaming further, he beheld the fullness of her bosom above the low-cut bodice of her shimmering, ice-pink satin gown and the fragile trimness of her waist and curve of shapely hips. Even the tiny pink slippers that peeked out from beneath the fullness of the pink skirts implied perfection.

"Wine would be delightful, Captain," Alisha responded. Looking up, she was held for a second by his consuming gaze.

Discovered in his bold perusal, Captain Frazer thought for a moment he was going to blush, something he had not done since his youth. "Yes, the wine," he murmured softly and hurriedly turned to the decanter and glasses on a small corner table. Taking a moment to gain control over his emotions, he poured two crystal, thin-stemmed glasses full of an amber wine and turned back toward his guest. "I hope you haven't found your first day aboard the *Velvet Venture* too tedious, Mademoiselle Whitlaw. Perhaps you're right, and tomorrow will bring sunshine."

"I brought along a few books I've put off reading, Captain, and entertained myself with one this afternoon. So indeed, no, I am not yet bored with the voyage. Though I do confess, I love the feel of the sun and will be glad to gain the fresh air above deck." She did not mention the fact that being left alone in her small cabin with little to do had invited morose thought of her father's death.

Captain Frazer was impressed. Other women would have complained about the confinement of a small cabin; besides being beautiful, she also seemed quite agreeable, he thought.

A knock upon the door interrupted their conversation and Benny entered bearing a large tray of food. "Good evening, Miss." He set the tray upon the low table before the settee, his eyes holding hers for a few lingering moments as he stood by to see if his Captain needed anything else.

Alisha smiled warmly. "The food looks delicious, Benny. Thank you." The boy seemed to glow with her every word.

"That will be all, Benny. I'll call if we need anything else." Captain Frazer watched the young boy from the corner of his eye, a small smile settling about his lips as he understood the boy's desire to stay near Alisha Whitlaw.

As Benny started to the door, he turned and for a few seconds more stared at Alisha before hurriedly saying to the Captain, "I almost forgot, sir. The cook says his supplies are falling about in the galley and Demetre thinks the storm is worsening."

For the past hour the rolling motion of the ship had increased. "Tell cook to secure everything and tell Demetre that I will be on deck shortly."

"Yes, sir." He straightened as though his mission were very important, as he went through the doorway and off in the direction of the galley to seek out the cook and first mate.

"I now know why Benny has asked me all day if there was any message I would like to send to your cabin." Captain Frazer smiled as he began to arrange their plates on the small table. With Alisha's questioning look, he added, "The boy is quite enamored of you."

Alisha's tinkling laughter filled his ears and seemed to pierce his very heart with its sweet sound. "Benny is a wonderful boy." Alisha was well aware that Benny was a bit smitten; she hoped the Captain would not mind. After all, he was but a young boy and all such youths were allowed harmless crushes. "Has he been the cabin boy on the *Velvet Venture* long?" she asked as she took up her fork and began to sample the delicious fare.

"Benny has been with me for almost two years now. His father is a close friend and hopes that Benny will take well to life at sea."

"I'm sure he will. He seems bright and willing."

"Now tell me about you, Mademoiselle Whitlaw. Your cousin's husband tells me you lived in France before you came to Martinique." As the Captain was questioning her, the ship lurched and seemed to turn a little upon its side as it rode atop a large wave. He had to reach out and steady their wine glasses to keep them from spilling.

Alisha looked at him with widened eyes as she felt the rolling motion. Never having been at sea during a storm, she was unused to the strange, disjointed movement. The rain had not bothered her but the crashing of the waves against the sides of the vessel and the rocking motion as the *Velvet Venture* was swept atop waves and then brought back down, was something very new. It left her feeling rather unsettled and made her forget his question and her food.

"There is nothing to worry about, Alisha. You don't mind my using your given name, do you?" He did not wait for an answer but went on. "The *Velvet Venture* is a fit ship and has ridden out many such storms."

Alisha could only nod as she felt the swaying and dipping of the vessel.

"Perhaps we should continue our conversation over dinner tomorrow night. I should see if I can be of help above deck. But don't forget there is still much I desire to know about you, Alisha. You're a very beautiful woman and I must admit that I'm intrigued."

Alisha did not answer. All she could think of was getting back to her safe little cabin and lying down on the bed where she would feel secure from the rocking movements.

Apologizing once again, Captain Frazer saw Alisha to her cabin. Once inside, she hurriedly stumbled about the room as she took off her pink gown and put on her nightdress.

Climbing beneath the covers, she lay awake for some time as she listened to the storm and the creaking timbers of the ship. All the stories she had ever heard of ships sinking at sea came to her mind and held her quietly still as she wondered about her fate aboard the *Velvet Venture*.

It was near midnight when Alisha awoke as she was thrown from her bed and rolled, wrapped in her blankets, across the cabin floor. Fear gripped her as she untangled herself and clutched the foot rail of the bed, trying to regain some semblance of balance. The ship swayed, lurched and shifted. Thunder crashed overhead, blending with the moaning and creaking of the vessel.

Again the ship turned and for a moment Alisha thought they were doomed as great shudders ran the length of the timbers and the chair and washstand in her cabin crashed to the floor.

I must escape this cabin, she thought. If they were to sink she would be trapped. In all the confusion, no one would think about her, hidden away in this tiny cabin. Pulling herself upright, she clutched the side of the bed and slowly made her way to the door. Clasping the knob and holding on for support, she pulled the door open and stepped out into the hallway. She stumbled to her knees several times as she made it to the entrance of the companionway.

Blinding sheets of rain lashed at her as she held to the inward rail on the side of the ship. If she could just find a safe place above deck, she thought as she inched her way along the rail; the rain fell in such a downpour she could see only a few feet in front of her.

Suddenly the ship was pushed upwards, rocking precariously on the very top of a gigantic wave and seeming to dance dangerously there for a few minutes in a soaring, plunging motion that left Alisha breathless and numb with terror. In the next instant she felt the downward plunge of the vessel, the crashing wave following the ship back toward the dark depths of the sea.

Chilling, dark water covered the decks of the *Velvet Venture*, her bow plunging upwards as though demanding to survive, but rushing sea water pulled at everything in her grasp.

Alisha felt her grip upon the side railing slacken and then her body being pulled beneath the surface of the devouring water. The cold depths enclosed her; she fought, her hands clutching at anything to save herself but all she felt was the cool liquid salt water as her body glided along with the crashing wave.

Alisha wanted to scream but some inner sense of survival warned her not to open her mouth. She was swept along as though weightless, with no control of her own body. Then suddenly she was being pulled downward.

An eternity seemed to pass as she fought the clutches of a watery death. Her head at last surfaced, and she gasped for air, her lungs expanding and filling with the invisible oxygen that nurtured life.

Feeling raindrops on her face and her heart beating wildly, she knew she had survived. She bobbed up and down along with the waves and looking through the downpour, she glimpsed the outline of the ship still being tossed about. Screaming for help, she tried to swim in the direction of the vessel, but the drenching rain, crackling lightning and crashing thunder drowned out her voice.

It was hopeless, she realized, as the ship disappeared. There would be no help forthcoming; no one even knew she had come out of her cabin. She would soon become exhausted and then the sea would swallow her up.

Bleak reality settled over her as she was swept along by a huge wave and then brought back down to the depths. Again and again she was carried along at the mercy of the sea. Her arms and legs began to tire as she tried to swim and keep herself afloat, her breathing ragged as she fought for life. Her head went below the surface and then she was spiraled back upwards.

When she thought she had fought with all her strength against the fate that awaited her, her hand touched something. She clutched whatever was there, willing her body to claim whatever assistance fortune granted her. It was the lid to one of the crates she had seen on the deck of the *Velvet Venture* when she had first boarded! It took all of her strength to pull herself atop its flat surface.

It floated! For a few minutes she wept with sheer relief at this miracle that had come before her. Her hands gripped tightly to the sides of the lid as the elements still fought a valiant fight to subdue her.

She was alive, she told herself. For the time being she was still alive!

Chapter Four

"Ahoy to deck! Tell Cap'n Fox there be something floating in the water straight ahead." A small, agile seaman clung to the rigging of the large ship known as the *Vixen* as the sleek, four-masted vessel skimmed across the ocean. His baggy, white breeches and red and white bulky shirt flapped in the wind like a piece of sail.

"The Cap'n don't be needing to be bothered about debris floating out there." A burly man with a sandy beard and hair mumbled as he sat cross-legged on the deck patching a piece of canvas sail. The Captain needed his sleep. Like most of the men that made up the crew aboard the *Vixen*, he had fought the storm the night through and had not found his head upon his pillow until late that morning.

"Let old Will himself climb down and take that bit of news to the Cap'n." Another rough-looking seaman sat with his back against the side of the ship next to Slade, who was patching the sail. He snickered aloud as though he would enjoy the sight

41

of the smaller man in the rigging awaking their captain with his news and the sure clubbing Will would receive with such a trivial announcement that something was floating on the water.

The larger man laughed as he took large stitches in the canvas. "Will never did have no sense no way. Remember that time he thought he saw the Spanish fleet and it turned out to be two French ships heading for the West Indies?"

"Yeah and remember when he swore he had seen an uncharted island?"

"It looks like a woman!" Will shouted with an excited voice as his hand shaded his eyes from the glare of the sun and he stared off in the direction of the floating piece of wood still some distance from the *Vixen.* The shapely form lying on the crate lid did not move and there looked like there was something tangled about her. It could be a mermaid, he thought. His imagination ran wild as he squinted hard to get a better look.

The two men sitting on deck laughed uproariously. Even Pete the helmsman, who was usually quiet and sullen, chuckled loudly at Will's report.

"Too bad we can't all be seeing a mirage like old Will's," the large man called Slade finally grunted after the laughter died down.

"The only mirage I be seeing of a woman is in me dreams at night. I be seeing Rosey dancing atop that table in that flaming red dress there in that little tavern on Grande Terre, every time I be shutting me eyes." The other fellow grinned widely.

"Now Rosey sure be the lass to be dreaming about, Danny me boy." Slade nodded his large head as he

42

pulled the thread through the canvas tight and bit it loose with his broken front teeth. "I heard the lass has the sweetest tasting lips on the whole of the Island."

"If ye be wanting the truth of that, ye can be asking Cap'n Fox. It be wide known that Rosey only has an eye for the Fox when the *Vixen* makes port on the Island; and she won't be having the time of day for any other."

"It be her hair that be wrapped about her body and don't 'peer as she be wearing any clothes!" shouted Will in amazement, breaking into the conversation the two men were having about the buxom tavern wench, Rosey.

"I think I be all fur seeing such a mirage meself," Danny chuckled, and stood up.

His heavy set, bearded mate put his work aside and also pulled himself to his feet. "There best be something out there or Will might just be finding his eyesight improved with the back of me hand when he climbs out of that rigging." The pair went over to the ship's railing and looked off into the direction Will was pointing.

"I'll be a tinker's damn if there ain't something out there!" Danny spoke with some surprise as he made out a dark shape floating atop the surface of the water.

"Do ya be thinking it be some kind of small raft?" asked the larger man as he also glimpsed something. "Can ya be making out a woman?" His voice held disbelief but the fact that there was something out there did add substance to Will's statements.

"I think she may be dead or something! She ain't moving!" exclaimed Will loudly.

43

"I reckon the Cap'n should be woke fur this," the large man stated as he continued to squint at the piece of wood that was slowly coming closer to the *Vixen*.

"Ye best be taking word to him then, Slade. I be staying here and keeping an eye out." Danny was not about to leave the rail. If Will somehow was seeing a woman out there on the ocean and she was naked at that, he was going to be one of the first to get an eyeful.

Slade would have also liked nothing better than to stay near the railing and watch as the object drew nearer, but thinking about Captain Fox's reaction if he were not informed that there might be a woman floating alone on the ocean, he turned and hurried to the Captain's cabin. Hoping that Will was right about seeing a woman and that he was not awaking the Captain unnecessarily, he knocked loudly on the door.

"Enter," a deep-timbred, groggy voice called. As Slade stepped into the cabin, pale brown, gold-flecked eyes looked from the bed across the room. "This had best be good, man." The Captain's large form rose up on an elbow as he tried to pull himself awake.

"I thought ye would want to know, Cap'n, Will sighted something floating in the water and swears that it be a woman."

At first the man in the bed had thought he had heard Slade incorrectly. "What did you say? A woman? If this is another one of Will's imaginary sightings, I'll have him flogged for disturbing my sleep."

"There surely be something out there, Cap'n. Me and Danny been watching from the rail."

"All right, Slade. I'll be on deck shortly. Tell Will to keep watching and tell Pete to get as close as possible to whatever it is out there."

"Aye, Cap'n," Slade said excitedly and hurried out of the cabin to give the helmsman and Will their orders.

For a moment the Captain of the *Vixen* lay back down against the pillows. "A woman!" he breathed aloud. "What next?" Will had best not be seeing things this time, he told himself as he sat up on the side of the bed. If not for the fact that Will was the most sure-footed of his men, he would not allow him in the rigging to keep watch.

Standing naked, he stretched his massive body and yawned loudly. He could have used a few more hours rest, for his temper was a bit darkened by not getting his sleep. Pulling on his dark, tight-fitting breeches, he went to the washstand and splashed some cool water on his face. After being on deck throughout the night and all of yesterday, he had done little more than strip off his clothes this morning before falling exhausted upon his bed. Now he looked into the washstand mirror for a second and gazed at his appearance. He had not even bothered to unbraid his hair. It still hung down his back, and his beard could well use a trimming, he told himself as he rubbed his chin.

Pulling on a loose-fitting white shirt, he tucked the tail into his waistband and buttoned it only halfway up. Dark, curling hair was visible on his broad chest. Not bothering with his boots, which had been carelessly thrown near the bed that morning, he started out of the cabin.

By the time the Captain of the *Vixen* arrived on deck, his entire crew was gathered about the rail shouting at one another as all eyes were fixed to the water below.

"She be a mermaid!" one crewman declared to the man standing at his side.

"Nay, a sea siren," the other breathed aloud.

"A naked goddess," another voiced as the entire crew vied to get a closer place near the railing and a better look at the form stretched out on the wood that was floating closer and closer.

"What the hell is going on?" demanded the Captain as he saw his men and wondered why most of them were not below getting their sleep. Their watch would start in a few hours and they would be too tired to do their work.

"There she be, Cap'n, just like Will claimed," Slade called when he heard the deep voice of Captain Fox. He had been the one who had told the cook about Will seeing a naked woman adrift upon the sea and the cook in turn had spread word throughout the ship. Not one crewman on the *Vixen* was not willing to give up his sleep for such a rare sighting.

Justin Martel, known to his crew and throughout the Caribbean as the Fox, made his way toward the railing as his men cleared a path for him near Slade. He stared with disbelief, just as each of his men had, when he peered over the railing and looked down upon the woman lying on the crate lid. He also thought she was naked, but upon closer inspection he saw that her abundant wealth of hair was wrapped about her body and all but concealed the short, skimpy material that covered only the upper half of her body.

"Drop the rope ladder," he ordered Slade. "And tell the helmsman to keep steady as he is." The crate lid was only twenty feet from the ship and drawing closer by the second.

"I be yur man to fetch her, Cap'n," a crewman shouted, starting to push his way toward the Captain and the rope ladder that was being lowered.

A larger man than he pushed the crewman aside and declared roughly, "I will see to this job, ye bloody infant. Ye be falling into the sea and drowning yerself and the woman trying to carry her up the ladder."

Mass confusion broke out as every man among them began to push his way to the rope ladder, shouting and shoving to be the one to get to the woman and be first to touch that golden flesh that showed beneath gleaming, copper-colored hair.

"Stand back," the Captain ordered, his golden-brown eyes angry. No one could mistake his meaning if they disobeyed.

"I can get the lass, Cap'n," Slade ventured as the rest of the crew backed off. He also desired just a simple touch of the woman's body.

"I will get her," the Captain said and pulled off his shirt and threw it to Slade. Climbing down the ladder and reaching the bottom, it appeared as though the girl was lifeless as the crate lid came within a few feet of the ship. Stretching out a long, muscular arm, the Captain pulled the lid to the bottom of the ladder.

Looking down at the woman for a second, Justin

Martel thought perhaps she was dead. She was so still, he could not even make out her breathing. Brushing away the strands of hair covering her face, he drew in a deep breath as he stared down at her angelic face. Touching the pulse at her throat he felt it beating and knew she lived. A soft sigh of relief escaped his lips.

The calls from his men as they wondered why he was taking so long brought him back to reality. Slowly he drew the girl to him and wrapped an arm about her waist as he held to the rope ladder and started the climb back up the ship.

She seemed so slight, he thought, barely a burden at all. Still she did not stir and he thought for a minute that perhaps she was ill. That could be the reason she had been set adrift on her own. He hoped that he was not making a mistake by bringing her aboard the *Vixen*. He had heard of more instances than he liked to recall when entire crews had been wiped out from the plague or an unknown illness. But he knew he had little choice. He could not leave her on the crate lid to the whim of the sea. It could be days or weeks before another ship would catch sight of her and by then surely she would perish.

Greedy eyes waited at the top of the ladder to feast upon the beauty in the Captain's arms. "Go on about your duties now, men," he called as he reached the top of the ladder and with one arm around the woman, he maneuvered his leg over the rail and stepped onto the deck.

"But, Cap'n Fox, 'tain't fair. We be figuring that she be a prize of the sea, like an offering to whoever finds her," one man in a dirty, faded yellow shirt

48

braver than the others spoke out. The rest of the crew nodded in agreement.

The Captain looked around at his rough, hard-fighting men and knew he was all that stood between the unconscious woman and their greedy lust. "Slade, throw my shirt over her." He looked at the large man standing near, and as he covered the woman's body, the tawny eyes went back to the men standing before him. "The woman is no prize from the sea. She could have been set adrift because she's sick."

The copper-hued curls flowed over her body and hung almost to the deck over the Captain's arm. As the crew looked at her pale face and immobile form, heads slowly began to nod in agreement; several of the crewmen stepped back. Sickness aboard ship could be disastrous. One touch of her skin or standing too close to one with fever could mean losing their own lives.

Captain Fox strode through his men and they cleared a wide path as he went toward the companion-way and his cabin. "Set about your work, men, and those with still a few hours rest coming to them, the sun will be setting soon and your shift will start again."

Amidst grumbles and complaints that the woman had so easily been swept out of their reach, the crew began to disperse. Some went down to the hold of the ship where they had their hammocks and others continued about their work.

With a wide grin on his impish face, Will called down to Danny and Slade as they started back to work on the piece of canvas. "Didn't I tell ya, lads, I be seeing a woman? Me eyesight ain't so bad, now is it? Maybe I be seeing another beauty out there floating about and we won't be so quick to tell the Captain this time."

The two men did not answer as they set about their sewing. They too felt the same disappointment as their fellow crewmen. The woman had been stolen from them!

Justin Martel laid the woman down upon his bed and pushed back the hair falling over her face. For a moment he sat down on the edge of the bed and gazed at her intently. Her features were not overly flushed and the touch of her skin had not been warm, so he doubted she was ill or fevered. He wondered at her stillness, though, but then reasoned that perhaps she had an injury that he could not see or perhaps it was merely exhaustion. There was no telling how long she had been on the crate lid before the *Vixen* had caught sight of her. If she had suffered through the storm on that small piece of wood it was impossible to imagine what she had been forced to endure.

Looking down at her shapely body, he marveled at such perfection. The damp gown she wore was as transparent as the finest gossamer, leaving nothing to the imagination. Her breasts were full, the tips darkened as they strained against the sheer fabric. Her small rib cage lowered to a small waist where he could glimpse a tiny indent. Her womanhood drew his eyes and he saw the curling of a dark triangle of hair. Pulling his gaze from this area he went lower to shapely thighs and long legs and finally his gaze rested on her tiny feet. And all that glorious hair, he thought. It surely must reach below her hips. For a moment, as his eyes went back to her face, he tried to envision the color of her eyes. A sparkling deep green or a violet blue, he thought, and was anxious for the moment when he would see for himself.

Brushing these thoughts away, he pulled her body forward to lean against his chest as he raised the damp gown off her body. Putting her back against the pillows, he pulled the silk sheet up beneath her chin. Her breathing seemed easy now, so perhaps she only needed rest.

Slipping into his shirt and taking the time to put on his black boots, he went out on deck to check on his men. Women were always the cause of some form of trouble, he thought with some irritation. Now he would have to take the time to smooth over any anger that his men were harboring because he had interceded between them and the defenseless woman. Once again his thoughts went to his cabin and the beauty in his bed; an angry scowl came over his handsome features. Of all the ships roaming the seas, why did the *Vixen* have to be the one to come across the woman?

It was shortly after the midnight hour when Justin closed the door of his cabin with thoughts of getting the rest he needed. He had come back several times to check on the woman but she slept on. Looking across to the bed he saw that she had not even moved from the position he had placed her in that afternoon. The sheet was still covering every portion of that incredible body and her shimmering, copper-gold curls fanned out over the pillows.

Going to the washstand, he pulled off his shirt and began to wash away the day's sweat and grime. Reaching behind his back, he drew the slim length of his long braid over his shoulder and began the nightly task of freeing his hair. The long, sun-streaked strands lay against his broad, muscled back.

Wearily he ran his large hands through his hair. Sitting on a chair near his desk, he pulled off his boots and as he rose to his feet and started to unfasten his pants, his eyes went to the bed. Glistening, silver-blue eyes stared wide at him from a pale, frightened face.

Slowly being pulled from her deep sleep by the sound of a door shutting, Alisha forced her eyes open. The first thing she noticed was that every inch of her body seemed to ache as she tentatively moved upon the down-soft mattress. She must have been rescued, she thought. The *Velvet Venture* must have come back looking for her and found her on the crate lid. By degrees her joy began to diminish as she took in the scarlet silk drapings encasing the large bed. This was certainly not her bed in the tiny cabin that had been hers aboard the *Velvet Venture;* nor was it like any bed she had seen before in her life! There were panels of mirrors lined within the canopy overhead and looking up she could see her own pale features and the red silk sheet draped across her body.

A small noise drew her attention and her gaze settled on the form of the largest man she had ever seen. His height was towering; the wide expanse of his back which was turned to her at this moment gleamed golden dark by the light of the lantern on the desk and bulging muscles swelled and rippled with his movements before the washstand. As he freed his hair from a piece of leather binding, it fell in a golden mane down his back. What was this massive man doing half-clothed in this room with her? Sheer terror began to make its way into her heart.

Slowly her body began to tremble as the man sat down and pulled off his boots. Had she truly been rescued, she questioned herself; or was this room some awful chamber in the pits of hell? Was this scarlet-draped bed her prison and this giant her jailer? With her heart hammering wildly in her chest, she watched as the giant rose to his feet and his hands went to the button to release his trousers. His head rose in that instant, his movement stilling as glittering, panther-like eyes went to the bed and beheld her. For a single minute Alisha's breathing seemed to stop as her entire body froze; her heart pounded in a raw terror that washed over her from those compelling eyes.

For a few short moments, the pair stared at each other. Justin Martel was totally captivated by her incredible beauty. The silver-blue eyes staring at him from the pale radiance of her ethereal face held him entranced where he stood.

Alisha was even more terrified as she stared into his face and could not look away. The searching, tawny eyes sparkled with a deep brilliance as she beheld the handsome outline of his bearded face, narrow, straight nose and sensual lips. Even the golden hair pulled back from his face and lying over his shoulders and down his back and the glimmering of

53

a small, golden hooped earring in his right ear bespoke raw, masculine power. He appeared at that moment merciless and overpowering and again the image conjured itself in her mind of hell's jailer. "Who . . . who . . . are you?"

With the sound of her trembling voice, Justin was pulled back to reality. Slowly he began to draw closer to the bed and at last he answered, "I'm Justin Martel and you're aboard my ship, the *Vixen*."

His voice was deep and seemed to vibrate in Alisha's ears as he stood next to the bedside. She clutched the scarlet sheet tightly over her breasts. "How did I get aboard your ship?" She searched her mind but had no remembrance of being rescued.

"My crew and I found you lying on a piece of wood, adrift on the sea. I carried you aboard my ship and to my cabin. Hoping that you were only exhausted from your experience, I left you to sleep." Justin could eaily read the fear and confusion on her features and as the wide, darkly lashed eyes stared up at him, he tried to make his tone gentle.

"All I remember is holding tightly to the crate lid throughout the storm and then the sun was so bright, so hot and I was so tired."

Her voice sounded so innocent, thought Justin. Wanting to find out more, he slowly eased his weight down on the side of the bed.

With his movement, Alisha clutched the sheet tighter and quickly pulled herself away from him to the headboard. Scooting her body to put a distance between herself and this frightful giant, Alisha felt the cool undersheet caress her naked flesh and in that instant realized she was entirely bare. "Where are my clothes?" she asked. Why was she naked and who had taken off her clothes? Who else would have done such a thing besides him? Had he not confessed to carrying her aboard his ship and putting her in his bed?

With a small smile, Justin vividly remembered the skimpy bit of nothing she had worn to cover her body when he had rescued her. "Your gown was damp when you were rescued and I thought you would rest better without it," he answered her. Remembering what he had seen when he put her in his bed, his gaze now roamed over her in warm appreciation. She was even more beautiful at this moment, he thought, with her eyes a deep shade of sapphire and her cheeks blushed with a pinkened hue.

"You mean, you . . . you . . . undressed me?" she stammered. Though she knew that it had to be he who had done the deed, still she could not believe any man could be so bold as to dare such a reprehensible act. "You had no right!" She imagined those searing, golden eyes roaming over her naked body, and as she glanced down at his large hands resting at ease on the top of the sheet, she wondered what more he had done to her. If she could not remember her rescue or his undressing her and putting her to bed, what more could she not remember? Her thoughts were plainly readable on her flushed features as her eyes rose from his hands.

"Have no fear, Madam. I do not take advantage of unconscious women. And as for your undressing, the gown you had on left little to the imagination. I saw little more without that bit of fabric."

Recalling the see-through nightgown she had worn when she had retired aboard the *Velvet*

Venture, her cheeks blushed brighter as she realized he had discerned her thoughts so easily. "I didn't mean you would have . . . would have . . ."

Justin sighed aloud. Women were all alike in their modesty no matter the circumstances. Even with the prospect of death, they worried over silly things. And this woman with her incredible wealth of burnt gold locks falling in disarray about her shoulders and trapped beneath her curvaceous body, was much like the rest of her sex. That wisp of a gown she had worn had more than likely been little more than an inducement to awaken some man's passions before she had somehow found herself adrift on the sea. It never crossed his mind that a woman with such a tempting body and delectable beauty could have any other reason for wearing such a revealing nightgown. "Why do you not tell me how you came to be on that crate lid, alone on the sea?" He would not make an issue now over her lack of virtue. There would be plenty of time to find out all he wished to know.

Alisha still did not trust this large man even though at the moment he appeared concerned enough about her situation. Keeping the few feet of distance between them and holding the sheet bunched in her fists over her breasts and her eyes resting upon him as though expecting him to lunge at her at any second, she began to tell him the circumstances that had led to her being aboard his ship. "I was aboard the *Velvet Venture* when I awoke during the storm. The sea was dashing the ship about so terribly, I left my cabin with the fear that we were sinking. When I reached the top deck, a huge wave swept me overboard. It was only luck that the waves had also washed away some crates that had been stacked on deck. A lid came near enough for me to grab it and all I could do was hold on to the piece of wood to keep afloat." Early in life Alisha had learned the benefit of using caution in her confidences; she told him only what she believed necessary. After all, she knew nothing about him. He could very well be working for the British. She had heard of privateers who were known as little more than pirates who held this fancy title and papers from the King allowing them to ravage the sea with their brutality and thievery. This bold and dashing Captain, with his scarlet-draped bed, certainly fit the image in her mind of a privateer or even a pirate. Again fear gripped her heart. If in fact she were not in the bowels of hell, was there a worse place than that heathenish pit of hades?

"What was your destination?" the Captain of the *Vixen* questioned as Alisha calmed down. His golden eyes had watched her intently, seeming to measure her every word.

"I was on my way to Yorktown, Virginia, sir," she allowed and hoped he would agree to see her to an Island port so she could continue on to her destination. At that moment the full impact of her destitution hit her. She was totally without any means. Everything she had owned was aboard the *Velvet Venture*. Her purse of gold, even her clothes. She could only hope she could somehow get word of her situation to Cordell.

"Then perhaps you can consider it some small luck that the *Vixen* rescued you, madam. I also am on my way to the American colonies." He also warned himself to be cautious. He knew by his correspondence with his friend, John Paul Jones, and also with Lafayette that General Cornwallis had set up his British command in Yorktown. This woman could be the wife of some British officer on her way to a happy reunion. He would give her no information to relay to the enemy. Again, distrust for all women rekindled in his heart and he swore he would be wary of her attraction.

Alisha was not sure at that moment whether it was luck, as he claimed, or ill fate that had set her in the path of this Captain's ship. On the one hand if he agreed to take her to the colonies, perhaps she could arrange to pay him for his inconvenience at a later date. On the other hand as she looked at the lean-featured, handsome face, she felt less control than she had always had in the past with men. There was something about this Captain that cautioned her to have a care. He was not to be taken lightly, and this frightened her more than the prospect of being set upon an Island without means.

Not saying anything further about going to the colonies, but still appearing unsure, he questioned, "What is your name?"

For a moment Alisha hesitated, but then finally confessed. "Alisha Whitlaw."

"Alisha," he breathed aloud. "It's a more fitting name than my crew bestowed upon you." He thought of the names he had heard his men shouting when she had been afloat—mermaid, sea siren, naked goddess—and a smile touched his lips.

Alisha was not brave enough to ask him what he was talking about, but remained quietly awaiting his next question or his next move.

"Well, Alisha Whitlaw, I guess we can say I will be taking you on to your destination." He imagined there would be some gentleman anxiously awaiting her arrival.

"Thank you," Alisha mumbled, not knowing what else to say.

Rising from the bed, Justin went over to his desk and extinguished the lantern's yellow light which left the cabin in semidarkness. The light from the moon fell through the window across the room.

Alisha expected the Captain to leave her to the privacy of the cabin and so was surprised when he stepped to the other side of the bed. As her amazed eyes caught his dim outline cast by the moonlight as he pulled off his breeches, she gasped in horror and started to leap from the bed. "What are you doing?"

"Why, madam, I am going to bed," came his easy reply.

"But you cannot! I mean you cannot sleep in this bed! In this cabin!" Her tone showed her outrage that he would dare such a thing.

"I can and will, madam. This is my bed and my cabin. You are the intruder here, let me remind you." Justin was tired and in no mood to humor her. What matter another man in her bed, he asked himself. After all, he was not going to attack her. He had never lowered himself to such measures in the past and he certainly would not do so now; though if she were to invite him he definitely would not refuse.

"You are right, of course." Alisha jumped from the bed as she felt his heavy frame easing down upon the mattress.

Justin peered across the bed, making out her form

standing there clutching the silk sheet about her body. "Where do you think you're going?"

"Why, this is your cabin, so I shall go to another." She lifted her chin a notch and expected that he would dress and show her to a cabin she could use until they reached her destination.

"If that's your desire, madam, I won't stop you, but let me forewarn you about my crew. They are a lusty lot. If you leave this cabin you may find yourself paying dearly for your wish to leave my bed."

His meaning was clearly taken. Alisha stared at the cabin door as though all manner of evil would beset her if she opened it. "But I cannot stay here with you!" she said in desperation, but wondered at the same time what else she could do as she observed him stretching out his length on the bed.

"I told you I am tired, woman. You're safe enough." As he leaned upon an elbow and looked at her standing there in indecision with the sheet tightly held around her, he spoke in a harder tone. "Come to bed, Alisha. It's large enough for you to keep your distance."

Not knowing what else to do and hearing the command in his voice and afraid to argue further lest he take the matter into his own hands, she slowly sat down on the side of the bed. As she did not feel any movement from the giant, she tentatively lay down, her back positioned to him, her body curled tightly with the sheet as her only protection.

With a sigh, the Captain also rolled over and within minutes his easy breathing told Alisha he was asleep.

It was some time before Alisha was overcome with

sleep. Her fear that at any moment he would reach out and take hold of her kept her in a state of frightened wakefulness.

Why did life keep handing her such impossible situations, she questioned herself, and for a moment felt as though she would cry. First, her father's death, then being washed overboard and now finding her rescuer a frightening man. She rebuked herself as she remembered Cordell's words, "Tears were wasted." She would not allow herself to become a whimpering mass of emotions! She had survived the worst she could have ever imagined at the hands of the sea. Could this man beside her be any more dangerous and heartless than the storm? A small portion of her mind warned her she may very well find this ship's Captain a more dangerous opponent than nature's elements.

In the morning when he was well rested he would take more pity upon her, she told herself. Perhaps then he would see that she had a proper cabin and the respect she was accustomed to receiving from gentlemen. Slowly she began to relax as he appeared to be deep in sleep and her own eyes became too heavy to keep open. Yes, tomorrow, she fell asleep with the thought. Maybe he could even find her some clothes.

Chapter Five

During the early hours of the morning, deep in the bondage of sleep, Alisha sought the warmth that her body was pressed against. The silk sheet had slipped to the floor and with the cool night air drifting through the open windows of the cabin, she snuggled her length against the heat that drew her like a magnet.

The touch of silken limbs entwined about his own and firm, full breasts pressed against his broad chest unknowingly fired Justin's blood within his veins and caused a tightening in his loins that slowly roused him from sleep. Clutching his breath as his topaz eyes roamed over the beautiful creature lying beside him, he glimpsed her fiery curls which were wrapped around his large forearm which she was using as her pillow. Her delicate features held a small pout about the petal-soft lips only inches from his own. Cautiously so as not to wake her, he drew back somewhat to better his viewing. The shapely swelling of her breasts pressed against his chest, her belly lying full against his ribs and as he felt the swelling of his manhood rubbing against velvet softness, his gaze went lower and glimpsed a shapely leg bent at the knee and pressed between his own muscled thighs.

Another light breeze circled the interior of the cabin and the woman in his arms snuggled even closer. It was only his warmth that had drawn her to him, Justin realized and a small smile came over his lips. If she were to awaken at this moment and find herself in this position, he could well imagine her embarrassment after her display of chastity last night. With a soft sigh he drew his arm from beneath her head and disentangled her tempting body from his own. There would be other mornings that he would awake with her lying next to him before he delivered her to the colonies. He would take things slowly for now. The seduction of this beauty should be savored.

With the heated contact being taken away from her, Alisha burrowed deeper into the down bed. Before putting on his clothes, Justin went to the other side of the bed and stood holding the satin sheet, his eyes fleetingly going over her form one last time before he covered the shapely figure lying in the middle of his bed.

After dressing quietly, Justin left the cabin. A smile of pleasure played about his lips as he made his way out on deck and began his day. Fate had set this woman in his path so he might as well make the best of it. They would part company soon enough and they would both quickly forget the encounter, he told himself.

*   *   *

Alisha had been dreaming. She was being held against a hard, masculine body. Immense muscles held her so gently and the warmth of the body enfolded her in a haze of security. She felt safer than she had in years, since the early years of her childhood. Her fingertips brushed against the flesh covering the wide chest and she felt her heart leap in her breast. Slowly her hand traveled up his chin, feeling the growth of a trimmed beard. She caressed the firm jawline and the high cheekbone, and from the depths of her dream, passion-filled, topaz eyes stared at her. She awoke with a start. Her first instinct was to jump from the bed as she realized who she had been dreaming of.

She was alone. Her heart hammered wildly as she sat up straight in the middle of the bed with the sheet drawn up against her body. Soft rays of sunlight were streaming through the cabin window as she looked about the room. She had slept the night through and had not even heard the Captain leave the cabin.

Holding the sheet about her, she wondered how long he had been gone and as a nagging reminder of her dream came to mind, she forced it to flee. It was just a dream, she told herself. She would never have gotten near enough to that man to touch his body. But why then was she in the middle of the large bed? The question came unbidden, as though to dispute her own thoughts.

Dragging the sheet with her, she climbed off the bed and stood in the center of the cabin. She was being foolish, she told herself. Even in sleep she would never allow herself to draw close to a man she knew no better than Justin Martel. It was but a dream!

She needed to find some clothes. Even her nightgown would be preferable to what she now used as clothing. Looking about the cabin she could not find the sheer gown she had worn when she was rescued. What could he have done with it? She spied a sea chest at the foot of the bed, and without thought she pushed open the lid.

The contents of the chest were obviously a man's. Pulling back the abundant supply of masculine clothing, Alisha did not find her gown. As her hand touched a white satin shirt with ruffles at the cuffs and collar, she admitted that the Captain did indeed have rather good taste. Perhaps he would not mind if she borrowed one of his shirts, she thought. Not allowing herself time to think about the consequences when he saw her, she pulled it from the chest and drew her arms through the sleeves.

It was quite large on her, the sleeves hanging down over her hands and the bottom of the shirt tail circling below her knees. Well, at least it was something to cover herself. She buttoned the collar, enjoying the feel of the cool satin against her naked flesh as she rolled up the sleeves. As she glanced down, she wished she had something to cover her legs as her calves and feet were plainly visible. There would be no sense in trying on a pair of the giant's breeches as she would never be able to keep them on her body.

Throwing the scarlet sheet back on the bed, she stood in indecision for a moment before going to the washstand and finding a clean cloth in order to wash. She felt very uncomfortable using the large man's toilet articles, but there was no choice. If he would not allow her another cabin, she would have to make do with what she could find here.

Glimpsing a brush on a small table near the washstand, she had no second thoughts as she took it up and sitting down in the comfortable chair near the desk, began to work the tangles from her copper curls. Feeling somewhat better, she began to make plans for what she would need to do now and in the days ahead.

If this Captain Justin Martel would take her directly to Yorktown her prayers would be answered. But since he had only said he was heading for the colonies, she was unsure of his destination. If she had to find other means to get to Yorktown, she was not sure how she would handle the situation. Perhaps she could borrow the funds from the Captain and repay him when she paid for her passage. Perhaps she would be able to get in touch with Amos and he would come for her or send her the funds to see her safely to Yorktown. This would be the safest way, she thought. She would send word to Amos the minute she was on shore. It would be wiser not to be too indebted to this Captain. There was no telling the amount of payment he would demand. *Nor could she be sure the payment he would desire for her passage would be in coins,* a small part of her mind whispered. Moving the brush quickly through her hair, she forced herself away from such thoughts. Had she not already survived a night alone with him in his cabin?

Again the images of her dream came to mind. The feel of his warm, firm body tightly held against hers, the touch of his beard near her cheek. She could even imagine his heated breath touching the pulse beat at her throat; and those consuming topaz eyes. Stop this, she ordered her rebellious thoughts, and jumped to her feet. Throwing the hair brush down atop the desk, she began to pace about the cabin.

What on earth was wrong with her? The man was probably a pirate! He had proved as much to her the night before by forcing her to abide his presence in this cabin. He had even disrobed her and admitted as much! But again that tormenting part of her mind questioned, *have you ever seen such a man in your entire life as this Captain Martel, Alisha? His size, his power, his handsome face, even his bold and demanding manner are all very different from any man you have known in your past.* "No!" She cried aloud to the empty room in denial.

A knock sounded on the door of the cabin at that moment and scattered Alisha's tormenting thoughts. Looking about fearfully, she dashed for the bed and pulled the sheet under her chin as she sat down on the side of the mattress. "Who is it?"

"It be me, mam, Will be me name."

"What do you want?" Alisha remembered the Captain's words last night about his lusty crew and she wished reverently that he would just go away.

"The Cap'n sent me, mam, with a tray fur ye."

"Oh." Alisha recovered somewhat from the terror that had taken hold of her.

"Should I be bringing it in, mam?" Will was unsure how to go about this job of serving a lady the midday meal in his Captain's cabin.

"Just a minute," Alisha called. Pulling her naked legs beneath the sheet, she made sure that little was showing but her face. "Yes, you may bring in the tray." Though she was embarrassed and still a bit terrified of the man who was to come through the door, she forced herself to set her chin firmly and behave like a lady.

The small-framed man who entered through the cabin door with a covered tray in his hand looked toward the bed and at Alisha with large, dark eyes.

Looking at the man, Alisha's fear lessened. He was nothing like the brutal crewman she would have expected. He was small and dressed in baggy seaman's clothes, his face childish with a gentle smile on his lips. "You can set the tray on the desk or that small table," she said and nodded toward the other side of the cabin.

She was indeed a beauty, Will thought as his eyes went over her lovely face and hair. "Yes, mam." He hurried to do as she said and after placing the tray, he turned to her once more. "It was me, mam, that sighted ye from the rigging and got word to the Cap'n."

"Then I wish to thank you, Will, for surely if not for you I would have perished." Alisha gave him a generous smile that made the little man blush from the roots of his dark brown hair to the neckline of his red and white striped shirt.

"It were me pleasure, mam." Will started to the door. Turning back toward her one last time, he added, "I be right glad the Cap'n didn't let the crew have ye like they wanted, mam."

Alisha stared after his retreating back and gasped aloud at his statement. *The crew had wanted her!* "My God!" she whispered aloud. What kind of horrible ship was she on? Now she knew the meaning of his words, when the Captain had warned she would pay dearly if she left his cabin!

Swallowing the large lump in her throat, she slowly rose from the bed. Had the Captain fought his crew over her? She could not imagine anyone challenging such a large man as Justin Martel, but his entire crew of men were surely impossible odds to stand up against.

Sitting down on the soft leather chair behind the desk, she uncovered the tray. She had not eaten in over a day and felt the full depth of her hunger at this moment. Her eyes lit up when she saw a small loaf of bread, a wedge of cheese, an orange and a full bottle of red wine.

Perhaps she was lucky to be in the Captain's cabin after all, she told herself as she took a bite of the cheese and leaned back in the chair. Though Justin Martel had not acted in the manner of gentlemen she had known, at least she had only him to contend with and not his entire crew. Pouring a glass of wine she drank the sweet liquid thirstily.

By the time she finished half the loaf and a portion of the cheese, she poured herself another glass of wine and peeling the orange with the small knife on the tray, she began to make some decisions.

When the Captain returned to his cabin, she would calmly discuss her situation. She would thank him for rescuing her and keeping his crew at a distance. Yes, she would be polite and appreciative of all he had done for her, she told herself as she finished the orange and sipped at another glass of wine. She would also promise him payment for taking her to Virginia. Surely with the promise of gold coins he would realize she was to be treated with courtesy and respect.

Finding herself relaxed after the meal and knowing that much of her fear had been soothed with the help of the wine that sent a warm lassitude throughout her body, she slowly savored the contents of her glass as though it were the rarest nectar. She would need all the courage she could muster, she realized. Though she often drank a glass of wine at dinner or social gatherings she had never imbibed as much as she had this afternoon. She looked at the bottle and discovered it was nearly half gone.

As she went to push the bottle away from her, a thoughtful pondering furrowed her brow. What did it matter, if the wine allowed her to be better prepared to face the Captain of the *Vixen*? Who else would ever know of her indiscretion? Once off this ship she would never again set eyes on Justin Martel or any of his crew. With this thought she silently refilled her glass.

The sun had set into a tranquil sea and a soft twilight slowly captured the day when Justin Martel left the running of the *Vixen* to his first mate and went to retire to his cabin.

All day Justin's mind had been consumed with the beautiful woman who had suddenly appeared in his life. Opening the cabin door, his gaze first went to the bed, as he expected to find Alisha wrapped in the scarlet sheet. Slowly his eyes swept the room and settled upon the vision of loveliness sitting in the chair near his desk.

She was wearing one of his white satin shirts, her long titian hair lying over her shoulders and lending her an air of a temptress. His daydreams did not do justice to the woman before him now. Gently he shut the door and drew further into the cabin.

Hearing the soft closing of the door, Alisha looked up, her silver-blue eyes resting on the Captain who did not seem as fierce and menacing as he had the night before. A soft, welcoming smile greeted him and though she did not know it, Justin's gaze was drawn to those tender lips as he fleetingly wondered how they would taste.

"I see you have made yourself comfortable in my absence." His words were softly spoken, the usual husky tremor hidden as though he feared he would somehow frighten her out of her pleasant mood.

The copper head nodded and the smile did not waver. "I was looking for my gown." A small hiccup escaped her lips and she quickly brought her hand up over her mouth in surprise.

Looking to his desk Justin noticed the empty wine bottle and a knowing grin came over his face. "So you were looking for your gown and thought to find it in my sea chest?" He drew still closer to her.

Alisha forced herself to remain calm. She was grateful for the wine that lessened the fear that she had felt the night before in this man's presence. Indeed she was at this moment feeling very relaxed, but as she felt the warming gaze of those golden eyes she felt herself beginning to tremble inwardly. *This*

Captain of the Vixen is but another man. Her mind aided her to bolster her courage. *Had she not flirted and bewitched men for the last few years? What difference that this man was larger and more handsome than the rest?* "Yes, I thought my gown was in the chest," she admitted. "But not finding it there, I borrowed one of your shirts." She felt no embarrassment at the moment over wearing the Captain's shirt. In fact, she rather delighted in the freedom that the soft material allowed. "I also used your hair brush," she confessed as she watched him stepping closer and closer.

What could he have expected, he asked himself. She had nothing of her own. Had he truly believed that she would sit on his bed the whole day through with the sheet drawn about her? What woman in need of a brush and clothing would not have done the same? "Feel free while aboard the *Vixen* to use whatever you need in my cabin." He went to the washstand, and as he stepped past her, his gaze swept over her entire form, lingering on the shapely beauty of her long, slim legs as she sat with one knee crossed over the other. "You don't mind if I wash? Our dinner should be brought in shortly." He began to unbutton his shirt even before she gave her response.

"Of course not, feel free." This was going better than she had anticipated. The captain was acting the part of a gentleman and would listen with reason after he was comfortable. Perhaps she could convince him to at least sleep with his men at night. She admitted to herself that his presence would truly not be too disagreeable during the daylight hours. As he pulled off his shirt and she had a clear view of his upper body, her eyes roamed at their leisure and lingered at each curve and on his muscles flexed with contained power. He was indeed more man than she had ever seen. Again her dream wavered before her eyes, but she did not force it from her mind as she had earlier. Instead she imagined the feeling of all that strength wrapped about her. The feel of that bronzed skin beneath her fingertips; and how it would feel to lightly touch those sensual lips. She felt heady, almost light-headed with these thoughts and had to force herself to get a grip on her emotions. It must be the wine, she told herself, for never had she allowed herself such fanciful thoughts.

She could not pull her eyes away, even while knowing she should. As he began to unbraid his hair she marveled at the thick, sun-bleached strands. Before stepping around her and picking up the brush she had used earlier, he pulled on a fresh, white shirt. Seeming to pay her little heed, he ran the brush through his hair and tied it back at the nape of his neck with a small piece of leather. Finished at last with his toilet, he turned toward her, catching a glimpse of warmth within her dove-gray eyes.

"I hope the midday meal was not too unfavorable. I'm sure that the fare aboard the *Vixen* is not what you're used to." He spoke as he went around his desk and placed the empty wine bottle on the tray that had not been retrieved after she had finished her lunch.

His actions brought a light, guilty flush to Alisha's cheeks for having consumed the entire contents of the bottle, but her present state of mind reasoned that there had been little else for her to do shut up in this cabin. Feeling somewhat entitled to her indiscretion,

74

she responded truthfully. "On the contrary, Captain, the meal was very welcome. I fear I was quite famished after my ordeal."

"Call me Justin, Alisha. I have hopes we can become friends. After all, we shall be sharing these quarters for the next few days while you're aboard the *Vixen*, and . . ."

There was a knock upon the door that brought a halt to his words and an angry scowl. He would have also added that they were both adults and perhaps they could seek whatever pleasure they were afforded since the hand of fate had brought them together. But as Will brought in the dinner trays, his thoughts took a different turn. Perhaps he was being a bit hasty. It appeared that the wine and her day alone in the cabin had mellowed her somewhat toward him. The matter might be better broached after sharing a meal.

Alisha also was disappointed at the interruption. She would have taken the moment to explain her wish to repay him for his rescue and for taking her to the colonies. She would have also requested that he allow her to pay him for the use of his cabin and to drive home the point that it was not seemly for the two of them to share his bed.

Will set about placing the two trays upon the desk, his dark eyes dashing quickly to Alisha and taking in her rare comeliness as he inquired of his Captain if there was anything more he would be needing.

Justin noted the appreciation in the little man's eyes as they roamed over Alisha and he wondered if it were the wine that made her appear unconcerned with her state of near undress in the presence of his crewman or if she was used to men looking at her naked legs? His distrust for women led him to believe the latter.

Alisha hardly noticed the little man as he rushed about the cabin. She was trying to remember all she had thought over during the day that she wanted to tell the Captain. It was rather difficult for her to concentrate while the Captain was so near and those tawny eyes regarded her so forcefully. Her mind did not seem as sharp as usual, and in fact she felt rather tired, a bit too relaxed. She hoped that the Captain would not linger too long in the cabin after dinner, even though she had to admit he was rather pleasing to look upon.

Justin told Will in a cool tone that he would be needing nothing else and when Will left the cabin, the Captain directed his full stare upon Alisha for an additional minute. She seemed unconcerned by what was taking place around her as she curled her legs beneath herself in the chair. A sigh escaped him and he forced himself to cool his stirring temper. "I hope you're hungry, Alisha, for there is plenty here on the trays." Why should it matter to him if the woman allowed other men to look at that golden flesh? When he dropped her off at the colonies he would forget her soon enough.

Alisha nodded but did not make the effort to move her chair around to face the desk to enable herself to join him. Waiting only a minute longer, Justin stepped from behind his desk and took it upon himself to assist her.

Bending over her as he placed both strong arms on the chair he proceeded to move it into place. Alisha was instantly assailed by the clean scent of soap and cologne. "You smell good," she murmured without thinking as she felt his warm breath on the side of her face.

Justin did not put the chair into position and leave her side. Instead he drew closer; his lips lightly touching her fragile jawline and so slowly stealing a tender path down the slim column of her slender throat.

Alisha sat mesmerized within the hazy illusion of his tender assault. The potent wine had dulled her reactions. She was unsure if this were reality or if she were caught up in her passionate dreams.

Slowly, Justin warned himself. Go slowly. They had the rest of the night ahead of them and she seemed willing enough for his advances. There was still dinner to eat and he had had little sustenance the day through. Pulling himself away from the tempting sweetness of her flesh, he went back around the desk. "I think you'll be better able to eat now." He sat down and began to set out silverware and plates.

Alisha was stunned as he left her side as though nothing unusual had happened and took his place behind the desk. Had she in fact been caught up in a dream spell cast by her imagination? Had he not been kissing her only seconds before? Had she not felt the warmth of his tender lips and the light brush of his soft beard along her throat? She looked at him as though expecting some word that would confirm what had just taken place. His sparkling, liquid eyes turned to a deep shade of topaz. Slowly she shook her head trying to clear her thoughts.

Filling his glass with wine, Justin looked at Alisha and as she did not speak but instead sat there looking at him with those incredulous slate-blue eyes, he filled her glass as well.

Trying to pull herself together, Alisha looked from the Captain to the plate before her. He had been right earlier when he had stated that the food aboard the *Vixen* was not what she was used to. It was more appealing to rough seamen, she thought, as she looked down at the plate containing potato chowder and a thick slice of bread. Her appetite had fled due to the turmoil. With little thought to the consequences of her actions, she reached for the glass of wine. Perhaps she needed a bit more of the heady liquor to bolster herself and regain a calmness over her shattered wits.

For a second Justin thought to give her warning to have a care, but instantly thought better of it. She was in a most amiable mood, due no doubt to the bottle of wine she had already consumed. Why should he restrain her? As far as he knew she had learned these drinking traits from the numerous men in her past.

Alisha had no notion of his thoughts as her eyes kept going to his firm, full lips as he ate his food.

"Are you not hungry, Alisha?" The husky tremor of his voice seemed to wrap about her and set her pulses rising.

"I . . . I thought we could talk," she stuttered softly and as his golden gaze held her. She seemed at a loss as to what else she should say. All her plans that day about approaching the Captain with her wish to pay for her passage and her desire for privacy had vanished from her mind without a trace.

"Perhaps we should make ourselves more comfortable then." Justin pushed away his half empty plate and gave her his full attention. Usually he did not pursue women to this degree. They usually availed themselves willingly enough from the beginning. But as she sat very appealingly at that moment across from him with her wide eyes looking at him and her bronzed curls lying free about her shoulders, he knew his effort would be a small price to pay. As she appeared not to object to his suggestions to make themselves more comfortable, he circled the desk and taking her hand he led her toward the bed.

Alisha felt as though her mind was numb. She could not speak, could not even turn her head in refusal as he drew her to the large, silk-draped bed.

"Since there's no sofa in my cabin, I think this will offer more comfort." He sat down on the edge of the mattress and, still holding her hand, pulled her down beside him.

Alisha was warned by a small voice in a corner of her mind: *this was not going as she had planned. This bed was one of the subjects she had wished to discuss with him.* But what was it she had wanted to say, she wondered as her heart began to beat swiftly and tingling heat suffused her body as she could not pull her gaze from his.

"What was it you wished to say, lovely Alisha?" He boldly reached out and lightly caressed the creamy flesh of her cheek, his hand brushing against the fine strands of hair that lay over her shoulder.

Alisha was paralyzed. She could not answer, nor could she push away the hand that was so tenderly touching her as no other had. *You should run! You should rebuke him!* The warning sounded again but she was powerless.

His hand brushed against the outline of her lips and made a slow, tantalizing path through her hair and drew her head toward him. Alisha was spellbound as she saw his sensual lips descend to her.

The touch of his mouth upon hers was magically soft, but slowly it grew more intense as he pressed fully against her. His hand wrapped around her head as the other eased her body tightly against his own.

The pressure of the kiss increased, his tongue traced her lips and without a will her mouth opened to oblige him.

Her taste was like the sweetest ambrosia. He sought out every hidden inch of the inviting crevice; his tongue swirled seductively around her, setting his blood on fire. "If it's the others you wish to speak to me of, there is no need," he whispered against her mouth as he drew his lips along her cheek and down to her jawbone. "Only this moment aboard the *Vixen* is of importance." As his lips sought the sweet flesh of her neck, he believed his own words. Only this woman in his arms right now mattered. Her beauty had entrapped him and left him thinking of nothing else from the first moment he had set eyes upon her. Her soft, tempting body stoked his desire until he was maddened with thoughts of possessing her.

His words made no sense in Alisha's befogged mind. She could not concentrate, she could only feel. His heated breath sent chills coursing over her entire body; his lips made a searing path from her chin to the small button on the white shirt above her breasts. She was mindless to do anything but feel every incredible minute.

"Alisha." The name caressed her in a breathless

spiral of passion, and with a slight movement the button slipped away from its holding.

No man had ever dared as much as this bold sea Captain, but Alisha did not push him away and reclaim her modest demeanor. Her every limb felt soft and pliable within his large arms. Her body trembled at his daring as her heart beat so rapidly in her breasts she thought she would swoon. As his lips lowered and he pulled away the shirt, his mouth plied her with kisses. She was lost in a whirling unreality.

With his head bent over her, Justin eased her back somewhat on the bed and then his tongue circled a rose tip crest on her breast and he heard a soft moan of passion coming from her lips. For a moment he satisfied himself with this loving play, his tongue leaving a damp path from one ripe peak to the other, and then he gently drew in a tempting nipple and slowly began to suckle.

This was beyond anything Alisha had ever felt. Her hands entwined in the long strands of his hair as though she feared she were about to tumble into a dark abyss. She felt steaming, molten fire starting from her breasts and cascading through every portion of her body, centering in the pit of her belly and causing an ache in her womanhood that left her throbbing with a need she had never known. Perhaps she was dying, she thought dimly, as Justin went to the other breast and set off the reaction even more fiercely. Could death be this all-consuming?

She had little more time to ponder her theory as Justin left her breasts and rose up to her lips once again. His kiss this time full and devouring. His tongue delved deeply and demanded a response.

Without will, slowly her lips complied. Her tongue touched his and was drawn into his mouth and tenderly he sucked it more fully into his warm, moist depths. This action sent her into deeper rapture. Everything he did, every touch he bestowed, kept her mindlessly aware of the new and powerful feelings storming throughout her body.

"You are so beautiful. Your skin is so soft and your taste so sweet." He tenderly nibbled at her neck and then his kisses showered her breasts. Lingering only a moment over the tender mounds, his lips went lower, raining kisses upon the delicate under flesh of her breasts and then languorously roamed over her ribs and across her belly and paused for a moment over the tiny indent.

His titillating seduction of her body left Alisha gasping, her hands clutching tightly to the scarlet sheets at her sides. His lips seared her with a consuming, branding fire and she was too caught up in the passionate web that he had cast about her to break away. It was no wonder mothers warned their daughters to keep themselves until their wedding night. These fires of passion could leap wildly out of control. As Alisha writhed under his thrilling assault, she knew she was completely out of control.

His heated lips scorched a trail over her rounded hips and as his hand boldly touched the crest of her womanhood, sparkling sensations shot through her body. His touch was so intensely earth shattering as he made contact with the nub of her very foundation, that Alisha clamped her teeth tightly together to keep from crying aloud.

With the moist, heated contact of his lips, a cry broke through the quiet of the cabin, torn from Alisha's mouth as she rose and clutched the long strands of hair in her fists. What was he doing to her? She was on fire. She was a cauldron of hot, trembling desire. She had not the strength to pull him away, she could only ride out the incredible journey, her mind void of all but the rippling waves of pulsating passion-induced shudders that filled her body and erupted into volcanic proportions.

Justin rose up, his hair free from its binding, his eyes a rich, golden brilliance and within seconds his shirt and breeches lay upon the floor at the side of the bed and as he bent over Alisha, warm, passion-laced amethyst eyes stared back at him; she inhaled raggedly, trying to recapture her breath. She was truly the most beautiful woman he had ever seen, he told himself, and surely the most passionate. Bending his head downward, he recaptured her honey-sweet lips. What man could resist such a woman?

Alisha had heard numerous stories from friends and Estelle about the pleasure to be received upon the marriage bed, but never could she have imagined such incredible rapture. Her wine- and passion-soddened thoughts fled as his mouth reclaimed hers and she was swept to the dazzling heights of desire.

His massive body was atop her, his golden mane hanging over them like a curtain of privacy. His hand roamed seductively over her body, lingering at her womanhood for a time and evoking a heated response as Alisha's body pushed against his probing fingers. Slowly he eased her thighs apart and his body poised atop her as his large, pulsing length brushed against her velvet warmth.

Alisha knew what he was about to do; she was naive only in having never allowed a man such liberty. The daring side of her nature was caught up too far in the moment for her to pull away. She felt the heated tip of his manhood touching her and easing into her tightness. A gasp of surprised pain escaped her lips as he pushed through the slim barrier of her maidenhead; her hands grabbed the firm flesh of his sides, her nails raking into his skin as the piercing pain chased away the earlier pleasure.

Justin stilled atop her as he felt the tightness of her virginity tear open. A virgin! His mind called out in warning, but it was far too late. She had been untouched! He was the first man ever to have lain with her! How could this be? He looked down into her wounded features in confusion. How the hell could he have not known? He had been so sure she had known other men!

As quickly as the pain had stolen through her body, it began to dull and Alisha moved her hips somewhat to adjust herself to her position beneath him. She had heard there was pain at first, she reminded herself, and the bolder portion of her personality questioned as she looked into his handsome face above her, *why not sample what more awaited her? After all, it was far too late to undo what was already done.*

With her slight movement, Justin's breath caught and his passions were inflamed to unbearable heights. There was no help for it now; he was ensnared by the feel of her enticing body and as his lips lowered to hers he moved deeper into her. He rained kisses over her eye lids and down along her cheek and over the softness of her throat. What was done was done. If he had known she was untried he would have kept a safe distance. He would have given her his first mate's cabin, taken her to her destination and been done with her. But now, the warning bells which rang sharply in his head that virgins were trouble sounded far too late. He could not stop, could not pull away.

Alisha's response as she pressed toward him and her hands eased their grip at his sides and traced a tempting path over the breadth of his muscled back, furthered his wild desire to fulfill his body's need for release; but he cautioned himself to have a care. Gently he moved his length in and out of her warm depths, holding himself back to keep from harming her unnecessarily.

All of the earlier pain had fled and in its place a pulsing filled her, sending rapturous delight stirring within her core as he moved in and out. Slowly her body began to undulate, her hips rising with his and keeping a steady movement that was breathtakingly pleasurable. From deep within her being a small spark was ignited and slowly grew into a towering blaze that skyrocketed and burst throughout every portion of her being. Her hands clutched tightly to his back, her legs rising about his hips to receive all of him and to taste the full depth of this unbelievable feeling. Her eyes enlarged and moans of passion escaped her lips as wave after wave of ecstasy's pleasure shuddered over her.

Justin was caught up in her passion as he looked down into her beautiful face and as her body shuddered and stirred beneath him, he was lost to all but the forceful raging within his own depths that drove him onward. He thought not of caution or gentleness as her legs rising above his hips tempted him beyond endurance and he sampled all that she possessed. With a deep, pleasurable moan, he was held for a timeless instant upon the brink of a towering climax. Another plunge and wildfire shot through his loins, leaving him shuddering uncontrollably. Clutching her tightly to him, he rode out the crest of his passion.

For a moment he lay still upon her. With disbelief he reviewed the beauty of the last few minutes. This woman was beyond belief! Never had he shared such glorious rapture. She filled his every need, his every desire. As he pulled up on his elbow and stretched out beside her, a portion of the hard, cold wall he had built around his heart softened.

A soft, exhausted sigh escaped Alisha. Her mind and body felt happily burdened and content with the Captain tightly pressed against her. She was too tired to question the new feelings she had experienced; too tired to question what she had done and what she had allowed him to do. For now she desired only sleep.

Justin would have apologized to Alisha for not realizing he was the first man she had known. He felt he had taken advantage of her and would have gently told her something of himself and that it was impossible for him to form an attachment to any woman at this time. There was something about her that touched him deeply where no other had been able to for the past four years. But as he turned and looked into her face, he saw that her eyes were tightly shut and her breathing was steady and deep. Perhaps tomorrow he would be better able to speak to her of all that he wished to share. He reached down and drew the sheet over them and, wrapping his arm about her slender body, he drew her near and shut his eyes.

Chapter Six

Even before opening his eyes to the new day, Justin savored the feel of the soft form tightly held in his arms and molded against his body. He inhaled the sweet, womanly scent of her hair and swiftly the memory of the night filled his mind, causing his blood to race hotly in his loins. Fate had never looked so favorably upon him, he reflected, as he thought of the days that were left before they would reach the colonies. Last night was but a prelude to the many hours they would spend on this silk-draped bed. For a moment his thoughts took him to his discovery that he had been the first, and again he regretted his hasty assumption that she had had prior experience with men. He would make it up to her, he told himself. Perhaps he would even go to Yorktown and seek her out after this war between England and the American patriots was at an end. He realized now that there was no husband awaiting her in Virginia, nor perhaps was there any gentleman of particular interest. She could very well have been on her way to her family when she was washed overboard and set adrift. A portion of his heart wanted to believe this, for deep down he wanted to be able to trust again.

Awakening to the feeling of being entrapped by something strong and unyielding, Alisha opened her eyes to find herself surrounded by Justin Martel's large body, his powerful arms wrapped about her. Instantly the dream that she had so fiercely fought off all day yesterday came to her mind. But this was no dream: She could feel his heart beating against her breasts, she could even feel his warm breath in her hair as her head snuggled against his shoulder and her cheek pressed against his neck. This was real: Terror the likes of which she had never known took a firm grip upon her and in desperation she pulled herself out of his arms and away from the heat of his large, naked body. "What are you doing?" she gasped, fighting for a portion of the sheet as she discovered she had no clothing.

Golden lion's eyes looked at her and in a tender tone, Justin said calmly, "Holding you until you awoke." He had truly hoped for a more pleasant morning greeting, but he quickly remembered that awakening next to a man was something entirely new to Alisha. But he would soon teach her that the morning hours in bed could be just as rewarding as the night.

"How dare you?" Alisha demanded, thinking he had deliberately waited until she slept to force himself on her. "Where is my shirt?" Her cool, silver-blue eyes held chips of sparkling ice as she glared at him.

Justin was a bit confused. She was not acting at all

as he had expected; she was furious at him. What had happened to the woman he had shared such passion with and held throughout the night? "Your shirt, or my shirt, Alisha, is over there on the floor, where it was discarded last night after we came to bed." She was treating him as though he were the worst sort of villain.

Something in his manner, or perhaps in the way he said the words, "after we came to bed," or the sight of that magnificent body as he wrapped an end of the sheet about his midsection and sat up against the headboard, brought fleeting images. She saw them wrapped in each other's arms, lost to all but a consuming passion. Slowly, bit by bit, everything that had happened the previous night came to her. Her eyes widened, her face paled and knowing that her prayers were wasted she still prayed that it had all been just another dream. Looking at him at this moment, though, she knew it had been real. She could even recall her own cries of passion, her own wanton behavior as she had kissed those full, sensual lips and cried aloud with pleasure as she touched that bronzed, hard flesh. Hot fire touched her cheeks and burned brightly down her throat to the tips of her breasts. "What have you done to me?" she whispered.

Watching her closely, Justin saw her anger turn to puzzlement and then in turn to realization and shock. She had not at first remembered what they had shared, he thought with a touch of humor mixed with disbelief that anyone could have forgotten the incredible ecstasy. Perhaps she had been a bit more taken with the wine than he had thought. As her accusations reached his ears, he felt a small spark of anger. Did she intend to blame him for everything that had happened? For if so, he would remind her how she had readily enough submitted to each of his advances. "I did no more than you desired, Madam." His tone was harder than it had been earlier as he defended what had taken place.

"What I desired?" Alisha's voice rose higher. "I did not know . . . I was . . . I was . . ." She could not even form the words to explain her behavior.

"Are you wishing to use the excuse that you were drunk, Madam?" His eyes were now as cold as hers as all the tenderness he had felt slowly began to slip away. He had thought this woman different, and now he felt betrayed.

"Yes!" Alisha shouted as she clung to this excuse and pulled the sheet from his lap and wrapped it about herself. Averting her eyes from his naked form, she hurried to the side of the bed to get the shirt she had worn the day before and to put as much distance between them as possible. Not daring to look back toward the bed, she quickly went to the other side of the cabin. Keeping her back to him and the sheet over her as best she could, she slipped her arms into the sleeves of the shirt.

Knowing that the morning was ruined, Justin also rose from the bed; taking his time, he strode naked to his sea chest and pulled out a pair of breeches and a shirt. "I would have you know, Alisha, you were not so besotted with wine that you could not have told me nay. You were very willing when I first kissed you, when I touched you. I did not have to force you to submit to me."

Alisha turned quickly to shout her denial, but as

her eyes took in his towering, naked form boldly standing next to the sea chest, she turned back around. "I was drunk and you took advantage of me. I did not know what would happen. I thought . . ." She would have said she thought herself caught up in a dream, but then she would have had to admit she had been dreaming about the very thing they had done. "You are no more than a knave! A beast! A brutal blackguard!" Her fury was running dangerously high as she called him every foul name she could think of. Hearing him finish dressing and splash water on his face, she at last turned to face him. "I regret the day your ship ever sighted me. I would have preferred to perish at sea than be rescued by you! You're the most unsavory man I've ever had the misfortune to meet!"

Justin had heard enough; spinning on a heel, his eyes met hers. "I also now regret that day when the *Vixen* came upon you, Madam. You are no more than a spoiled, unreasonable child; and to think that for a time I thought you a warm, desirable woman."

"And you're no more than a rapist!" Alisha shouted back in her fit of temper and stomped her foot. She would have liked nothing better than to leap upon him and scratch that too-handsome face to pieces; but with the fear that coming within reach would again allow him to take hold of her, she restrained the impulse.

For a full minute Justin did not speak but glared across the cabin at her. Her cheeks were bright pink and her shimmering eyes sparkled with a glow, her hair wildly in disarray about her shoulders and down her back. Even with his anger now raging, he had to admire her beauty. "It was not rape, Madam, that brought you to my bed last night. Nor was it rape that brought about your cries of passion and the shudders of pleasure that I felt when you discovered the full depths of being a woman at my hands. Nay, what took place upon that bed last night could never be called rape! You were more than willing to have an end to that precious jewel you women value so highly!" He did not await her response, but instead stomped angrily to the cabin door.

With the truth of his words tormenting her very soul, Alisha grabbed hold of the nearest thing and threw it as hard as she could toward him, hoping that somehow she could hurt him as his words had hurt her.

The book hit the portal above his head, and as he continued through the open door, his deep, masculine laughter filled her ears in mocking torment.

"Oh you . . . you . . . demon from hell!" she shouted as he slammed the door.

Left with nothing to vent her fury upon but the cabin, Alisha turned back to the desk and without a thought she swept ledgers, charts and maps to the floor in a heap. How dare he treat her in such a highhanded manner, she fumed, stomping about the empty cabin. He had abused her and violated her. Forcing her to stay in this cabin and to lie in his hellish red bed! She stood before that great monstrosity and with a hate-filled glare, began to attack it with a wrathful vengeance. Slinging the pillows to the floor, she grabbed hold of the sheets, their vibrant color seeming to burn fiercely in her heart as she threw them to the floor and kicked them out of her way. Even the silk drapings were not safe from her onslaught. One by one she tore them from their holdings at the top of the canopy, and with that finished, she took a deep breath. Her chest was heaving with exertion, as her glittering eyes burned and darted about to find something else to vent her wrath upon.

Finding nothing in her path, she surveyed her handiwork and felt only mildly relieved. She was still enraged. If she ever calmed down she knew she would have to face the reality of the truth of his words. She had wantonly given herself to the Captain of the *Vixen*.

As the remembrance of his warm, golden eyes filled her mind, she could easily have allowed herself a moment to dwell upon the handsome sea Captain. Instead she forced herself to move about the cabin, seeking something to occupy her thoughts. Noticing the sea chest, she pulled back the lid to retrieve another shirt, this time feeling no guilt or worry over Justin Martel's reaction. After removing a shirt much like the one she was wearing, on impulse she pulled out more of his clothes and threw them in a heap upon the floor. Anything that belonged to the Captain of the *Vixen* at this moment was a target for her wrath.

Going to the cabin door, she firmly locked it. She should have thought to take such steps yesterday afternoon before he had returned to his cabin and taken advantage of her intoxicated state, she told herself belatedly. At the washstand she yanked off the shirt she was wearing and slung it with the rest of the debris upon the floor. Picking up the rough sponge, she lathered it with the soap lying on the washstand

and without sparing a single portion of her flesh, she scrubbed until her golden-tanned body glowed with a bright pink hue. She attacked her face, neck, breasts, legs and arms to wipe away all evidence that Justin Martel had ever touched her, had ever held her so tenderly and kissed every part of her body.

Pulling on the fresh shirt, she looked around at the mess on the floor for the hair brush she had knocked aside earlier. With hard, demanding strokes she calmed the wild disorder of her brass-colored curls. Her toilet complete she began to pace about the cabin once again, not allowing time to settle her thoughts; for if she did, she knew she would be troubled by the fact that she had given herself to a man whom she knew little about, a man she now believed she disliked intensely. He was heartless, she told herself. He had deliberately taken advantage of her, awaiting the most vulnerable moment to seduce her! Alisha's anger and denial over her own part in her deflowering kept her from becoming a whimpering mass of regret.

A knock sounded upon the outside door, and swinging around Alisha stood as though ready to defend herself from Justin Martel or anyone else who would dare to come through that portal. "What do you want?" she demanded, holding little fear of retribution. What more could anyone do to her?

"It be me, Mam, Will. I be bringing ye a tray." The little man could discern her cool tone through the door.

"Go away!" she shouted back.

"But, Mam, the Cap'n thought ye might be hungry." Will wondered what had taken place between the woman and his Captain. Captain Fox had been in a dark mood from the moment he had come on deck this morning; and now the woman was acting strangely, too.

"Your Captain can go straight to hell, for all I care! I want nothing from him!"

"Yes, Mam," Will murmured as a frown crossed his usually happy-go-lucky face. Cap'n Fox wouldn't be liking this none at all when he reported that the woman sent him away without taking the tray. If there was one thing he knew about the Fox, it was that he didn't take kindly to being disputed. As he left the companionway, he hoped Captain Fox wouldn't be too hard on her. A beauty like her should be treated with kindness, no matter what happened between them.

Alisha kicked out at the pile of clothes near the sea chest as she heard the little man's steps lead away from the cabin door. Who did this Captain Justin Martel think she was? Some shallow-minded twit? A woman he could ravish, say all manner of cruel things to and then calmly offer her a breakfast tray? Her anger was full blown now as she stormed about. How dare he! . . . How dare he! In her mind he was the worst kind of miscreant, the most dishonorable man she had ever met. Her indignation knew no bounds—she felt like screaming the walls of the cabin down and lashing out at anything around her.

With her emotions at last spent, she slumped in the chair near the desk, two bright spots of crimson staining her cheeks and her small fists clutched tightly together. With her last bit of strength she pounded the arms of the chair. How could she have ever allowed herself to be such a fool? And with this question, for the first time she was forced to acknowledge her own actions. It was the fault of that ridiculous dream! That was the reason she had drunk so much from the wine bottle and had been dull-witted enough to allow that pirate to take such liberties. Liberties, ha! He had stolen her virginity! *Thievery is a very strong charge, Alisha,* she thought to herself. *Do you not think you would have fought against such a crime even in your relaxed state?*

Perhaps he used a gentle nature to do his misdeed, but it was thievery just the same! She fought to keep her anger directed at Justin. What he took was hers to give to the man she loved, the one she would one day marry! *But he did not take it, you gave it freely to him. Remember your cries of passion while lying beneath him on that silk-draped bed? Remember the heat of his lips? The fire of his touch? Your own body opening to receive him?*

"Nooooo," Alisha cried aloud and her hands grabbed both sides of her head tightly as she tried to force these thoughts from her mind. She wanted to remember none of that. But she could not force the vivid remembrance from her thoughts, as she recalled to mind the incredible feelings he had awakened in her.

Throughout the remainder of the day, Alisha had bouts of rage and then periods of quiet distress as she fought an inner war with her own emotions. She wanted to forget that passionate side of her nature she had discovered last night; she wanted to keep a slim hold on the fantasy that she had been the helpless victim, blaming Justin Martel totally for what had taken place.

The wild, hard-to-control side of her conscience raged a relentless battle reminding her that, *she had only to tell him no. She could have fought him; she could have said something that would have kept him at a distance. She also was to blame.* Forcing the hurt and anger to remain in her heart, she had to curse that bold and dashing rogue of a ship's Captain; for if not, she would believe herself little better than the garishly over-painted women of little repute she had always thought of as contemptible. Mistresses, women of the streets and abundantly endowed tavern maids who gave their favors to any man. She was not like any of them; she protected herself with the thought that it had not been her fault.

It was late in the afternoon when Justin finally made his way back to the cabin, his mood still not improved from the morning with Will's reports that Alisha had not allowed him into the cabin with her meals. He had hoped by this time she would have cooled off and he would be able to talk sensibly to her, but as he tried the knob on the door and found it locked, he knew her anger had not abated. Boldly he knocked upon the door. "Alisha, enough of this foolishness! Open the door!" He fought to keep a grip on his temper as he realized he had been locked out of his own cabin.

"Go away!" Alisha shouted as she recognized the deep voice of the one who had brought her so much misery. "Go somewhere else and leave me in peace!" Alisha was not about to open the door. He could very well find some other quarters aboard this ship.

He had had enough! If this woman thought she

could keep him out of his cabin or any other place he desired to go aboard the *Vixen*, she would soon enough learn that she was mistaken. Bracing his powerful shoulder against the door, he pushed hard. The lock gave, slamming the door inward.

Alisha stood wide-eyed in the center of the cabin amidst all the clutter of her morning's destruction. "Get out!" she screamed. "How dare you intrude upon my privacy!"

Justin could not believe his eyes as he stepped into the cabin. It appeared as though every one of his possessions was scattered about the floor and in the middle of this great calamity, Alisha stood defiantly before him. Her silver-blue eyes piercingly brilliant, her cheeks enflamed and her stance proud and unyielding. "Your privacy, Madam? Do you not mean my cabin? Let me warn you now, Alisha, I will dare what I please! Lock that door against me again, and I will have it removed." In truth Justin knew he would not take such a strong action. She was much too tempting a prize to put on display for his men. He would rather not have to kill or maim a member of his crew over a woman. But at this moment he used a strong enough threat to keep from having to break into his own quarters every time he wanted entry.

"You are despicable!" Alisha seethed aloud, but the threat of his removing the cabin door and thus allowing his crew to look within the room had the desired effect. She would not lock the door again. This large man was enough to have to contend with. Putting on a brave front, she shot back at him. "What does it matter if you remove the door and your crew are able to enter this cabin? What more could any one of them do to me than you have already made me suffer?''

She was being totally unreasonable, Justin realized and his mood grew darker by the second. She was not about to admit what had truly taken place last evening. She wanted to blame him and nothing he could say at the moment would change her mind. "I will say again, Alisha, that you were as willing as I. You can play the part of injured maiden as long as you like, but if you think your game will entrap me in any fashion, you'll find out you're mistaken. I'm not the man a young woman would care to take as husband." Justin thought to warn her now that if this was her ploy it would not work. He had no intentions of marrying any woman, let alone being trapped into a state of wedlock by tears, anger, or pleas.

Alisha looked horror stricken. Did this man truly think she had actually considered the thought of wedding him? He must be totally insane, she thought. Raising her chin proudly, she looked directly at him. "You, sir, have nothing to fear in that regard. I hold no intentions of marrying any man, let alone you!"

Justin glared at her, his golden eyes dangerously bright. He should have been heartened by her words, he told himself, but her quick, adamant refusal only heightened his displeasure. Wanting now to lash back at her, he commanded in a hard tone, "Put my cabin back in order. If you cannot keep that nasty temper of yours under some control, I'll see that you're removed from this room and placed some-

101

where on deck for the rest of the voyage!" Turning, he stormed out.

Alisha fumed and kicked out at everything in her path. Who did he think he was? He was not her master! He could not order her about as though she were one of his crew! He had wronged her! She believed herself entitled to her anger and the destruction she had caused. If he wanted his cabin back as it had been, he could very well do it himself! She sat back down in the chair in a raging huff, her arms crossed beneath her breasts.

It was only a few minutes later that simple reason slowly returned. What choice did she have but to do as he had ordered? If he forced her to leave his cabin, she would be easy prey to any of his men.

With slow, halting steps, she forced herself to begin the arduous task of straightening the room. It was much easier making the chaos than it was to put it back in its original order, she thought as she bent down and began to fold his clothes and put them back into the sea chest. After arranging his desk to a semblance of how it had been before she had scattered his possessions, her eyes went to the bed. She would be damned if she would put those horrible scarlet drapes back up or touch those silk sheets! She did not care what threats he used, she refused to go that far!

Her cleaning finished, Alisha sat back in the chair, her temper cooled somewhat. As she looked about the cabin she now felt somewhat guilty over the mayhem she had inflicted upon Justin Martel's cabin, even though she had put it back to rights. He had, after all, rescued her from the sea and protected her from his crew. If only she had some time to sort out all of her conflicting thoughts. So much had happened in a course of only two days and she was beginning to feel the full strain of it all.

It was only a short time later when Will knocked lightly on the cabin door and entered with Alisha's dinner tray. "The Cap'n said ye would be hungry, Mam." He smiled toward her as he placed the tray upon the desk. "The Cap'n also told me to be bringing these." He held up a fresh set of linen sheets and quickly his gaze turned from her toward the bed and the sheets and drapes on the floor. "I just be taking these away, Mam." He gathered them into a pile and left them on the floor as he set about making the bed with the clean linens.

Alisha felt her face flush scarlet as she watched the little man make up the bed that she and Justin Martel had slept in the night before. She wished she were anywhere at this moment but in this cabin.

Turning back toward her after finishing his chores, Will smiled with genuine warmth. "Ye best eat now, Mam. The cook done made something special fur ye." Taking up the bundle from the floor, he tucked the scarlet sheets and drapes beneath his arm as he headed for the door.

"Thank you, Will," Alisha murmured softly, truly appreciating the crewman's kindness and at the same time feeling her anger rekindling over the fact that she had been put into this situation. She could only imagine what Will and every other member of the crew of the *Vixen* thought of her!

Clean sheets and a tray of food, she thought bitterly. Whatever the Captain ordered he received. She could not lock the door of the cabin and she could not vent her anger. All she was allowed to do was sit quietly and await his return.

Justin Martel stood at the rail of the *Vixen* and gazed out to sea as the darkness encroached upon the blue-green depths and a million stars appeared over head on the dark velvet backdrop of a clear night sky. His thoughts carried him back in time, to a different life when he was a different man. Alisha had somehow reminded him of another woman whom he had believed himself in love with a long time ago.

Chelsea—he allowed the name to remain in his mind without chasing it away with dark, murderous thoughts as he had done for the past four years. Chelsea Winthrop, one of the high-born Winthrops, and before he had learned the truth of her nature, Justin had believed her to be the fairest of them all. Her beauty had captured him from their first meeting at a ball given in honor of Lord Winston Elsbey. Her flashing, emerald eyes and raven hair won him over that same night and inside of a week he was more than ready to swear his undying love. It was but a half-year later they were engaged to be married; he made plans to purchase another ship to add to the merchant ship he already owned and believed she was making plans also—for their wedding day and their future together.

With their wedding date two weeks away, Justin arrived home earlier than expected from a sea voyage. He had not planned to arrive in the London ports for another week, but with thoughts of Chelsea burning in his mind, he had pushed his crew and his ship so he could spend as much time with his love as possible.

Arriving at his London town house, he noticed lights throughout the bottom portion of his home and expected to find his friend Mark Stevenson in residence. Mark had been staying at the town house while Justin was at sea.

Feminine laughter reached his ears as he climbed the stairs to his bedchamber. He thought little of this as he imagined that Mark was entertaining one of his latest conquests. It was only as he passed the open door and heard the familiarity of the female voice that he stopped in stunned disbelief.

"I've told you often enough, dear Mark, that there's no need to fret about Justin." The deceitful words of the woman he thought he loved still burned in Justin's memory as though he was hearing them for the first time. "After our marriage, I'll see that he takes plenty of voyages, and we'll be able to share many more nights such as this."

"I still don't see why you're going through with this marriage," a masculine voice, belonging to the man Justin had believed to be his friend, stated with some emotion.

"We've gone over all this before, my love. You know my reasons. My father has great hopes that Justin will add to the family coffers with the ships he owns. He would never allow us to wed and I've grown tired of living under the same roof with my father's third wife. If your love of the gaming tables were not so widely known, perhaps he would consider you a suitable husband; but alas, it's far too late for that. He has selected Justin Martel and there's nothing I can do to change his mind." Chelsea seemed to purr as Justin had never heard her do in his presence.

"We could always run away together. Your father would relent in time." And then Mark added in a rush of emotion, "You know, Chelsea, I cannot bear the thought of any other man touching you."

"Why should we run away? We'll have everything we want right here; everything will work out perfectly." Chelsea spoke sweetly with that cat-like, purring tone. "You're Justin's close friend, so no one will think much of your visits to the town house. Even Justin won't be suspicious. I promise that after the vows are spoken, I'll demand my own bed-chamber and have so many womanly maladies that Justin will soon tire of knocking upon my door and will willingly take to the sea at every opportunity."

Justin could scarcely believe his ears as sheer, torturous pain seared his heart. He began to step into the chamber and confront them, but he held himself back, knowing that he would have killed them. Instead, he turned and made his way back down the stairs, Chelsea's betrayal burning like a lance through his heart.

That very night he left London. He made a new life for himself in the Caribbean as a privateer and in time thought himself purged of any softness toward women. Alisha Whitlaw had once again made him realize he could be vulnerable if he did not keep up his guard.

If not for the fact that King George had revoked his privateer's commission, outlawing him and his crew for preying upon British ships, Justin would not

106

have been in the area to find Alisha. The accusation by the Crown had been a lie; Justin Martel held his oath dear, and would never have attacked a British ship while his allegiance was sworn to England. But with the release of his commission he and his crew were now free to join in the battle between England and the American Patriots. His plan was to see John Paul Jones near Richmond and from there he would meet Lafayette. He had never planned on rescuing Alisha Whitlaw and being reminded of the bitter memory of his past, but his thoughts of Chelsea Winthrop brought him face to face with a grim warning. Women were not to be trusted!

Justin rebuked himself as he stood there alone on deck. It had been easy over the years to maintain the wall he had built around his heart, but the woman in his cabin had softened his resolve. Alisha was like all the rest, he told himself sternly. Perhaps more beautiful and more spirited but like all other women at heart. The fact that she had been a virgin only added to his distrust. Women were a faithless lot. Alisha more than likely knew that she could never be faithful to one man and that was her reason for swearing so righteously that she would never wed!

As the hour grew late, the crew retired and the upper deck grew quiet. Justin made his way to his cabin with slow steps. He was not able to chase away his heated thoughts of the copper-haired beauty. The image of her sleeping upon his bed, her shimmering curls upon his pillows and her soft body hidden beneath the sheets played boldly in his mind.

Chapter Seven

The lantern on the desk had burned down to a dim, yellowish glow and as Justin's eyes were drawn to the bed a thankful smile played about his lips. Alisha appeared to be sleeping peacefully, her body curled and facing away from him. He would not have to endure any more of her accusations and tantrums. He also noticed that the drapes were still down and both they and the scarlet sheets were gone. Justin had never truly cared for the outlandish draperies, but he had never bothered to change them and they thus reflected the original owner of the *Vixen's* flamboyant tastes.

With quiet steps he went to the washstand and washed and combed out his long hair. Extinguishing the lantern, he shed his breeches and eased himself onto the bed next to Alisha.

She did not move in her sleep and as his eyes adjusted to the darkness, for a breathless moment Justin studied her face by the moonlight that stole through the window. Even in her sleep she was beautiful. Each feature of her face appeared perfectly outlined. As his eyes were drawn to the petal-sweet lips, he was pulled toward them like a moth to flame. In his mind he was prepared for her to lash out at him as he placed his lips gently over hers; he was not prepared for the softly yielding moan that came from deep within her throat, nor was he prepared for the feel of her body pressing against his.

In sleep, Alisha moved closer to the man in her dreams. Sleep had been hard to gain earlier that evening because of her thoughts of what she and the Captain had shared the night before on this large bed, and also because of her determination to remain awake to guard against him. But as the hours passed, exhaustion slowly claimed her and in the bonds of sleep, her mind wondered at will, paying little heed to her refusal to think about Justin Martel.

The kiss grew sweeter and fuller. Her hand reached up and entwined in his golden strands of hair and as Justin gently unbuttoned the front of her shirt and began to ply her neck and breasts with kisses, she slowly began to stir.

"No." The word sounded almost drugged, even to her own ears. Her body wanted him even if her mind denied it.

His lips rose back to hers and before she could say another word, he ravished her mouth. For a lingering minute she tried to push him away, to fight him off, her mind screaming that she did not want this, but the sweet assault of his mouth and the touch of his hands slowly melted away all reality. She was totally lost in a mindless, heady force that engulfed her. *Why not take this small interlude into paradise?* that bolder part of her questioned. *What harm is there in it, when you are in truth no longer a virgin?* Though she knew this was not right, she was powerless to resist the aching need deep within her body. As though her defenses had been broken down, she softly moaned and her slim arms drew up around his back.

Justin knew the minute her resistance waned and his heart sang as he felt her arms entwine about him. His lips brushed ardent kisses over her face, her throat, her breasts and Alisha was pulled deeper and deeper into the all-consuming feelings that only this man had awakened. Without a will of her own, she responded hungrily, her own lips feathering kisses along the side of his jaw and upon his neck, her body surging against his.

Justin was on fire, burning to possess her supple essence and quench the flames licking wildly through every part of his being. She was a strong elixir to his overwhelming desires; he could not seem to get enough of her taste, the feel of her in his arms. Not able to prolong the agony raging through him, they came together in a maelstrom of rapture.

As he filled her with a heated, pulsating fullness, Alisha cried aloud as her body welcomed his lance into her moist, quivering sheath. Her mind and body were totally consumed in the utter pleasure of the moment. There was no right or wrong, only this vast need. She was swept over the threshold in a wondrous display of swirling brilliance, his powerful strokes holding her in the clutches of an earth-shattering explosion of passion that raged through the very nucleus of her soul. She cried his name aloud without realizing it, as her body shuddered uncontrollably beneath him. Not able to prolong the mounting tide of his own scalding ecstasy, Justin was also swept up in the vortex of overwhelming passion.

For a breathless minute they clutched each other as their bodies trembled in the aftermath of their union. But as quickly as her body was sated and her mind once again under control, Alisha pulled out of his arms and away from him. "Please, just leave me be," she said in a strangled whisper. On the verge of tears, she pulled away from him and curled up as though to show her resistance to him and also to herself. How could she have been so weak? she asked herself, fighting back the tears. She had been powerless to fight him off from the moment he first touched her. There had been no defense; her own body had betrayed her!

Justin would have reached out in an attempt to soften Alisha's feelings toward him, but seeing the rigid outline of her back and remembering vividly the tirade she had unleashed upon him this morning and afternoon, he knew the effort would be wasted. She would only blame him—even for her cries of passion and the glorious fulfillment she had discovered. He rolled over and away from her, telling himself he would be glad when he delivered her to the colonies and the temptation of that beautiful body of hers would no longer be near.

The following days aboard the *Vixen* were but a constant reminder to Alisha of her own body's lustful betrayal. Each night toward the late night twilight hours Justin came to her; his touch caused her to cast aside all her planned defenses. Her body not only submitted but enjoyed fully the pleasure that his large, virile body offered. Each night after the searing finish of their coming together, Alisha would turn her back to him and lie awake until the early hours of the morning, her emotions in a turmoil. The war between her inner self and the power of his heated touch kept her in a state of constant agitation.

The few times she had seen Justin during these days when he ventured to the cabin to retrieve a map or the ship's ledger, she had been cool, not willing to allow him to know of the inner fight she had daily to fight off her attraction to him.

Her only hope throughout these days was in the knowledge that they were heading for the colonies and that this nightmare would one day end. Once she arrived in Virginia she was determined never again to see Justin Martel, or be reminded of the nights she had given herself over to her raging desire. She would devote her time to finding her father's murderers and bringing them to justice. There had to be a way to bring the killers out in the open, she thought each day as she planned her revenge.

With the knowledge that those who had killed her father were brought to justice, perhaps she would return to Martinique. Estelle and Cordell would welcome her and once she was back on the Island and with those who love her, in time she would be able to put her father's death and the events that had happened aboard the *Vixen* behind her. She might even find the man she would wish to spend the rest of her life with there on Martinique.

With little else to do, she mentally reviewed the young men she had met on the Island. The Governor's son, Jeffery SaintClair, had pursued her for the last year, sending her flowers and poetry frequently and inviting her to every event on the Island. There was also Dory Rollins and several others who had been very attentive. Surely it would not be too hard to find the right man out of this group. She had just not given the matter much thought. Even during these thoughts of the future Justin Martel's bold and dashing image intruded and he seemed to overshadow all the gentlemen she had ever known. Harshly she rebuked his image. She would one day find the right man! He would be kind and understanding, not a bit like this Captain, she vehemently told herself. The man for her would have none of the recklessly overpowering qualities of Justin Martel!

As she sat there debating with herself, the cabin door was pushed wide and the man who provoked this wild torment in her soul stepped into the cabin.

For a full minute Justin's gaze devoured Alisha. It was no wonder he could not seem to stay away from his own cabin. Her incredible beauty set her apart from all other women. Pulling his thoughts together, he started to his desk. "I've brought your dinner tray," he said, placing it on the corner nearest the chair she was sitting in.

Alisha would have much preferred Will to have brought her dinner as he usually did. Justin's presence reminded her too vividly of what had gone on between them and she felt her cheeks turn pink as she held her head high with a prideful tilt and turned away from the Captain and the meal he was offering. Perhaps he would quickly get whatever he had come to the cabin for and leave her to her solitude—and to her dangerous thoughts of him.

Justin seemed unconcerned as he sat down behind his desk and silently shuffled through papers, making notes in the ship's ledger. Setting these aside, he spread out a map and thoughtfully studied the diagram before him. Raising his eyes to Alisha after a few minutes, he looked at the tray that remained untouched and frowned. "Are you not hungry, Alisha?" he questioned softly. Getting no response, as she dared not look in his direction for fear she would be lost in his golden eyes, he added more sternly, "Don't be foolish, Alisha, for you'll only spite yourself. You may well be famished before you get another meal."

What were his intentions now, Alisha wondered. Was he tired of her attitude? Was his plan to withhold her meals? Deep inside she felt a searing pain from his words and the conclusions she drew. Bracing herself, she took a deep breath. Well, his plan would not work! He could starve her if he wished but he could not force her to receive him with open arms! Perhaps her body could not resist his touch but her mind and soul would fight him off with every last ounce of strength she possessed. Her posture grew more rigid as pride gripped her.

"So now you would starve me." Her tone implied acceptance of such an ordeal if it were forced upon her. Turning in the chair she faced him, her features flushed and her silvery eyes aglint.

Never had Justin met such a headstrong woman! It was too bad, he thought once again, that they did not have more time for him to break through that icy reserve she had in the daylight hours. The woman that he held in his arms at night responded to every touch, every kiss with a passionate nature beyond any he had ever known. At times throughout the day, he wondered what it would be like to be greeted warmly by her when he entered his cabin, or to feel her silken arms slip about his neck without knowing that her mind was fighting her body. If not for the fact that he had obligations he felt honorbound to keep, he would keep her with him until he won over her mind as well as her body; until he was freed from this spell, the feeling that he could not get enough of her. With a sigh of regret, he spoke calmly. "I would never starve that beautiful body, Alisha. An overly thin frame in my bed is not to my liking." Glimpsing the bright scarlet of her cheeks he would have relented and explained his reason for cautioning her to eat the meal, but before he could say more, there was a knock on the door and two large crewmen entered carrying a large sea chest.

The pair was very much the image Alisha had built up in her mind of the crew of the *Vixen*. They were both unshaven, rough-looking men and looked directly at her with awe and greed as they placed the chest in the middle of the cabin. Alisha quickly tried to pull the hem of her shirt down as far as possible over her bare legs.

"Here be the chest ye wanted from the hold, Cap'n," the larger of the pair stated, his glance leaving Alisha for the briefest second as he looked toward Justin.

"Thank you, Slade." Justin noticed the way his men looked at Alisha and he felt a spark of anger. Did this woman have the power to bewitch every man she met?

"You can both leave now." The Captain's tone was cold and commanding. Neither man willing to test his anger, they turned to leave.

"Tell Matthew to hold our course and keep the men ready," Justin added before they closed the door behind them.

Thank God Justin had not left her to the mercy of his crew, Alisha thought. Once again she realized her good fortune that he had stood between her and his crew and that he had brought her to his cabin after the rescue.

Pushing aside thoughts of the men's reaction to Alisha, Justin rose from his chair and went to the sea chest. Opening the lid, he rummaged through the wealth of woman's clothes until he found what he was looking for.

"I think this will do," he stated as he turned toward her with a gown of rich taffeta overlaid with a delicate black Spanish lace. In the other hand he held a pair of black, high-heeled shoes.

Alisha sat dumbfounded as she watched him open the chest and glimpsed the abundance of woman's clothing inside. Her first reaction was to wonder why he subjected her all these days to wearing nothing but his shirts, when he had a chest full of clothing she could have worn all along!

Reading something of her thoughts as she stared at the gown in his hand and then at his face, Justin hurriedly tried to explain. "I had forgotten the chest was in the hold, Alisha." But as she still stared at him with disbelief he tried to make light of the situation. "If you prefer my shirts, Alisha, I can always have the chest taken back." He moved as though he intended to put the gown and shoes back.

"No," Alisha cried aloud and jumped from the chair snatching the gown and shoes from his hands. Perhaps all that she had left was her pride, but she knew she would be better able to serve even that slim emotion if she did not have to wear his silk shirts while having every portion of her figure outlined for him. Holding the dress against her bosom, she at last gave vent to her rage. "I can't believe you would be so mean as to force me to wear your shirts when you had such a chest of clothing aboard!"

In truth Justin had forgotten about the chest. He had gotten it months ago when the *Vixen* had attacked a Spanish vessel and he had thought at the time that perhaps he would make a present of it to Rosey, the tavern girl on Grande Terre. It was not until this afternoon as he had been wondering what Alisha could wear when they arrived at the colonies, that he had thought about the chest. "I would still prefer you wearing only my shirt, Alisha, but I am afraid it will be a bit too revealing when we reach the colonies."

"The colonies?" She breathed the word aloud as though she dared not believe him. Was this his reason for coming to his cabin so early in the evening? Was she at last going to be able to find out the full circumstances of her father's death and once again see Amos's dear face?

Misreading the hopeful thought on her face, Justin felt anger stirring in the pit of his belly. She certainly did not hide the fact that she was anxious to be away from him. "Aye, this very night should see you stepping your dainty feet on dry land once again. Though I hope you'll not be too inconvenienced, my lady, that the *Vixen* will not be delivering you to your doorstep." His words could not conceal the unexpected anger he was feeling at her reaction to his announcement.

"We're not going directly to Virginia then?" Alisha questioned anxiously as she wondered where he would leave her.

"I'll leave you near enough to Yorktown to please you," he stated sharply. He could not tell her where his ship would make anchor for he dared not trust her. She had told him little about herself or her reason for going to Yorktown. As far as he knew, she could be awaited with open arms by Cornwallis himself.

"Any place will be fine," she said absently, giving little heed to the anger that had beset him. As far as she knew he was anxious to be rid of her and able to concentrate on his own affairs. She would need to make plans. She would contact Amos as soon as possible and he would come for her or send her the needed funds to get to Yorktown. Then with a generous reflection, she offered, "I'll pay you, of course, for rescuing me and also for this gown and shoes. You need only tell me where to send the money and as soon as I reach Yorktown, I'll see that you receive payment."

"I have already been paid in abundance!" His cold words lashed out at her and brought a swift remembrance of what they had shared and a pang of guilt-ridden anger.

"Of course you have, and the price was met whether I willed it or not!" Her haughty demeanor returned as her blue-gray eyes glittered with shards of crystal and the excitement of the moment was dashed.

"Admit it or not, Alisha, your body did not object to payment in full!" With these words Justin stomped out of the cabin, leaving Alisha to face the full magnitude of what had happened between them.

Wanting to return his taunting, she glanced down at the gown in her hand and instantly grew calm with the thought that she would soon arrive in the colonies. She would not think about his words, she told herself as she pulled off her shirt and quickly settled the lustrous gown over her hips.

Finding the gown to be a perfect fit and the shoes as though they had been made for her, she glanced down at the full contents of the chest. As her eyes glimpsed the variety of woman's apparel, she wondered where the Captain of the *Vixen* could have acquired such a bounty? Why would this chest be aboard his ship? Surely they belonged to some woman. They were much too valuable to have been discarded. Justin Martel would not just simply carry a chest of woman's clothes in case of an emergency, such as a woman being rescued at sea!

A wife! The most obvious answer and as the idea grew in her mind she felt somehow betrayed. She sat down slowly as though she doubted her ability to stand any longer. He had told her nothing of his past or even his reason for going to the colonies. Perhaps he was returning from a voyage to his home and family. There was no reason for the aching throb that filled her heart, but suddenly she had no peace. Was this the reason he had told her not to try and threaten him into marriage? He was already married! Could she have so wantonly given herself night after night to a man who already had a wife? For the first time since leaving Martinique, after all she had been through, she felt the swift sting of tears. She dashed them from her cheeks with the back of her hand. What had she expected, she asked herself. He had never made any promises nor had he declared his undying love!

"I want nothing from him!" she cried aloud to the empty cabin. But deep within she felt pain sear her heart with the thought that another woman laid claim to that large, virile body which had awakened all her dormant desires. "He's nothing more than a womanizing rogue!" she hissed aloud. She was glad now that she had not allowed herself to show how vulnerable she had been to his charms. She thought of the times she had almost weakened her resolve and admitted to him after their passions had been slaked, that she did not fully blame him for the awakening of her body's needs. She was glad now that she had not let down her guard and admitted that he was right, that she had wanted him as much as he wanted her!

Enough of this! The stronger side of her nature

that had enabled her to survive and endure all manner of pitfalls pushed aside her weaker emotions where Justin Martel was concerned. What did it matter if he had a wife and family waiting for his return? She would never see him again after tonight! Taking up the hair brush, she swept her long curls into a tight knot at the back of her head.

When Justin again entered the cabin Alisha had her feelings tightly under control and was sitting stiffly in the chair near his desk. She had little to do now but await word that she was at last free to leave his ship.

Justin stood and marveled at her as he shut the door of the cabin. The darkness of the lace gown enhanced her golden skin and set off her copper hair and cool, silver-blue eyes. Even the set of her firm chin and her imperious manner enhanced her beauty. "The gown becomes you, Alisha," he complimented, his earlier anger pushed to the back of his mind with the sight of her.

Alisha would not acknowledge the compliment as she held him guilty of deceiving her in her own mind.

With a weary sigh over the constant confrontations that went on between them, Justin went to his desk and pulled out a small purse of gold coins from the top drawer, setting it before him. "We should be making land soon, Alisha. Will shall find a vehicle and see you to Yorktown." Still no response, but what did he expect, he asked himself. He was the worst sort of villain to her. "Take these coins in case there's a need, Alisha."

This statement earned him a response. Her dark

glare gave him her answer. *She would take nothing from him!* He had already given her more than she wished to remember. "I only want to be off your ship. You don't need to worry any further. I can arrange for my own transportation." She certainly did not need one of his crewmen to see her to Yorktown. In her mind this man had betrayed her completely and she wanted nothing more from him.

Justin's patience was truly strained. Alisha Whitlaw was the most unreasonable woman he had ever met. With a loud slam, his fist hit the top of the desk. "Until I say otherwise, Madam, you're my responsibility. You will do as I say and you will suffer the presence of my man when you leave this ship. Once you're safely to wherever it is you're going in Yorktown, you will then be left to your own fate. But not until then!"

Alisha dared not argue further in the face of his cold fury. Swallowing the retort on the tip of her tongue, she stiffly nodded.

A few minutes later a young man with a seemingly clean and well groomed appearance entered the cabin. "We have reached land, Sir, and Will has left the ship to do as you instructed."

Justin was thankful for his first mate's interruption. Alisha always seemed to rub him the wrong way and though he knew this would be the last time he would ever see her, he had hoped their parting could be somewhat more cordial. After all, what they had shared would not be easily forgotten. "As soon as Will returns bring me word and have Slade and one of the boys come for the chest."

"Yes, Sir." Matthew Collins, the first mate,

answered his Captain and before turning toward the door, he hurriedly cast a glance at Alisha. He had heard much about the woman who had been rescued from the sea. It was unfortunate, he realized now as he glimpsed her, that he had been the only one aboard ship who had slept through her rescue. It was no wonder the entire crew of the *Vixen* had seemed to speak of nothing else for the past days.

Had his entire crew been too long at sea, Justin asked himself as he watched his first mate look toward Alisha and his dark brown eyes enlarge with disbelief. "That will be all, Mr. Collins," Justin declared in a chilling tone.

"Yes, Sir. Sorry, Sir." Matthew heard the hard tone and knew instantly his Captain was not pleased that he was standing and gaping at the woman. But what man could help it, he wondered as he hurriedly left.

It was just as well Alisha was leaving the ship this night, Justin told himself as he looked at the delicate outline of her profile from where he sat. Whatever this woman had done to him, whatever spell she had cast, he would be well rid of her. He had never snapped at one of his own men over a woman, nor had he had any desire to strike out at one for only a glance. This woman was playing havoc with his insides and at the moment he welcomed the thought of getting his life back to normal.

It was only a few moments before Slade and one of his mates came into the cabin to retrieve the chest. Having been warned by the first mate not to even glance at the woman, they set about their task as quickly as possible, to the relief of Alisha and Justin.

As the minutes passed, Alisha sat as patiently as

possible awaiting the announcement that she would be free to leave the *Vixen*. She tried hard not to glance at Justin or even think about him, but with little else to do, her eyes were drawn again and again to where he stood before the washstand.

Having taken off his shirt and freed his braided hair, Justin also tried to force thoughts of Alisha from his mind. He could not put a reason to it, but the thought of allowing her to leave gave him a hollow feeling in the pit of his stomach. He had as yet not tired of the fire of their passion together, he told himself as he finished trimming his beard. If given more time she would become as all the others that he had known over the past few years. Perhaps this way would be better, he admitted. There would be no tearful goodbyes. Nor would there be any needless hurt or anger if he found another to take her place. But even with this thought, uncertain doubt tormented him.

Looking at his massive back, Alisha could not forget the times her own fingers had laced over those corded muscles. This would be the last time she would ever see his magnificent body, she thought wistfully, forgetting for a moment that she believed him already married. She allowed her eyes to stray over his sun-streaked hair and the outline of his handsome, bearded face. He was not looking toward her as he finished his toilet, but she could envision those warm, gold-flecked eyes with a thrilling fire of passion in their depths. A rush of heat traveled over her entire body as she thought about his lips touching her own and how they had roamed over other portions of her flesh so deliciously.

A knock upon the cabin door pulled her back to her senses and with Justin's command to enter, the first mate reappeared, this time not daring a glance in her direction.

"Will has returned, Sir. He has brought a wagon back to the ship."

"Thank you, Matthew," Justin answered in a mild tone now that he believed himself at peace with his decision to release Alisha. "We'll be out on deck shortly."

Matthew Collins knew when he had been dismissed and as he left the cabin, Justin turned to Alisha. "If you're ready, your transportation awaits."

Pushing her thoughts of him to the farthest recesses of her mind, Alisha stiffly nodded and started to the door.

Before she reached out a hand to open the door, Justin took hold of her arm. "I would demand one more payment, Alisha." Before she realized what he was about his head lowered toward her and his mouth settled over hers. He could not allow her to leave without tasting her sweetness once more. Perhaps he even hoped that with this kiss he would discover once and for all that she was no different from any other woman.

At the first touch of his mouth, Alisha struggled in his arms, her hands pushing against his large chest. But given no choice in the matter since he seemed to surround her and pay little heed to her futile struggles, within seconds her arms moved from his chest and wound around his neck.

This kiss was without equal, as though Justin would brand her as his own forever. His tongue plundered her moist, warm depths and his body pressed tightly against her. At that moment Alisha thought she would surely melt with desire for him. Nothing else mattered.

As quickly as he had taken hold of her, he released her. "When your thoughts plague you, sweet Alisha, think of this kiss and know the truth." He turned his back and silently opened the door and started down the companionway. He had thought to purge her flesh from his soul with that kiss, but he had not succeeded. He had had to use all his force to draw away, knowing that if he did not at that moment, he would have kept her aboard the *Vixen* and in a rash moment cast his honor aside to keep her as his own.

Alisha's knees felt weak and her mind seemed to swirl in a hazy illusion of unreality even as his words touched her ears. It was only as he stepped through the door and started down the companionway that her anger washed over her. What kind of person was he? Why did he not just leave her in peace and allow her to leave his ship without being forced to submit this one last time? Did he extract his greatest pleasure from proving to her over and over again that her body could so weakly succumb to him? Gathering the stiff taffeta and lace folds of the black gown in her fists and forcing her chin to rise with her determined pride, she angrily followed him out on deck.

The entire crew of the *Vixen* turned out for Alisha's leave-taking as they had for her arrival; but this time there were no crude remarks, no lustful shouts or arguments over who would be the first to touch her. The gazes that beheld the regal beauty of the black clad vision that came from the companionway were held in awe as Alisha kept her head high and did not allow her eyes to waver from Justin Martel's back as she followed him across the deck. The comments whispered among the rough group standing about were held in the lowest voices of admiration.

Alisha would have desired nothing more than to run across the gangplank and to the wagon waiting for her as she felt the eyes of the crew upon her. She forced herself to go slowly, following the Captain across the deck and down the gangplank—then at last she felt the firmness of land beneath her high-heeled shoes. She had nothing more to fear, she told herself with a deep breath. She would soon be on her way to Yorktown where she would be safe.

Justin helped her into the front of the wagon without a word. Everything had already been said between them with that last kiss. For a few minutes he spoke to Will as the two men stood behind the wagon. In short order Will climbed into the front seat and took the reins. As he called out to the pair of horses, the wagon began to pull away slowly.

Justin stood silently watching the wagon until it was no longer in sight. She was gone at last, he thought to himself, wondering why he didn't feel relief. She had been a thorn in his side from the moment he set eyes on her; she couldn't stand the sight of him, and her feelings had never been concealed. Even with these unpleasant reminders, he could not halt the feeling of loss deep in his soul.

Knowing Justin to be watching with those warm, golden eyes as they pulled away from the gangplank, Alisha did not experience the heady sensations of relief that she expected. It was not the fact that she would never see him again, she thought. Why should this bother her after all she had suffered? Nay, it was only because she was still unsure of her safety that she held this empty feeling within her breast. The feelings of thankfulness that she expected the moment she was free of Justin Martel would come as soon as she reached Yorktown and Amos McKenzie!

Chapter Eight

A bright, full moon illuminated the rutted dirt road as the couple in the wagon made their way toward Yorktown. After an hour of silence as Alisha tried to put thoughts of Justin from her mind, she at last turned to the little man on the seat next to her.

"Have we much farther to go, Will?"

"Not too far." Will smiled at her, his usual gift for gab having fled this night. With her question Will remembered the instruction he had been given by Captain Fox. The *Vixen* had put into a little-used cove below Yorktown, the perfect spot to avoid notice from the British. But Will was to tell Alisha none of this for fear she might let something slip to the enemy about their use of the cove. His instructions had been to drive the wagon as slowly as possible to make it appear they had landed farther away from Yorktown.

Alisha noticed that Will did not seem very talkative, so she kept her thoughts occupied with the first steps she should take when she reached Yorktown. It was just as well that no one would see her arrive. If things were as bad as her father had described when he wrote to her about Cornwallis and his troops having taken over the city, she knew it would be wise to speak with Amos first about her father's death before stepping headlong into the path of the enemy. Her thoughts of the murder forced Justin Martel to the back of her mind for the time being.

At the slow pace Will was going it was an hour later when the wagon reached Yorktown. The Whitlaw house was near the main section, not far from the newspaper office. Will directed the vehicle down the deserted streets and pulled up in front of a large, two-story, brick house.

The lower portion of the house was alight and Alisha also noticed there was a lantern burning in the small carriage house to the side, near the kitchen garden. Amos must still be up, she thought, anxious once again to be in the house filled with so many childhood memories of happiness and love. Eager to see Amos, who had been like a second father, she hurriedly climbed down from the wagon seat.

"The Cap'n said I was to be leaving the sea chest, Mam," Will stated as he climbed down from the other side of the wagon.

"What?" Alisha spun around to face him. "What sea chest?" She had expected Will to be on his way as soon as he dropped her off.

"The chest the Cap'n had put in the back of the wagon before we left the *Vixen*." Will nodded toward the sea chest that Alisha had not noticed until this moment.

It was the same chest that had been in Justin's cabin, the one filled with women's clothing. Why on earth would Justin Martel give her this chest which she believed contained his wife's belongings? She shook her head in bewilderment as Will climbed onto the back of the wagon. "Take the chest back to the ship, Will. You can tell your Captain I need nothing from him." Once again anger leaped into her heart as she wondered if Justin thought of this as payment for those passion-filled nights.

"No, Mam. I can't be doing that," Will declared as he firmly shook his capped head. "Why, if'in I brought back the chest, the Cap'n himself would come into Yorktown and deliver it. There surely ain't being no sense in all that."

Knowing his Captain for the stubborn man he was, Alisha knew Will spoke the truth. If she refused to take the chest, Justin Martel would arrive on her doorstep if only to prove once again that he would have his way. "All right, Will," she sighed. "Drag it into the house and have done with it."

Will bobbed his head and grinned at her as though they shared an understanding of his Captain. The days she had spent with the Fox had taught her what most men learned about Justin Martel in a short time: he gained what he wanted one way or the other. Hurriedly Will began to pull the chest from the back of the vehicle and dragged it along as he followed her up the stone walk to the front double doors.

Turning the knob, the full realization of her father's death seemed to overcome Alisha. Charles Whitlaw would not be here to greet her after so many years of separation. The outside portion of the house now seemed like a looming fortress, the warm, welcoming feelings she had known as a child vanished with the knowledge that there was no longer a mother or father to welcome her.

As the door eased open and Alisha stepped into the front foyer with Will following closely on her heels, a manly voice called out.

"Why, lass, is it truly you? You have come home at last?" A medium-framed man with a graying beard, small paunch and balding pate came rushing toward them from down the hall. Within seconds, Alisha was being fiercely hugged by Amos McKenzie.

Alisha knew she had come home when she saw the older man hurrying toward her. This wonderful, kind man who had always been there for her was still here, his arms wrapped about her as his gentle voice filled with love reassured her that she was not alone. "Oh, Amos, it has been so long." She choked back the tears that threatened to engulf her as she hugged him in return.

Silently Will left the chest near the door and turned away from the happy reunion. He would hurry back to the *Vixen* so the ship could get underway while it was still dark. A large grin split his face as he reflected that he had saved this beautiful young woman from a sure death at sea and it was he who had delivered her safely home.

Before he left, Alisha spied him silently leaving the foyer and introduced him to Amos. She also remembered that if not for Will she would surely have perished on the crate lid at sea.

A few moments after Will left, Amos wrapped his arms around Alisha's shoulder and led her to the front parlor. "Come in here, lass. I was going over some ledgers, but that can wait for another night. Make yourself comfortable and I'll make a pot of tea."

Leading her down the hall and settling her in a comfortable chair, Amos let his eyes roam over her, taking in every detail of the beautiful young woman she had become and scarcely believing she was truly here once again at the Whitlaw house. "You just sit here now and relax, lass, while I go and fetch the tea. Mandy has already gone to bed, but it won't take me a minute to heat up some water."

"Mandy is still here?" Alisha questioned in surprise. She had expected that the old black woman who had been her father's cook and housekeeper for years would have decided to go elsewhere after Charles Whitlaw's death.

"Aye, lass. Mandy and I both knew you would be coming home one day and would be needing us." Amos patted her cheek lovingly with his work-worn hands, and then hurried off to make the tea.

Looking about the parlor as she realized how fortunate she was to have dear friends like Mandy and Amos, Alisha noticed that everything looked just as it had when she had left for France. The warmth of the room seemed to reach out and surround her with a nostalgic sense of homecoming. Her mother's spinet was still in front of the French doors; the rich, dark wood and warm, flower-printed furniture seemed to be the same as when she had seen them last. Even the paintings on the wall had not been removed or changed. It was just how she remembered the cozy parlor, just how her mother had decorated it years

135

ago. Her father had always said he could not abide changes in his home; Alisha realized now with a woman's heart that he could not bear the thought of disturbing anything that his dear Linette had touched. A deep sadness filled her with the thought of how lonely her father must have been after her mother's death.

"Now, lass, tell me how it is that you arrived without sending any word?" Amos broke into her thoughts as he set the tea tray upon a small table and pulled a chair up closer as he poured the tea and handed her a cup. "I would have come for you at the docks. There was no reason for you to have gone and hired a man to bring you home." Amos was referring to Will, whom Alisha had introduced only by first name, and he had him assumed to be a driver hired at the docks.

Alisha took a sip of the strong tea. "I didn't even think to send word, Amos. As soon as I received your letter, my cousin's husband booked passage for me aboard a French ship heading for the colonies."

"I understand, lass. I should have thought as much." Amos had known she would have taken the news of her father's death hard and should have expected her to give little thought to anything but getting to Yorktown.

"I did not hire Will, Amos. The ship I was on when I left Martinique ran into a storm and I was swept overboard. Will was from the ship that found me afloat on the sea." Alisha could speak about her ordeal now that she was safe here in this house. Though she could tell no one about her nights in

136

Justin Martel's arms, she could at least tell Amos about what she had endured at sea.

Amos stared at her in wonderment, not able to imagine all that she must have gone through. "Thank God you did not drown, lass!" he exclaimed as the full magnitude of her ordeal hit him. "And praise the saints you were rescued and brought home to us healthy and sound."

Sound of body but what of mind, Alisha wondered as she was vividly reminded of what had taken place aboard the *Vixen* in the Captain's cabin. "Tell me of my father, Amos." She did not give herself a chance to dwell on Justin Martel.

Amos sighed deeply and his light green eyes filled with a sadness that could not hide his feelings. There would be no way to make this easy on Alisha. Charles Whitlaw's death was a direct result of the British rule here in Yorktown. "Your father and I were not blinded to what might happen, Alisha. Since the take-over of Yorktown by Cornwallis and his troops, every day the *Yorktown Press* was released to the streets we expected reprisals for what we printed about the injustices committed by men under the General's command. I swear to you, lass, I never imagined that even the British could be so cruel. I would never have left Charles alone that night in the office, even for the short time I did, if I had known the British would pick that night to descend upon the newspaper office. Charles was my oldest and dearest friend." Amos's voice caught and tears were clearly visible in his eyes.

Alisha's heart went out to this man who had stood

so steadfast beside her father for so many years. The pain he was feeling nearly broke her heart. "Father always knew of your devotion, Amos. I am sure there was nothing you could have done to prevent what happened, and father would not have wished you to be harmed." Giving this kind man strength and comfort helped Alisha to accept what she was being told.

Her words seemed to have the desired effect, for Amos slowly nodded his head and pulling out his handkerchief and wiping at his nose, he soon calmed down.

"Are you sure it was the British, Amos?" she gently questioned, not wishing to add to his misery but needing to know everything for her own peace of mind.

"Aye, lass, it was the bloody tyrants! I saw about a dozen of the red-coats walking away from the office when I was returning with the coffee."

"Did you see who the officer in charge was?"

"Nay, lass. I thought little of them until I got to the office and found Charles. Over the past two months I've been asking questions all around Yorktown, but no one has talked much. The British are being close-mouthed about the whole affair."

Bracing herself for his answer, Alisha questioned, "How did my father die, Amos? Tell me everything."

"Charles never believed in violence, lass, but he must have tried to stop the soldiers from destroying all that he had built up through the years. The office was a shambles and when I arrived Charles was lying in the middle of the floor with a sword wound in his chest." Amos knew there was no way to soften the horror that had been inflicted upon the Whitlaws.

Alisha gasped aloud, "A sword wound? What crime could father have committed that would warrant such punishment?"

"Your father printed the truth about men such as Benedict Arnold and Banastre Tarleton who have ravaged the southern colonies without control. Burning down houses, destroying acres of crops and confiscating as much tobacco as possible to weaken the South's economy, even going so far as killing whole families of patriots. Such men are under Cornwallis's command here in Yorktown and the fact that the *Yorktown Press* described all their crimes to the populace of Yorktown rankled the British no end. Even the Tories were beginning to complain that the British were too harsh."

"So the best way for the British to quell the opposition was to silence the bearer of the truth," Alisha supplied bitterly.

"That is about the size of it, lass. Without a newspaper reporting the victories of the patriots and the atrocities of the British, the townspeople believe the British in full control and there's little opposition to Cornwallis or his men."

Alisha realized for the first time the full extent of the tyranny that England was inflicting on the colonists and with the realization a spark of patriotism flamed within her soul. "I want to go to my father's office, Amos."

"It has been left as I found it that night, lass. I have not been able to bring myself to clear out your father's things."

"That's just as well. I would see for myself what

these brutal men did to my father's place of work."
Alisha stood, feeling her hatred of the British strongly in her heart, enabling her to direct her hurt and anguish over her father's death at the ones responsible.

"We could go in the morning, lass." Amos looked at her with a frown.

"I wish to go tonight, Amos. There are other things I would attend to tomorrow." Like confronting those responsible for this horrible tragedy, she thought angrily.

"But Alisha, there is no one about at this time of night except the British soldiers. It may go hard if we are seen."

Alisha could well understand his caution, but she was determined to go to the newspaper office this very night. She needed this added reminder of all that her father had suffered to hold within her heart when she faced those who had done the deed. "I'm sure I can remember the way to the office. If you will give me the key, I can do this alone."

Alisha had always been a headstrong child, but now Amos was confronted with a very determined young woman who would not be swayed. "You will not be going there alone, lass. I will go with you." Alisha was far too beautiful to be left alone on the streets of Yorktown with soldiers running rampant.

Alisha did not argue. She did not relish the thought of going alone to the newspaper office at this time of night; but she knew in her heart she would go, with him or without him.

"The air is a bit chilled tonight, lass. Do you have a cloak?" Amos looked at the fine gown she was wearing but her shoulders were bare and he did not wish her to take sick.

"All of my clothes were on the ship I was on when I left Martinique."

"But the trunk in the foyer?"

"A gift from the Captain of the ship that rescued me," Alisha replied stiffly as she was once again reminded of Justin Martel.

Amos noticed the change in her voice, but thought better than to ask. She had been through some very hard times which he assumed would be better forgotten. "Perhaps I can be finding something for you then." He hurried out of the parlor without hesitation.

Alisha had seen a woman's cloak in the sea chest earlier that evening but she refused to accept another gift from Justin Martel. She would make do with what she had until she could have more clothes made here in Yorktown.

Amos returned with a man's cloak that was rather large on Alisha's frame, but only caring for the warmth Alisha smiled. "This will be fine, Amos. I hope to have some things made as soon as possible."

"That may be a bit longer than you expect, lass." Seeing Alisha's puzzled look, he added, "With Cornwallis and his troops of nearly five thousand here in Yorktown there is little to be found, and that which is available is so high priced a body can't afford it. Things were bad enough when Charles was still alive and the paper brought in an income, but now Mandy and I are down to watching every coin we can gather together."

Alisha had not realized how hard things were nor

how bad they had been for her father. He had never mentioned such problems in his letters, and had faithfully sent her funds for her expenses. Alisha had done without little in her life, but listening to Amos she knew there would have to be some adjustments on her own part. She would worry about clothes tomorrow, she told herself as she followed Amos out into the cool night air.

The walk to the newspaper office was short and without event. As Amos inserted the key into the lock, he looked at her and questioned softly, "Are you sure, lass, that you're up to this?"

Alisha quickly nodded before she could change her mind. This was the place her father had spent most of his time. All the memories returned in an overwhelming flood. Watching her father and Amos as they labored to get the paper out each day, sitting on the top of her father's desk, legs dangling over the side as she would excitedly tell him about her lessons each day. Each of these good memories now were overshadowed by the fact that this office had also seen the end of her father's life and all of his work.

Amos eased open the door and allowed Alisha to step in before him. "Stay right here by the door while I light the lantern." He hurried to do this so she would not trip over something on the floor.

Alisha's eyes were wide with amazement as light filled the office. It looked as though a tornado had turned the place upside-down. Nothing was in order—everything movable had been sent crashing to the floor. "My God, I don't believe this," she murmured as Amos stood by and watched.

"I'm sure the soldiers were under orders, lass."

"You mean orders given by Cornwallis?"

"Who else has such authority now in Yorktown?" Amos had known from the moment he found Charles on the floor surrounded by this destruction that Cornwallis had ordered the assault, but what could he do when all the colonies were being subjected to such horror?

Taking a deep breath, Alisha stepped further into the room. Her father's desk was tilted on its side and the paperwork he must have been working on that evening was strewn across the floor.

"The only thing that seems not to have been destroyed is the printing press, lass," Amos reflected as he walked about and for the first time took a closer look at the upheaval.

"We should take it back to the house, Amos, before vandals do something with it." Even in the grip of the terrible shock she was suffering, Alisha thought rationally. "Why should we allow vandals or the British to have anything else of my father's?"

"I guess I could get Mandy's boy Ben to help me." Amos stood near the printing press and lovingly ran his hand over it. "Ben stays down near the waterfront nowadays looking for extra work loading and unloading ships."

"Do you think you could find him this evening?" For some reason Alisha preferred that they do this deed during the night hours. She wanted none to know that the printing press was to go to her father's house.

Amos was surprised at the request, but slowly

nodded his head, learning already that Alisha was formidable when she set her mind to something. "After I see you back to the house, I'll hitch up the wagon. I'm sure I can find Ben."

Looking around the office one last time, Alisha felt her insides turn over. She had to get out of here—she was beginning to feel sick. Heading toward the door, she forced her eyes away from the dark stain in the center of the floor, knowing without being told that this had been where her father had been slain. Once outside in the fresh night air, she took deep breaths to calm the overpowering feelings of loss and fury that swept over her. *I will make them pay, Father*, she swore inwardly as she stood and waited for Amos to lock up.

True to his word, after seeing Alisha home and carrying the sea chest up to her room, Amos set out in search of Ben to help him load the printing press and bring it to the Whitlaw house.

Having no tangible reason why she wanted the printing press to be brought to the Whitlaw house, only knowing she had to do this for her father, Alisha climbed the stairs to her bedchamber. Perhaps one day another newspaper would start up in Yorktown and she could give the printing press as a donation in memory of her father, she thought as she opened the door to the chamber that had been hers as a child.

Amos had left a lantern burning and as she looked around the small room, a smile of reminiscence touched her lips. As in the rest of the house, everything in this room was just as it had been years ago. Her bed, the desk where she had studied so diligently, even her shelves lined with fashionably dressed dolls. It was as though she were stepping back into another time, another life.

She felt as though she no longer belonged to this world, this safe and secure life. She was no longer that innocent little girl who had known nothing of hardships. Over the years she had changed and though she desperately tried to deny it, she knew that most of the changes had been brought about by Justin Martel. If nothing else could teach her, those nights aboard the *Vixen* had impressed fully upon her that she was no longer a child or an innocent.

Thoughts of Justin attacking her relentlessly, she made her way down the hall and opened the door to the bedchamber that had belonged to her mother.

Linette Whitlaw had been a delicate beauty with fashionably good taste. She had decorated this room for her own use, but rarely occupied it, preferring instead to share a chamber with her husband.

Alisha stepped into the room and lighting the rose and gold leaf-painted glass lantern on a corner table, she looked about at the beige, gold and white contents of the chamber.

This room definitely belonged to a woman, she thought. The large white bed in the middle of the chamber was covered in a white lace, ruffled coverlet; the sheer white, gold-trimmed draperies accenting the hand-painted headboard. The furnishings were delicate pieces of workmanship and definitely French. A touch of her mother's homeland seemed to linger in the room and reach out with a welcoming embrace to the daughter.

This bedchamber would suit her much better, the woman in her claimed as she walked over the plush

145

beige carpet and stood before the white marble fireplace which had not seen use in years.

Feeling tired from all she had endured this day, Alisha looked down at the black gown she was wearing. She went to the wardrobe with the hope that there would be some clothes of her mother's left unnoticed by Mandy, who had long ago packed up Linette's personal belongings and given them to charity.

The hangers were empty, the wardrobe holding only the scent of fragrant rose sachet to keep musty odors from setting in. Now what was she to do, Alisha wondered, feeling totally impoverished. If what Amos had told her earlier was correct there would be little money for new clothes any time soon.

The sea chest remained in her mind and though she felt ill at ease with the notion of using anything more from it, she knew with a sinking feeling that she would have to. She could not possibly wear this gown every day, and what was she to sleep in? The only alternative was something of Mandy's and, if her memory served, the black cook was at least twice Alisha's size.

With a sigh of resignation, she made her way back to her old chamber. The chest was far too large for her to drag into her mother's room. She would have Amos bring it tomorrow. For now she needed only a nightgown and robe.

Pulling the lid back, again Alisha was struck by the wealth of rich fabrics. There were several nightgowns and as Alisha went over the delicate handiwork, she wondered if they were from a young bride's trousseau.

Gathering the gowns she went back to the room. With the feminine apparel lying across the bed, she realized that none appeared to have ever been worn. At least this was some small concession, she reasoned with her belief that the clothes in the chest had to belong to Justin Martel's wife. Picking a nightgown of pale, bronzed satin, she hung the rest in the wardrobe.

Tomorrow she would have a leisurely bath, a treat after her days at sea when only weeks ago it had been an everyday event. Stepping out of the black dress, she slipped into the satin nightgown, which seemed to mold sensually over her body. She would not be so foolish again as to have her gowns shortened. She thought of her rescue at sea and the gown she was wearing and a bright flush of scarlet touched her cheeks.

Trying to distract herself from thoughts of Justin, she freed her hair from the knot at the back of her head, the burnt copper curls reaching below her waist. Realizing that she did not even have a hair brush, she hoped there would be one left from her childhood in the other chamber.

Retrieving the brush Mandy had used to calm the wild mass of impudent waves when she was a child, Alisha sat before the gilt dressing table and stroked through her hair.

It was strange, she reflected as she looked into the mirror, that the woman staring back at her had not changed drastically over the past weeks. She was still Alisha Whitlaw, with only a touch of hard-won knowledge in her gray-blue eyes and a new tilt of determination about her chin. Still, the difference

147

was hard to discern. There was no visible evidence of the woman she had become during the nighttime hours aboard the *Vixen*. None could determine by a look the incredible passion she had discovered in the arms of a sea Captain, whom she called a pirate for his trouble. To look upon her one would see the same Alisha and think of her as she had been before she left Martinique: innocent and untouched.

"Drat!" she swore, and slung the brush down upon the table top. What did it matter now? She had survived! She was at home and she was safe! The fact that she was no longer a maiden was of little importance. She had never been the type to dwell over a deed long after it was done, so why did she have to keep thinking about him now? If not Justin Martel then another might have been the first to show her those earth-shattering feelings.

Pulling back the covers on the bed, she forced herself to lay aside her thoughts of the audacious sea Captain. She was weary of mind and body, she realized, as she went to the lantern and turned down the flame. Tomorrow she would go to British headquarters and confront the enemy that had so heartlessly turned her whole world upside-down. There would be a reckoning of her father's death whether those responsible realized it or not. But for now she was so tired, the downy soft, feather mattress engulfed her as she stretched out. Sleep quickly claimed her.

A warm, masculine body sought her out within the sleep-crested images of her mind. Strong fingers roaming over her flesh and the searing flame of lips blazing a path left her moaning softly with desire. As

148

his body rose above her she could feel herself opening to welcome his hardness. Her hands became entangled in golden strands of hair and as her bright blue eyes looked into the handsome features of Justin Martel, he lovingly returned her gaze. Her sob of torment filled the empty chamber: "Why do you not leave me alone?"

Chapter Nine

Dreams are often hard to separate from reality as Alisha discovered as she was slowly awakened by the bright sunlight streaming through the chamber windows.

Before opening her eyes to the new day, she stretched on the soft mattress, her flesh tingling as she remembered the strong hands that had so tantalizingly caressed every inch of her body; the searing, languid play of heated lips. "Justin," she said as the name escaped before she could stop it. Turning on her side to face his side of the bed, Alisha opened her eyes sleepily. He would be above deck with his men as he was before she awoke every morning.

With a start of surprise that forced her to total wakefulness, the full impact of her whereabouts hit her. She was no longer aboard the *Vixen*! She felt her body flush all over—even in sleep she was not free of Justin Martel!

It was but a dream, she told herself. And as she sat

on the side of the bed she reasoned that the dreams would soon stop. They were only a lingering aftermath of all she had been through. She would not allow herself to revel in her feelings of contentedness. Catching a glimpse of the sea chest, she clung to any diversion that would take her mind from her thoughts of Justin Martel.

Almost as tired as she had been before going to bed, she forced herself not to think about her restless night as she went to the chest and began to pull out gowns and lacy undergarments. There was a rich, dark cloak with fur lining and also one of a lighter material of jade green. Beneath these were shoes and an assortment of beautiful hair adornments. At the very bottom of the chest Alisha spied a familiar gold-threaded purse.

Reaching out tentatively, she lifted the heavy purse in the palm of her hand. Opening the small latch, she saw the glitter of gold coins. It was the same purse that Justin had offered her in his cabin, the same purse she had refused! Anger filled her breast as she stared down at the wealth in her hand, fighting a strong temptation to hurl it across the room. But Amos's words about their financial circumstances came back to her. Not only would she be depriving herself if she cast the coins aside but also those who were depending upon her. Mandy and Amos would both need help in these times of hardship. Both were now too old to find employment elsewhere, and there was no telling how long this British occupation would last.

Her sensible side finally won out. She would keep the gold coins and the clothes but only out of necessity. As soon as possible, and when she was better off financially, she would make inquiries to find out where to send Justin Martel payment in full. The fact that she was forced to keep what he had so arrogantly thrust upon her filled her with an even deeper frustration.

With her mind turned now to survival, she looked with more interest at the contents of the purse. If they were careful with their spending perhaps there would be enough to see them through six months or even a year. She could sell the hair ornaments to a jeweler, she thought, and if there was still need she would sell the dresses. There had to be women in Yorktown still able to purchase such treasures.

Taking a few coins out of the purse, Alisha tucked the remainder securely in the top bureau drawer and covered it with the undergarments from the sea chest.

Deciding upon a royal blue gown which boasted a full skirt and a bustline low enough to catch the eye but modest enough for day wear, Alisha was determined to look her best when she stepped into the enemy camp.

No one would ever guess her financial state, she thought, securing a diamond-encrusted hairpin at the crown of her head to capture her curls, leaving soft tendrils about her neck and against her temples. Nothing about her appearance bespoke the Whitlaw's poverty.

This gown, the one Justin had picked for her, fit her perfectly. The sleeves puffed at the shoulders and tapered tightly to her wrists. The bodice molded over her breasts to a tiny waist and a full skirt, the matching slippers peeking out beneath the hemline.

Indeed, she looked the part of a wealthy lady on her way to town.

As Alisha made her way downstairs, Mandy was the first to catch a glimpse of her as she reached the bottom step. "Why Lordy, child, if'in ye ain't a plum beautiful vision!" the old black woman declared. She was obviously amazed that the young girl who left the Whitlaw house as a child had come back as this ravishing young woman.

"Why, so are you, Mandy," Alisha grinned as she hugged the rotund figure. "I'm so glad you stayed on, Mandy," she added as they drew out of each other's arms.

"Why, child, this old black lady ain't got nowhere to go. I done been too long working fur Master Charles to be taking any uppity notions of going off somewhere else."

Alisha grinned widely as she had as a child at this unshakable fortress that was Mandy. The plump, black woman had a cheerful nature and was always willing to speak her mind. "Well, I see you're still just as sassy as ever!" Alisha laughed.

"Why, yes, Mam, I reckon I is. I 'spect if the good Lord had wanted me to change fur some reason, He would have done made the changes Hisself." Her dark brown eyes twinkled merrily and the large belly jumped with her mirth. "Now, child, I gots some of them thin little flour cakes ye used to not be able to get enough of when ye was a youngun. There ain't no honey to pour over 'em, but they be filling just the same." Mandy started toward the kitchen as though there was no doubt that Alisha would follow.

154

Alisha was delighted that the old woman was still here in her father's house. She had forgotten the care and attention Mandy bestowed upon those she loved. Once in the kitchen and seated at the small wooden table that served as a working counter and where Mandy and Amos ate their meals, Alisha drew out some of the coins from the small drawstring purse.

"Mandy, I want you to get the food supplies that are needed." She held out the coins as the older woman poured Alisha's tea.

Mandy looked with wonder at the outstretched hand. "Yes, Mam, Miss Alisha, I do just as ye say." She hurriedly wiped her hands on her apron before taking the treasure. "I done told that old Amos and my boy Ben that when ye be coming home, everything would be just like it was when yer pappy was here. I be knowing where the best bargains in Yorktown can be found and ye can be believing I won't be letting a single coin slip from my fingers for no good reason."

"I hope we can get some honey and lemon." Alisha smiled as she sipped the strong brewed tea.

"Why, child, I be getting everything we be needing with this here gold," Mandy said, grinning widely.

"Has Amos eaten his breakfast yet?" Alisha questioned as she bit into one of the light, fluffy flour cakes. There were still some things she needed to ask him and she would need the carriage readied for her trip to the British headquarters.

"Why no, Mam, him and Ben were down in the basement real early this morning, but I reckon Ben's done gone down to the docks and Amos be back at the carriage house. I spect though that it won't be long before he be in here wanting something to fill his belly."

True to the older woman's prediction, before Alisha had finished her breakfast, Amos was sitting across from her with a plate full of Mandy's delicious flour cakes. "Ben and I put the printing press in the basement, lass," he said as he poured himself a cup of tea.

"That's fine, Amos." Alisha gave little thought to the printing press this moment as she distractedly tried to figure out how best to approach Amos with her plans for the day. She knew he would not be pleased with her going to the British, but she would have to tell him for she needed him to drive her. She had no idea where in town she would have to go.

"You're looking mighty pretty this morning, lass." For the first time Amos noticed her appearance, his green eyes taking in the blue gown and her upswept curls. "Were you planning to go out?"

"I wanted to talk to you about that, Amos." There was no way she could skirt around her plans. She would need his help. "I thought I would go to British headquarters and talk to someone. I might be able to find out something about my father's death."

Standing at the large, wood-burning stove, Mandy rolled her eyes heavenward at Alisha's announcement. "Why, child, there ain't no call fur ye ta go around that pack of red-coated heathens. Ye ain't gonna learn nothing more from them good-fur-nothings about yer poor pappy. Why there ain't a one of em gentleman enough ta look ye in the eye and tell ye the truth." When away from the Whitlaw house, Mandy tried to stay as far from the soldiers as possible. And that was with considerable maneuvering, considering that the Yorktown streets were full of the red-coated heathens, as she and Anna Bell, the Holcomb's cook, had named them.

Amos looked at Alisha with new respect. Most women would sit back and bemoan the fate that had befallen them, but not Alisha Whitlaw; she had enough daring to brave the lion in his den. "Mandy is right, lass, you won't be hearing the truth of what happened that night. It's more than likely you won't do no more than stand outside closed doors and be put off by one officer or another. There are rumored to be over five thousand British here in Yorktown and Cornwallis won't be bothering himself with any of the internal business of the town. He delegates problems to others and spends his time hatching up new torments to inflict upon the colonists. He intends to bring us fully under British rule!"

"This is not an internal problem, Amos. My father was murdered and I intend to find out who is at fault and for what reason; and if I have to cool my heels out in the halls, I will do so until they tire of looking at me and let me talk to someone. If I'm told only lies, at least I'll be told something." Alisha would not be put off or swayed from her decision.

Amos was learning that Alisha was much like her father. When she set her mind to something she believed in there was no diverting her. "I will take you in the carriage to where you want to go, lass. I only warn you to have a care. These men are ruthless and care for naught except to see a means to their own end."

Mandy pouted at Alisha's refusal to listen, but she could see there would be no arguing with the girl. The only thing she could do now was pray that the Lord above would keep Alisha from becoming another victim at the hands of those red-coated heathens.

The morning wore on and Alisha's nerves grew taut. She paced back and forth in front of the desk set up in the hall outside the door of General Cornwallis's private domain. The young sergeant behind the desk, who served as the general's errand boy and sentry, had told her in polite enough tones at least a dozen times in the past two hours that the general was in a meeting and could not be disturbed.

Her patience was wearing thin. Perhaps she had not made her desire to see the general quite clear enough; or perhaps she had not made her request in the right fashion. She could feel the young man's eyes rise from the paperwork on his desk and go over her in an appreciative manner each time she paced before his desk. What could she lose trying a different approach to gain an audience with the general? After all, she was getting nowhere standing out here in the hall.

"Excuse me, Sergeant." Her tone was honey-laced as she set out to beguile the young man. Placing both hands atop the desk, she leaned over to display the swelling tops of her bosom. "Perhaps I did not make myself clear about my reason for wishing to see the general. You see, General Cornwallis and I are old friends. In fact, very good friends! He will wish to see me as soon as possible." She batted her thick, long lashes over her sparkling, blue-gray eyes. Her cheeks flushed slightly as she told the lie.

Caught under her spell, the sergeant was speechless. Reading much into the meaning of her words, he at last stuttered, "I . . . I have these papers to take into the general. I will tell him of your presence, Mam." He quickly grasped a bunch of papers from his desk, his eyes lingering on the lovely face before him for just an added moment before he started toward the general's office. The general was one lucky man, he thought with some envy as he opened the door.

Going this far, Alisha would not be made to wait any longer. Without another thought she lifted her skirts and followed after the young sergeant. Taking a deep breath, she pushed open the door and stepped into the large, well-appointed office.

There was a group of six uniformed men sitting around a large desk and with the opening of the door, all eyes turned upon Alisha.

There was no backing down now, she told herself, and sweeping boldly into the room with a dazzling smile, she looked directly at the bewigged gentleman sitting behind the desk. "Why, General, I do hope I'm not intruding?"

With the sound of her softly musical voice each man rose to his feet as though on cue.

"That's her, Sir, the woman who has been waiting to see you," the young sergeant whispered in the general's ear.

General Charles Cornwallis and his officers were transfixed by the blue-eyed, raven-haired beauty.

Clearing his throat as though allowing time to regain his composure, Cornwallis at last remembered his men who were standing about in awe.

"You men are dismissed. See that what we have been discussing is carried out." The general stepped around his desk and with no further thought to his men approached Alisha. "You wished to have a word with me, Madam?" His tone softened with appreciation.

As the officers began filing out of the room, Alisha slowly nodded her titian head. "I do hope I'm not imposing on you. I daresay I can imagine how busy you are, General." Alisha had never been adverse to flirting with a gentleman to gain attention, and in this case it could mean getting the information she desired. It was a game that women had played for centuries, and Alisha had perfected a style all her own. Her voice was flattering, her gray-blue eyes like glittering crystals beneath lush lashes.

The effect upon General Cornwallis was immediate. "Nonsense, my dear, I'm never too busy to spare a few minutes. Why do we not make ourselves comfortable over here on the settee?" He reached out and gently taking and kissing the back of her hand, led her across the office to a small corner with a settee and two comfortable chairs arranged before a fireplace. "Would you care for a glass of wine?"

Alisha found General Cornwallis to be a very charming gentleman, but she could not forget her warnings from Amos nor could she forget that little went on in Yorktown these days without his knowledge. If he was not directly responsible for her father's death, she held no doubt that he had had a hand in the deed. "Your offer is very kind, General, but no, thank you." The last time she had drunk wine she had lost her maidenhood. She could not afford to lose her wits in this man's presence.

Charles Cornwallis rested his slightly overweight frame on the settee a small distance from Alisha. "Well then, perhaps you can tell me how I can be of service, my dear." The General could not remember when he had been so attracted to a young woman so quickly, without even knowing her name. The death of his wife had affected him deeply and it had been some time since he had felt any form of attraction toward another woman.

Alisha sighed softly with the hope of putting him off guard. "General, I have only just arrived in Yorktown. I have been abroad for the last several years."

"Yes, yes, I understand," the General eagerly replied. He had already realized that he had never seen her in Yorktown and she was far too lovely to have escaped his eye.

"Upon my arrival I received some very distressing news." At this point Alisha had to restrain herself from hurling accusations at him and demanding some form of satisfaction for the murder of her father, but she knew that approach would get her nowhere. This man sitting so attentive to her every word held full authority in Yorktown. Why, he could even have her imprisoned if she dared to defy him. With a firm grip on her emotions, Alisha lowered her eyes so he would not be witness to the burning hatred in them. "My father was slain, General, and his office and much of his livelihood destroyed by some villainous men." Alisha forced herself to raise her eyes, the dampness of unshed tears misting her gaze. "I had hoped you could somehow help me to find out who the murderers are."

Charles Cornwallis felt his heart wrench at her plight. "Of course, my dear, I will do whatever I can. Tell me the name of your father. Perhaps I already know something of his fate. Times in the colonies are most disturbing these days, but much of what takes place here in Yorktown eventually reaches my ear." He patted the hand resting in her lap, desiring to show his sympathy.

Alisha wished nothing more than to strike out at the hand placed over hers. She had little doubt that he knew what happened to her father, since it was his men who had attacked him. But knowing she had to continue to act the innocent victim, she sighed softly. "My name is Alisha Whitlaw, General, Charles Whitlaw was my father; he was the owner of the newspaper here in Yorktown called the *Yorktown Press*."

Charles Cornwallis was caught by surprise. The hand covering Alisha's tightened somewhat as his puffy dissipated features paled visibly. She silently watched his reaction.

"Um, yes I did hear something of the incident." He drew his hand away and slowly rose to his feet, turning his back for a long moment as he poured a glass of wine from the sideboard.

These British were as guilty as sin, Alisha thought as she watched his every movement. The mention of her father's name had caught him off guard and by

162

his nervous reaction, she knew he was now trying to pull his wits together.

Reviewing all that he remembered about the newspaperman as he poured his wine, Charles Cornwallis recalled that he had turned the affair of Charles Whitlaw over to Banastre Tarleton. His orders were to put a halt to the daily paper that attacked the British. Tarleton in turn had given the orders to Lieutenant Jefferson, who had carried them out to the letter. Cornwallis had been more than satisfied with the fate of the trouble-making news-paperman. Since Charles Whitlaw's death there had been little opposition to British rule here in York-town.

Faced now with Whitlaw's daughter, a stunning woman who attracted him greatly, he drew in a deep breath before turning around. He certainly could not admit that he knew what happened the night Charles Whitlaw was killed—or in fact that the British had any hand in the matter. Just the thought of the hurt and betrayal that would fill her beautiful eyes left him numb around his heart. It had been far too long since he had found a woman who could capture his interest.

Regaining his seat on the settee with the wine glass loosely held in his hand, he forced a sympathetic tone as he claimed no part in the deed. "It was a surprise to us all to hear the sad news. I had met Charles and found him very agreeable." The truth was he had detested the man for his daily attack against the Crown and his constant pleading to the populace of Yorktown to stand up against British tyranny.

Forcing her anger to remain under the surface, Alisha said with wide eyes, "Who could have done such a reprehensible thing?"

Believing himself free to tell her whatever he wished because she had not been in Yorktown to know the truth for herself, he readily appeared to supply what information he could. "Most of what I have learned about the affair points to the patriots. Your father's newspaper was daily exposing their crimes against loyal colonists."

"The patriots?" Alisha breathed aloud with surprise and could have easily exploded with fury that he could dare blame others for his own crime. He surely must take her for a complete fool, she thought.

"I tell you, my dear, there is no end to what these outlaws will do! They fight against all that the Crown stands for and no law-abiding man or woman is safe from their viciousness!"

There was little Alisha could say to refute this powerful General's accusation. She would have her revenge, she swore, even while sitting in his presence; but she knew she would have to bide her time. If she could only get information about that night from someone who had witnessed the soldiers entry into her father's office, or perhaps from one of the soldiers themselves. "Well, General, if there is no more information you can offer, I will not take up any more of your time." She started to rise, anxious now to be away from him, as she feared she might not be able to hold her mounting temper much longer.

General Cornwallis also rose to his feet, feeling somewhat disappointed that she was leaving so soon. He could have spent the rest of the afternoon in her company. He presumed that she was unwed for she had made no mention of a husband and he would think that if she had a spouse he would be here at her side. "I wonder, Miss Whitlaw, if you would consider having dinner with me this evening?"

Alisha's features showed her surprise at the request and as he gazed into her wide eyes, he hastily explained. "I am having a small dinner party with a few of my officers and would deem it an honor if you would agree to be my guest." He had made no such plans but he would soon enough remedy this slight obstacle if she would but agree. As many officers as he requested, even upon such short notice, would without complaint show up at his doorstep if he gave them the order. "I will be able to ask around about your father and may have more information this evening."

Alisha's first instinct was to refuse coldly, but upon reflection as she looked at her so anxiously with his dark eyes, she slowly nodded. If there were to be other officers at the dinner party perhaps she would hear something about the night her father was killed. She gave no regard to his promise to get her more information.

"Dinner would be most pleasant, General." Alisha forced her voice to sound soft. "I must admit it has been some years since I was last in Yorktown and I know few people socially."

Charles Cornwallis puffed out his chest with her answer. It would be more than a pleasure to appoint himself her guardian. He would see that she went out socially, but he would be the one to monopolize her appointment book. He thought her the very essence of womanhood, a breathtaking creature who had set his blood flowing within his heart again. "I shall send a carriage for you then at eight." He needed no instructions to find her house. The Whitlaw home was a large, attractive building not far from the main section of town.

Alisha nodded and without another word she turned away, gliding out of his office with his dark eyes riveted upon her until she disappeared.

Once outside British headquarters, Alisha let out a long, pent-up sigh and glimpsing the carriage and Amos across the street, hurried toward them.

Inside the vehicle where none of Cornwallis's officers or soldiers could hear her, she was free at last to give vent to the fury welled up inside her. "How dare that pompous, over-indulgent scapegrace stand boldly before me and tell such lies! The patriots indeed!"

She had won this first round with the over-inflated monster. He believed her a timid, little innocent who could be easily swayed by his deceit, but she would have revenge over her father's murderers and the British would somehow rue the day they ever lifted a hand against Charles Whitlaw!

Chapter Ten

Lord General Cornwallis's carriage arrived in front of the Whitlaw house at the appointed time and Alisha, after assuring Amos one last time that she would be careful and return home early, hurried out and climbed into the waiting vehicle.

Alone within the handsomely appointed carriage, she had little to occupy her but her thoughts. She reflected over her conversation with Amos when she had announced her intention of having dinner with General Cornwallis.

"Are you daft, lass?" had been his first outburst. "You can't be taking dinner alone with that man! A lamb does not gather with lions, lass. The larger, more powerful beast always devours the innocent. Cornwallis is a man that has ordered the looting and sacking of entire townships and is the cause of the death of many. You should stay as far away from such men as possible. You sought him out and asked your questions and we both know that you were lied to. What good will further involvement with the likes of him be doing you?"

It had taken Alisha some time to convince Amos to hear her out as he already had his mind set against her going. "I will not be alone with the general, Amos. It is to be a small dinner party with other officers. I only agreed with the hope of hearing some small information about my father."

Viewing the firmness of her jaw, Amos soon realized that Alisha would not change her decision to go to this dinner party even in the face of his objections. But he did not withhold his warnings even as she came down the stairs and started out the front door. "Be careful, lass, and don't be losing your temper no matter the circumstances."

Alisha had kissed his finely wrinkled cheek and hurried out to the waiting carriage. As the vehicle turned off one of Yorktown's main streets and onto the long drive of the old Danford mansion, which Cornwallis had confiscated shortly after his takeover, Alisha drew in a deep breath to calm her nervousness. Perhaps Amos had been right about fraternizing with the enemy, she told herself, now that the moment was so close. Keeping a steady grip on her emotions, she concluded that she had no other means to get the answers she so desperately sought.

The downstairs portion of the three-story, colonial house was ablaze as the carriage pulled up before the front steps and the massive double doors swung open. A uniformed doorman hurriedly came down the steps to open the door and help Alisha alight.

It appeared that the general's home lacked few comforts, Alisha thought, as another carriage quickly appeared and another doorman stepped to assist the occupants. She would be surprised by little this night, she told herself with an inward feeling of loathing for these British who could afford this splendor. She knew in her heart that the evening would be in stark contrast to the hardship and suffering that Cornwallis and his troops had forced upon the populace of Yorktown.

As the doorman led her into the front portion of the house, General Cornwallis himself greeted her in the great-room off the foyer. As he glimpsed her entrance which he had been awaiting over the past half-hour, he quickly made his way toward her. Outfitted in a strikingly tailored red jacket with large, gold buttons down the front and a sash of gold thrown over one shoulder, he set himself apart from his fellow officers.

"My dear Alisha." He gallantly took her hand to his lips as his dark eyes took in her pale, dusty rose gown. "I have done little this afternoon but count the hours until we would meet again."

Alisha felt herself blush as much from her dislike of the man and the way his eyes roamed over her, as from the rather familiar words he used. Stiffening somewhat, she drew her hand back and as elegantly as possible made her reply. "It is a pleasure to be here, General. It was very kind of you to invite me."

Charles Cornwallis was enthralled. He reveled in her seeming innocence as he was witness to the blush that stained her delicate cheeks and the lowering of her gaze before his scrutiny. Drawing her hand back within his own he lightly placed it in the crook of his arm and brought her further into the central room where his other guests were gathered. "Ladies and gentlemen, I would have you meet Miss Alisha Whitlaw. She is newly arrived in Yorktown." He quickly introduced her to his company who were seated about the elegantly furnished room. The men all wore officer's regalia and the women a variety of colorful, fashionable gowns.

Alisha smiled becomingly. The gentlemen returned smiles and glances of appreciation; the women for the most part were young and attractive but their cool, appraising looks silently told Alisha that she was an intruder and the competition of another beautiful woman in their midst was unwelcome. It was only later that Alisha realized that their attitudes were due mostly to the fact that most of the women were mistresses to the officers. Their fear of being rejected for another woman was genuine.

Aware of the interest in his officers' glances, General Cornwallis smiled as he led Alisha to a wingchair across from the settee and sat in a matching chair at arm's distance.

"Well, General, I hear that more Hessians have joined Clinton in New York. Perhaps now there will be an all-out attack on Washington and his rabble of followers." A platinum-blond woman wearing a pale green satin gown spoke up from the settee after the general appeared comfortably seated.

Feeling very generous this evening due to the fact that Alisha Whitlaw was by his side, Lord Cornwallis decided to answer the woman. She was sitting next to Lieutenant Williams and lightly tracing a circular pattern along the side of the Lieutenant's thigh with her long, red fingernail. Under normal circumstances he would have mumbled some inau-

170

dible reply, but this evening he did not wish to appear lacking in good will in front of the woman he wished to impress. He slowly nodded his bewigged head. "Twenty-four-hundred Hessians have added their number to Clinton's command, but I daresay it could still be some time before Henry Clinton rallies an assault against the riffraff at his back door."

"Clinton is not as aggressive as General Cornwallis, my dear." The officer at the woman's side lightly placed his hand over the one tracing a pattern on his tight-fitting, white pants. "There are men who are quick to make a decision and then there are others who ponder for some time." The Lieutenant tried to explain to his mistress that Clinton was one of these men lacking in decision-making abilities.

"They say that Clinton's reason for not attacking Washington is his fear that he will somehow lose New York. And then where would Mrs. Baddeley be?" Another woman added to the conversation and at her words a tittering went around the room.

Alisha had no idea who this Mrs. Baddeley could be and how Clinton's attacking Washington could affect her. Interested in the conversation, however, she softly questioned the woman sitting upon the settee. "Whoever is Mrs. Baddeley?"

With sparkling green eyes and a wide grin, the woman was more than happy to supply her with the information. "Why, my dear, everyone knows that Mrs. Baddeley is Henry Clinton's mistress and the mother of several of his children."

Looking about at all the grinning faces, Alisha could only stammer her reply as she felt her face flush. "I am afraid I had no idea . . . that . . . that . . ."

"Of course you could not have known," said Charles Cornwallis, coming to her defense. His dark eyes circled the room and quickly put a halt to the grins upon his officer's faces. Perhaps it had been a mistake to bring Alisha into such a group, Charles thought to himself as he looked at the boldly painted features of the women. Alisha Whitlaw was a rare and pure innocent; these women held much in common with Clinton's doxy, Mrs. Baddeley. "I do believe dinner should be ready by now." He stood and offered Alisha his arm, hoping to put her at ease and stop such common conversation.

Alisha was more than glad to go in to dinner. These British were a bold lot, she told herself as she noticed that neither the men nor the women seemed in the least embarrassed by this Mrs. Baddeley's lifestyle.

The cavernous dining room was as lavishly formal as the rest of the house. A large table ran the length of the room with two lighted crystal chandeliers overhead. The table settings of fine china, gleaming crystal and sparkling silver were displayed upon a fine linen tablecloth draped with an overcloth of hand-embroidered, Irish lace.

General Cornwallis escorted Alisha to a chair at his right at the end of the long table. A long retinue of servants dressed in starchily crisp, white and navy blue uniforms began to enter through a side door with platters and trays.

The first course was a delicious lobster bisque, and as Alisha sampled the savory dish, she carefully listened to the conversation around her. She was more than a little surprised that there was so much information freely passed around about British military affairs.

"Have there been any further reports about the French fleet heading to the colonies from the West Indies, General?" an officer questioned between mouthfuls of the creamy soup and sips from his wine glass.

General Cornwallis would have wished for the evening to be spent on a livelier note. It would appear that his officers and their ladies were little concerned this evening with the art of pleasant conversation. He had hoped to impress Alisha with a wonderful dinner and some light discourse and then perhaps later in the evening a walk through the gardens.

Looking toward Alisha the general felt some of his concern leave him as he noticed her mild interest in the conversation at the dinner table. "If there is indeed such a French fleet, Hood and Graves will head them off before they ever reach the colonies and make short work of them. And if somehow, God forbid, they do indeed elude our naval forces, here again will be another decision for Henry Clinton. The rumor is that the fleet will be heading in his direction."

Alisha listened attentively as she picked at her food and wondered how the British had ever gotten as far as they had in this war with the colonists. They seemed so unconcerned and so inflated with their own superiority that it appeared impossible for them to come together and decide upon a course of action that would benefit England. Looking around the table as the servants refilled wineglasses and placed large platters of meat and bowls of vegetables upon

173

the table, Alisha felt her anger simmer beneath the surface.

A woman began talking to no one in particular but her words instantly caught Alisha's attention. "Did you hear? They caught the ringleader of that group calling themselves the Sons of Liberty in Richmond. He was in the process of handing out handbills that protested the British occupation in the south. A small troop of soldiers caught him in the act and arrested him and two of his accomplices. The three of them are on their way to Halifax to stand trial for treason."

"The sooner all these traitors learn their days are numbered, the better off all the colonies will be." This came from a rather stocky, darkly handsome man. Alisha had learned earlier his name was Banastre Tarleton.

As she looked across the table toward him, his piercingly bright, coal-black eyes held hers for a moment; then they slowly dimmed to a warming glow that was not lost upon Alisha.

Forming her bright red lips into a pout in a rather bored fashion which implied to all that she had heard these same sentiments time and again, the red-haired beauty at Tarleton's side said in a voice loud enough for all to hear: "Banastre, darling, everyone knows your dislike of the patriot rabble here in the colonies."

The look that Tarleton gave the woman was nothing like the one he had directed toward Alisha; this glance was laced with an intense warning to keep her thoughts to herself.

Taking up her wine glass rather quickly, the

woman swallowed the sweet, amber liquid in one gulp. Her pale features took on an even lighter shade as she instantly realized she had made a grave mistake in speaking to Banastre Tarleton in such a manner before others. She had felt the cruelty of his large hands upon occasion and with the look he had bestowed upon her, a shudder coursed up and down her spine with the knowledge of what lay in store for her.

So this was Banastre Tarleton, Alisha thought to herself. Amos had told her much about him and Benedict Arnold and how this pair of officers, with Cornwallis's blessing, had pillaged townships throughout the southern colonies without mercy. At that moment Alisha would have liked to ask him about her father's death and watch his reaction, but as she saw the fear upon the face of the woman at his side she thought better of it. There was a ruthlessness in those black eyes and a hardness about the lips that told her more than any words could that this man was not to be taken lightly. Pulling her gaze from the pair across the table, she turned toward the general and said in a soft tone, "Has any of these handbills that the Sons of Liberty were passing out reached Yorktown?"

Charles Cornwallis smiled adoringly at Alisha. Even her soft phrased question held a touch of innocence that seemed to warm his heart. "Why no, my dear, none of these handbills has reached Yorktown. There is certainly no need for you to worry over such matters. We British have full control of Yorktown and I would never allow such propaganda to be distributed throughout our township."

The general took this opportunity to impress upon her the power that he held.

Why the arrogant nerve of this over-dressed, over-fed jackal, Alisha thought as he finished. *He would not allow such propaganda to be passed out here in Yorktown!* She fumed inwardly but kept a small, gracious smile upon her lips. If only she could do something to make him eat those words, she thought to herself. As the conversation kept up a lively discourse around her, the spark of rebellion that had begun with the news of her father's death began to ignite in the farthest corners of her mind. Just how hard could it be to start up a campaign to put together such handbills and get them out to the people of Yorktown?

By the end of dinner, Alisha had endured all the British arrogance she could withstand for one evening and was beset by a throbbing headache. As the group made its way out of the dining room and toward the drawing room for brandy and wine, Alisha drew Cornwallis's attention outside in the hallway by asking to call the evening short. "I am afraid, General, that I must beg off the rest of this pleasant evening. I do not wish to appear unpleasant company, but I fear that of a sudden I feel a bit unwell. Since my arrival yesterday in Yorktown, I have been quite overwhelmed."

The general showed his disappointment, but hurriedly assured her in the most solicitous manner that he understood entirely. With just the two of them standing outside the drawing room door, he took her hand and kissed it softly.

"I can well understand the tremendous strain you

have been under, Alisha." Once again he made free with her given name and again it had an annoying effect upon Alisha. "I myself will gladly see you home. I need only a minute to take leave of my guests." Those in the drawing room held little importance for Charles Cornwallis. The only reason he had invited his officers and their women into his home this evening was because of the need to have a dinner party which Alisha Whitlaw could attend. Now that she desired to go home, he could easily enough dispense with the party and enjoy a carriage ride with this beautiful woman.

Alisha had no desire to suffer his company any longer. "Oh no, General. I wouldn't think of allowing you to call such a wonderful party to a halt so early in the evening. I wouldn't wish any of your delightful guests to think ill of me. If you would just have your driver take me home, I would be very grateful."

Once again the general's disappointment showed, but not wishing her to be put off by ill manners toward his guests, he slowly nodded. "You are right of course, my dear. It would be rather rude of me to leave my other guests unattended. I ask only two things of you, and then I will seek out my driver." His dark eyes studied her face with an intense yearning.

Alisha tried to ignore the sable eyes looking down at her. "What is it that you wish, General?"

"First, that you call me Charles and second, that you agree to have dinner with me at the end of the week. I know of a charming little inn on the outskirts of Yorktown that boasts the most fabulous cuisine."

177

At that moment Alisha would have agreed to almost anything to be out of his company and away from this house. Her headache was worsening by the moment and she needed time alone to think about steps she would take to begin her revenge against these high and mighty British. Putting on a false smile that belied her true feelings, she addressed the general in the agreeable fashion she knew he expected. "Of course, General, I mean Charles, the end of the week will be fine for dinner." She did not wish to alienate or discourage him. After all, she had already found out a wealth of information this evening about the British that she would otherwise not have known.

General Cornwallis was more than pleased with her answer. With a wide smile, he patted her hand lightly once more before hurrying off to find his driver.

Once inside the carriage, Alisha sighed with relief and found her headache miraculously disappeared. Sitting back against the leather cushion, she could not wait to get home and tell Amos about her plans to print up flyers and distribute them around Yorktown.

Of course they would have to be extremely cautious. It would be impossible to hand out such flyers denouncing the British on the open streets of Yorktown. But they could pass them throughout the town under the cover of the night hours.

A small smile played about her lips as she imagined the anger that would beset the British and General Cornwallis over the fact that someone would dare to take such action against their law and order; with such thoughts an inner feeling of triumph over the wrongs the British had committed against the colonists began to take hold of her.

The same night as Alisha began to formulate her plans for revenge, Washington and Rochambeau began their crossing of the Hudson river at Dobbs Ferry and King's Ferry. Their objective was to meet DeGrasse and the French fleet along the Chesapeake and then launch an all-out assault against Cornwallis in Yorktown. With this objective in mind, Washington left a remnant of a command base along the Hudson to distract Henry Clinton.

With Clinton's history of indecision and the ploy that the Continental troops were still a threat to New York, Washington's and Rochambeau's forces moved out of the area and headed south with seemingly little hindrance.

On the outskirts of Charlottesville, in a little tavern called the Pidgeon's Roost, a small wood sign above the portal boasted of fine food and spirits as it rocked back and forth on rusty chain hinges before the onslaught of wind and rain. Justin Martel leaned back in his chair at the finish of his meal.

The small corner table in the front common room offered the most privacy for the meeting that had been arranged for himself, Lafayette and John Paul Jones. Between mouthfuls of beef and potatoes and crusty, warm bread, Justin had been made aware of the state of affairs here in the colonies.

"If all goes well, Washington will have begun his

march away from New York this very night." Lafayette spoke in low, guarded tones, not wishing their conversation to carry. "All of our forces will meet in Williamsburg at a designated time and if our luck holds, DeGrasse will be sailing up the Chesapeake with our fleet." The young Frenchman, who looked barely twenty, gazed at the two men sitting across from him with a hope-filled, excited gleam in his dark eyes.

"So Washington thinks his ruse will work and Clinton will sit tight in New York, does he?" John Paul Jones questioned thoughtfully after listening to the plan that had been put into action this night.

"This is our last chance, John Paul." Lafayette left off the last part of the large Scotsman's name that had been added in order to avoid British naval authorities after he had settled in Virginia in 1774. "If anyone can pull this off, George can. He has left a sizeable number of men behind to give the appearance of a normal camp—and give Clinton pause to wonder if New York is not their true objective. He also sent out word to the taverns and into the streets that Clinton and his main body of British in New York are the target of our assault."

"It has merit, I'll be saying that for you, lad." John Paul Jones nodded his dark head. "If Cornwallis and Yorktown can be brought to heel, the rest of the British will soon follow. They say Clinton and his officers up there in New York are a bunch of gluttonous drunkards and that's the real reason for his slow reactions to what's taking place around him."

"That's what we're counting on for the time

being." Lafayette grinned charmingly as he took a drink from the mug of ale at his elbow. "Only this morning some of my men caught a British officer on his way to Yorktown with a letter to Cornwallis from Clinton himself. The contents held the assurance that there was little threat to Yorktown from Washington and that the main force of British troops would be staying in New York in case of an assault and Cornwallis was not to worry."

"By the sound of the letter it would appear that Clinton is trying to reassure Cornwallis not to be too concerned with rumors," Justin added.

Lafayette agreed but admitted they had gained little information from Yorktown. "Most of our news about the British comes from New York. Washington and I have corresponded about trying to improve our spying network in Yorktown and now at this critical time it is even more important, but the British command in the south is not easy to infiltrate."

"Perhaps the right man has not as yet given it a try," Justin volunteered with the belief that anything was possible if done properly.

Lafayette had liked this large man from the moment of their first meeting only an hour or so ago. He seemed intelligent and capable and from what John Paul had told him, he was more than willing to lend himself to a cause that held only this one last hope that Washington had put into action. "You may well be right, Justin. The outcome of much in the days ahead could weigh heavily upon the right man being placed in Cornwallis's camp. The information that a spy could gather in Yorktown could greatly benefit us if we knew Cornwallis's plans and thoughts—and perhaps were privy to any correspondence between him and Clinton." Verbalizing the need for a spy set off a spark of an idea in Lafayette's mind.

As both Justin and John Paul Jones agreed it would indeed be wise to place a man in Cornwallis's camp, Lafayette's dark eyes focused thoughtfully on Justin.

"The officer who was captured this morning had light hair, similar to yours, Justin, and he was rather large of stature, though not as big as you. I think with a few adjustments you could take his place and carry the letter to Cornwallis." As Justin sat up straighter in his chair and John Paul Jones also appeared to pay closer attention, Lafayette hurriedly continued. "The officer's papers state that he is newly arrived from England and had only been there a short time after being in service to the Crown in India with his father. I know it could be risky, but the odds are in our favor that no one would recognize you as an impostor."

"I had thought I would add my ship and my crew along with John's as a blockade-runner against the British," said Justin, caught off guard by Lafayette's proposal.

Quietly watching the two men, John Paul Jones felt assured that Lafayette would have to find another man for this job. Justin Martel was a man of the sea like himself and he was sure he would prefer to do his fighting with a ship beneath his feet.

After the initial surprise wore off and as Lafayette awaited an answer, the first thing to come to Justin's mind was the fact that Alisha was in Yorktown. He had not been able to get her out of his mind and even now, as he knew both men awaited his response, he could not chase her lovely face from his thoughts. If he went to Yorktown as a spy for the cause, he would be filling a vital position. It was easy enough to convince himself to go when he thought of the alluring Alisha Whitlaw. Perhaps his agreement to spy would even bring about peace of mind. If he were to see Alisha in a different setting among other women, he was sure he would be able to forget her. With this in mind, his large arm reached across the table and he took Lafayette's hand in a strong grasp. "I hope I'll prove to be the right man then, General."

Lafayette grinned boyishly as he shook the hand gratefully, feeling assured that indeed he had made no mistake. Known as the Fox of the Caribbean, Justin Martel would be a valuable man to have on their side. "I don't wish to minimize the risk that could be involved in this venture, Justin. Your life could well be at stake if you are found out."

Once he had committed himself Justin would not back out. He lived daily with risk upon the sea and the fact that he could lose his life was nothing new when he plunged headlong into a situation. Each time the *Vixen* had come upon a Spanish ship, his fate and that of his crew depended solely upon their strength and cunning. This situation in Yorktown would be little different when it came to risks.

Seeing that Justin was not going to change his mind, Lafayette, for all his young years, instantly took charge. "See to your ship and crew then. I'm sure John Paul can help you. Tomorrow morning I'll have your papers ready and will tell you then who your contacts in Yorktown will be."

John Paul Jones was mildly surprised by this evening's outcome and shortly, after Lafayette had left the tavern, turned to Justin. "Well, old friend, I guess we should return to the *Bonhomme Richard* (John Paul Jones's ship, named after Benjamin Franklin's *Poor Richard's Almanack*). "I have a very fine bottle of old brandy that I laid claim to after capturing a British ship. I've been saving it for a rare occasion, and I must admit I know of none rarer than a privateer-sea captain taking to land to become a spy."

Chapter Eleven

Amos McKenzie was not as receptive to the idea of printing flyers and circulating them around Yorktown as Alisha had expected.

"Taking such strong action against the British is far too dangerous," he argued. "If you're caught, lass, you could go to prison or worse—hanged for treason." He gave little thought to his own fate if he were caught, but the prospect of the daughter of his old friend being labeled a traitor to the Crown filled him with dread.

"It will work!" Alisha cried aloud, determined to go through with the plan she had conceived after leaving General Cornwallis's house.

"Lass, how will you get these flyers around town? Will the British not suspect that your father's printing press is involved?" Amos tried to reason with her, halting his work of cleaning and reassembling the printing press. He and Ben had taken the entire machine apart to bring it down to the basement.

"We shall distribute the flyers late at night, Amos. Perhaps Ben will help us. I have already decided to drop a comment to Cornwallis about vandals breaking into my father's office and stealing the printing press."

As Amos wiped a rag at the ink on his hands a frown darkened his features. "You will do well to stay away from these British, Alisha. There's little you can gain from them. Set your mind to starting a new life for yourself." He hoped she would find a young man and put the past behind her.

"I'll get the information I need for my flyers by accepting the general's invitations." Alisha did not back down even faced with Amos's anger and his words of caution. "How can I start a new life? Can I forget my father was murdered by these men who freely strut around Yorktown and impose their insufferable presence upon the colonies? I cannot sit back and do nothing when I see a way I can help, not only to avenge my father's death but also to help the cause our patriots are fighting for—freedom!"

"Even if the price could be your life? Do you truly believe your father would approve, lass? Charles sent you away from these war-torn lands to keep you safe."

"Was ever a child so well loved?" Alisha asked the question aloud but it was aimed inwardly as she knew that everything her father had done had been because of his love for her. "My father gave his life for his beliefs, Amos. Can I do less for his memory and my own beliefs?"

Amos sighed aloud, once again feeling the force of her determination. She would have her way with his help or without it. He wearily nodded his balding head. "The printing press will be ready to roll by tomorrow, lass. When you've made up a copy of what you want written on these flyers, I'll set it to print."

Alisha was overjoyed. She could not imagine how she would have operated the printing press without Amos. In a burst of excited happiness, she threw her arms around his neck and kissed him on the cheek. His face and the top of his balding pate turned a bright red over her display of thankfulness. "You'd best get your rest now, lass," he stammered softly, a small smile on his lips.

Alisha readily agreed, as she indeed felt weary to the bone. With a restless sleep the night before and then her tension-filled day and tonight in the company of General Cornwallis and his officers, she was more than willing to do as Amos bid her. With an added thank you and a fond good night, she left the basement and made her way to her chamber.

For the first time Alisha felt fully in control. Tomorrow she would take her first steps toward avenging her father's death.

As she began to pull off the rose satin gown and brush out her hair, she reflected over some of the information she had gained at the general's house. Besides much talk about Clinton and the rumored French fleet, there had been mention that Benedict Arnold had returned to New York and it was not likely that he would return to the south. The general's comments plainly left one with the belief that he held a strong dislike for the man everyone spoke of as a traitor. First Arnold had been in the services of the Continental army in the colonies and then turned in favor of the British. There had been mention that Arnold's wife's family were loyalists and this was the reason for his back-slide, but it was obvious that those sitting around the general's table still thought the man untrustworthy.

Tomorrow morning, Alisha thought to herself, she would put all her information together and write out a handbill that Amos could set to print. She was excited at the prospect of what the following day would bring, her spirits heightened by doing something positive at last.

Pulling out a pale, almond-colored nightgown from the wardrobe, Alisha slipped the sheer material over her body. As quickly as the gown settled over her limbs, her mind was beset with thoughts of Justin Martel.

She had forced thoughts of the sea captain from her mind throughout the day, but now with the prospect of getting a good night's sleep, he seemed to come—bold and ever-dashing—into her thoughts.

Perhaps it was the feel of the gown against her flesh that stirred thoughts of the handsome pirate. Justin's hands had the same seductive feel as they had roamed over her those nights aboard the *Vixen*.

With a groan of frustration, she paced about the bedchamber. Then she stopped as her entire body seemed to tingle with awakened desire as the gown caressed the sensitive points of her breasts and only added to her discomfort and her need.

Sleep for Alisha Whitlaw was hard-won this night. Each time she shut her eyes images of the handsome sea captain appeared. No matter how successfully she controlled her thoughts during the day, her nights were filled with a longing she could not deny.

"Damn you, Justin Martel!" Alisha cried aloud in torment as the image of his golden eyes seemed to mock her.

Justin's own thoughts were equally tormented with the remembrance of those days and nights shared aboard the *Vixen* with the ravishing sea-siren he had plucked from the sea.

Leaving the Bonhomme Richard after helping John Paul Jones finish the bottle of brandy, he had made his way to his bed aboard the *Vixen*. As he restlessly awaited for sleep to claim him, visions of the copper-haired beauty with her sparkling, slate-blue eyes and honey-sweet lips played provocatively through his weary mind.

Somehow this woman who had come so unexpectedly into his life had a hold on him which he could not shake. Even his decision to spy had been made with her in mind. If not for the fact that she also was in Yorktown he would never have agreed to leave his ship to play the part of a British officer.

"Damn!" he swore as he plumped his pillow with his fist and tried to get more comfortable. Alisha Whitlaw had affected him more than he liked to admit—even to himself!

Take heart my fellow countrymen! British tyranny will not last forever! The day is fast coming when we shall be free from a greedy Crown that cares not for the plight of the colonists but only for the coins that

189

*are added to King George's coffers. Rise up and stand
firm! These British tyrants are little more than
gluttons getting fat on our misery. This yoke will be
cast aside soon; but we must band together to gain
our independence, as the French forces have joined
with the American militia. There is word that a
French naval fleet is heading toward the colonies to
give aid to our cause. Let us not be lax on our own
part. The cause needs all the men and women who
are willing to add their arms and voices in this stand
for freedom!*

Alisha reread the handbill one last time. All
morning she had sat at the small writing desk in her
chamber and worried over the words for this first
flyer.

She knew there was a need to awaken the people of
Yorktown, to rekindle a yearning for freedom that
had been squelched since the arrival of the British
forces. She hoped that this flyer would give them
hope and encourage them to look at what was taking
place around them.

As Alisha prepared to take the piece of paper to
Amos, on impulse she scribbled the signature of
The Vixen on the bottom of the page. Without allowing time for second thoughts about her false
endorsement, she hurried downstairs.

Finding Amos with Mandy in the kitchen, Alisha
handed him the piece of parchment and sat down as
Mandy got her a small plate of sweet rolls and a
steaming cup of tea.

"Amos here has been telling me what ya got
planned to do, Miss Alisha, and I be thinking it be the
right thing. It peers there ain't a soul anymore in

190

Yorktown that ain't a'feared of these red-coated heathens and somebody should be telling the folk hereabouts just what a pack of devils they be!"

Having this large, determined woman on her side was a relief to Alisha. Mandy could be stubborn as a mule and Alisha did not welcome the thought of having to convince Mandy as she had Amos. "Thank you, Mandy. I'm glad you agree, and if all goes well by tomorrow morning Yorktown should be having much to talk about." And the British too, she told herself as she imagined General Cornwallis's anger when he discovered these flyers being circulated throughout a township he believed to be fully under his power.

"This looks good, lass," Amos said after he had read the paper. "I'll start setting it and we should have the flyers ready to go out this evening." Amos gave no more argument, as he knew that now he would have two strongly determined women to stand up against.

Alisha felt heartened and confident that all would go well. "Have you spoken to Ben about our venture? Perhaps he could tack some of the flyers along the docks and on the warehouses on the waterfront."

Hearing the excitement in the young woman's voice, Amos smiled fondly as he nodded his head. "Ben will meet us here after dark. He seemed as enthusiastic about the idea as you and his mother."

Mandy beamed with the mention of her only son. "Benjamin be a good, God-fearing boy, Miss Alisha. He be right happy to be doing his part to get these red-coated heathen soldiers off of our streets so that decent folk don't got to be fearing fur their lives."

191

Mandy held a true patriot spirit from the top of her graying, short-cropped head to her threadbare slippers and she would have her son no less willing to take up the banner and fight for what was right. Even if that fight meant flyers tacked up in the dead of night.

"Good then, we should get to work. I'll be going into town this afternoon. I thought I would stop by and mention to General Cornwallis that my father's office has been vandalized and the printing press stolen." Alisha had thought to mention this to the general before the first flyers reached Yorktown and before a suspicious eye was cast in her direction.

"That be the only part of this whole affair I don't rightly cotton to, child."

Already knowing her sentiments toward the British, Alisha quickly stood before she could say more. Stepping around the table, she kissed the old black woman affectionately. "Everything will be fine, Mandy. Try not to worry." Turning toward Amos, she spoke on a lighter note. "It's such a pleasant day, I think I'll walk. I saw some shops yesterday when we went to the British garrison and perhaps I'll browse on my way back home."

Both Mandy and Amos knew they would be instantly overruled if they protested, and Alisha was not of a mind to give them the time. With a pretty flash of her turquoise skirts, she turned and started out of the kitchen.

Shaking her large head, Mandy could not suppress a smile. "I swear that youngun be just like her pappy."

Amos, more of a worrier than Mandy, agreed with

a troubled frown. Alisha might have inherited her mother's lovely looks, but she had definitely been blessed with the Whitlaw stubbornness.

Alisha's day had gone much as she had initially planned. She visited the general at his office for only a short time, relaying to him the news that vandals had broken into her father's office and stolen the printing press. Before taking her leave, she was reminded by the general of his invitation to dinner at the end of the week.

It was not until later in the afternoon as she was leaving a small dress shop that Alisha was made more aware of the type of man she was to come up against.

Blocking her progress with his tall, swarthy presence, Banastre Tarleton bowed from the waist as he greeted her, his coal-black eyes raking over her from head to slipper.

"Miss Whitlaw, this is quite a pleasure to see you again so soon after last evening."

To add to all the horrors that Alisha had heard this man had committed over the southern portion of the colonies, there was something else in his manner that disturbed her. Perhaps it was the way his dark gaze seemed to devour her with an intensity that left her feeling chilled even though the midday sunshine was bright. "Good afternoon, Colonel Tarleton," she replied in a cool tone, hoping to give him as little encouragement as possible.

"I see that you've been shopping." He looked behind her to the dress shop she had just left and, appearing in no hurry to be on his way, he added, "I was told that you're newly arrived in Yorktown and I also heard about your father's untimely demise. I wish to extend my condolences and offer my assistance if you need an escort or a sympathetic ear in your time of grief."

Alisha saw no remorse in the lustful gaze that lingered upon her face. For a moment she even wondered if this man could in fact have been her father's murderer. There was a visible cold-heartedness about this man that left her feeling ill at ease. "Thank you, Colonel, but the General has been good enough to offer his help in looking into my father's death and I have friends I can depend upon for anything else." She desired to have as little as possible to do with this man. She could hold General Cornwallis at a distance with her feminine flirtations, but Banastre Tarleton was a different sort entirely. The thin line of his lips as he smiled down at her and the ill-concealed hardness in the dark eyes that held nothing of the softness of his smile, gave warning that this was not a man to be easily outwitted under any circumstance. "I . . . I am afraid, sir, that I must be on my way," she stammered softly as she tried to step around him.

With a quick movement Banastre Tarleton halted her with a light hand upon her arm. "For now, Miss Whitlaw, I will say farewell, but I will also pray that soon we shall be afforded the time to further our acquaintance." His words implied much and left Alisha feeling even more uncomfortable.

Pulling her arm from his grip. Alisha turned and hurried down the sidewalk, without replying to his brash comment.

With each step that took her closer home, her fury mounted. The man was an insufferable brute. Justin Martel had never filled her with such loathing. In fact, Justin, for all his high-handedness, had been warm and giving. He had saved her from the sea and even from his crew and had given her clothes and a purse of gold. She was certain there would be no such generosity from a man like Colonel Tarleton. He was dangerous and ruthless and she would do well to avoid him whenever possible. Unknowingly Alisha was beginning to compare the men she met in Yorktown with Justin Martel and in her mind all seemed lacking by comparison.

The flyers had been printed and stacked in three piles on a small work table beside the printing press, and with the arrival of Ben the small group began to make their way to the Yorktown streets in the darkness of the night.

With last minute words of caution, Ben started off toward the docks with his batch of flyers and Amos and Alisha, both dressed in dark clothing, cautiously made their way through town.

The hour was late and the streets deserted as the pair tacked the flyers on buildings and doorways. The townspeople's houses were dark and silent as flyers were shoved beneath doors.

The pair silently kept to the shadows, afraid that at any moment the British might come upon them and accuse them of treason. It was not long before they found themselves on the edge of town.

Clutching Amos's arm, Alisha looked up a long

drive off the main street and whispered, "This is the house that Cornwallis now claims. I think it only fitting that the general should see the work of the *Vixen* when he awakens tomorrow morning." Her heart hammered wildly in her chest at such a daring thought; but the prospect of General Cornwallis's rage made her all the more determined to tack a flyer to his door.

"There may well be guards watching the grounds, lass," Amos warned in a low voice, but seeing the glint of excitement in her eyes he was also caught up. "I'll do the deed, lass. You stay hidden near that group of trees." He pointed to a spot at the end of the drive.

Alisha gave him no argument, knowing that if there were guards Amos would have a better chance of eluding them if he were alone. She knew without doubt that he would never agree to her tacking the flyer to the general's front door.

Slowly they made their way up the long drive, staying within the shadows of the hedges that grew on either side of the well-kept lane.

There was little light cast by the moon and the large house at the end of the drive was dark and still as Amos stopped near the group of trees at the end of the lane and nodded for Alisha to stay hidden. As she silently stepped into the shelter of the looming trees, he bravely made his way to the door of the general's house.

Without hesitation, Amos tacked a flyer on one of the large wooden columns a few feet from the door. As he started away from the house, his more daring side took over and he pulled forth another flyer and tacked it on another column. Just in case some of the general's men might wish to take a look, he thought with a wide grin.

Returning to Alisha's side, the pair hurried back down the lane. It was not until they drew close to the Whitlaw house that either could breathe a sigh of relief.

All the flyers had been given out and Ben had been cautioned not to return to the house in case he were followed. By the time Alisha and Amos entered the house, they were greeted by Mandy who ushered them into the kitchen where she had a steaming pot of tea warming on the wood-burning stove.

"I hope the general enjoys the flyer, for it will be the last one that he'll have hand delivered." Alisha smiled rather weakly as she sat down and sipped the tea. Now that they were safely home some of her pent-up fear finally caught up with her. As she reflected on their daring, she felt herself beginning to tremble.

"Are you all right, lass?" Amos asked with concern as he noticed her hands shake.

"I'm fine, now," Alisha said in a small voice. "I hope Ben didn't run into trouble." Now that they had posted their flyers, the full enormity of what they had done was dawning upon her.

"Don't ya be worrying none about Ben, child. He be a smart boy. I done told him to send his friend Terrance to the house if he got himself into a tight spot. Terrance was going to be hanging around the docks tonight just in case," Mandy said with reassurance. "Ya just be worrying about them red-coated heathens now that yer a'stepping on their toes. They'll be like an old mule with a burr under his saddle trying to get shed of his torment. They won't be a'resting till they be finding whoever this Vixen is!"

Alisha knew that Mandy was right, but she was too committed to her vengeance. They would have to catch her and prove her the Vixen. Until then she would not let up with the flyers or her desire to rid the colonies of the British. There would be no going back to yesterday. She had started this venture and she would see it through to the end!

Chapter Twelve

Charles Cornwallis sat comfortably in the dining room eating his breakfast and reflecting upon his favorite pastime of late, Alisha Whitlaw. It seemed that awake or asleep his thoughts centered upon the beautiful young woman. As he was about to pour his second cup of coffee, one of the soldiers who kept watch over the outside grounds of his property timidly entered the room with a piece of parchment clutched in his fist.

"Sir, I thought you should see this." The young man spoke nervously as he was afraid of the general's reaction. He and his two friends who had been given the duty of guarding the general's house, must have been sleeping when the flyers had been tacked to the columns at the front door. He did not relish the general finding out that they had been remiss in their duty.

"What have you there?" Cornwallis questioned in an easy tone.

"Well, sir, this was tacked outside your front

door," the soldier replied as he offered the handbill and stood at attention awaiting the chastisement that he knew was coming.

General Cornwallis scanned the contents of the handbill and as the meaning of the printed words dawned on him, his features began to cloud with anger. Wadding up the paper in his tightly clenched fist, he slammed it down against the table, causing his coffee cup to rattle and the young soldier to jump backwards. "You mean that this . . . this . . . Vixen came to my front door and delivered this while you, Higgens and Bates were on guard duty?" The general rose to his feet as he choked out the words in a rage that threatened to consume him.

At that exact moment Banastre Tarleton entered the dining room with one of the flyers. "I see that you have already seen this, General." His dark eyes observed Cornwallis's angry features and slowly turned to the wad of paper in his fist.

"I could just as easily have been murdered in my sleep here in my own house!" Cornwallis raged. "I am beset with incompetents! This Vixen comes right to my front door and no one sees or hears a thing! Why, the scoundrel could have come up those stairs and shot me in my bed and my own guards would have slept on peaceably!" Cornwallis was thinking only about his own security and the fact that one of the enemy had come so close.

It took Cornwallis a full minute before he turned his attention from the young soldier, who stood at attention with head lowered, and spoke to Tarleton. "What do you mean? Are there more of these pieces of rubbish?" He brandished the wadded paper about in the air.

The young soldier who had been under verbal attack moments earlier was not about to tell him there had been two of the flyers tacked outside the general's front door; he would let Cornwallis discover it for himself.

Noticing the piece of paper in Tarleton's hand, Cornwallis turned back to the soldier. "You and the other two soldiers can report to headquarters this morning. You will be replaced without delay and I hope the stench of your new position at latrine duty will help you stay awake!"

The young man knew when he had been dismissed and as he left the dining area, he groaned inwardly. Guarding the general's house had been the best position he could have asked for. The food was delicious and there was little to do. The prospect of latrine duty filled him with disgust and misery.

A lazy, contemptuous smile settled over Tarleton's features as he watched the soldier leave the dining room. He had always believed Cornwallis too easy with the men under him and this was just another case in point. Latrine duty would teach the men little. If left up to him he would have found a much more fitting punishment for the three men: they were to stay awake! Turning back to the general, he held out the flyer. "These have been tacked up throughout Yorktown, sir."

Banastre Tarleton's dark eyes crinkled with amusement as he watched his commander's reaction. Cornwallis stomped about the Persian carpet in his slippers, his houserobe flapping about his legs. Without his wig, strands of dark and graying hair stuck out at odd angles; Tarleton thought he looked like a squat, pot-bellied rooster working up a full-fledged tantrum.

"I want this . . . this . . . Vixen stopped! Find out who he is and who is helping him and put an end to these outrageous lies! I thought that once that trouble-making newspaperman was out of the way, this sort of foolishness would no longer trouble us here in Yorktown."

With the mention of Charles Whitlaw, Tarleton was instantly reminded of the dead man's daughter and the laughter in his dark eyes turned to greedy yearning. "What are your exact orders, General?"

"Make a house-to-house search for this Vixen or anyone helping him. If the culprit is in Yorktown, I want it known this very day. And have your men gather up as many of these wretched flyers as possible. Anyone having one in their possession is to be arrested for treason! If we allow this sort of slander to go on, the colonists here will believe themselves capable of forming groups against us. We must nip this affair in the bud before it has a chance to take hold and flourish. This Vixen must be stopped and set up as an example to our good townspeople before another one of these damning pieces of paper reaches the streets! We must make a quick stand and show the people that we British will not allow such treason under our very noses!"

Tarleton nodded in agreement with the general's decision. He and his men did not mind in the least terrorizing the populace of Yorktown. "This flyer was printed on a printing press. Before coming out to your house, I stopped by the Whitlaw newspaper office and found the press gone." Tarleton was not above holding anyone suspect and as he supplied this information to Cornwallis his inward thoughts were upon Alisha Whitlaw. Since the printing press was her father's, of course she was the most likely suspect and he would make sure that he was the one to hold an interrogation with the winsome beauty.

"Yes, yes, Alisha, I mean Miss Whitlaw, already reported that vandals broke into her father's office and stole the printing press." Cornwallis absently sat back down at the table and with a more leisurely perusal went over the crumpled flyer. "Perhaps the vandal is this Vixen. Ask questions. Maybe someone saw them break into the newspaper office and recognized someone."

Well, perhaps he would not interrogate Alisha Whitlaw as a traitor against the Crown, Tarleton told himself, but before this day was at a finish, he would certainly have the pleasure of her company.

Within the next hour Tarleton and the British troops assigned to him were carrying out Cornwallis's orders. Combing the town, they conducted a thorough search of the taverns and inns, every shop and warehouse and then finally each house that was not occupied by the British. The occupants were bullied and harassed with questions pertaining to the flyers and the outlaw known as the Vixen. At the conclusion of questioning each building was turned upside-down as the British troops forced their way in and searched every corner to find the printing press.

As Tarleton, flanked by his soldiers, rounded a block in the business section of one of the main streets, he glimpsed two men standing along the sidewalk holding one of the flyers. With their attention held upon the handbill, he quickly ordered several of the soldiers to place them under arrest for treason. The most likely way to make a point, he reasoned, was by making a firm example.

The two men were middle-aged and had found the flyer tacked on the side of a building. As the soldiers descended upon them, they both stepped back on the sidewalk in surprise.

"What is the meaning of this?" one man cried in outrage as his upper arm was gripped firmly by a soldier.

Hearing the cries of the gentlemen, Tarleton walked slowly into the group of soldiers and with a leering grin, answered the gentlemen's questions as they stared in horror at the soldiers around them.

"You both are under arrest for treason against the Crown!" Tarleton's tone was cold and unrelenting.

"But neither James nor myself are traitors! We both support the Crown!" one of the men gasped aloud, his eyes growing wider with fear by the moment.

Tarleton snatched the handbill from the man's grip. "This, sir, is your undoing! Anyone found with one of these traitorous flyers in their possession shall be arrested for treason! Now take them to the guardhouse," Tarleton ordered his men before turning his back on the loud protest as the men were dragged away.

Those people standing about and watching the two gentlemen being taken off to the guardhouse made haste to step back and allow the soldiers to pass them on the sidewalk. There were whispered comments about the flyers as all were witness to this new horror from the British.

One woman standing by automatically placed her hand in her apron pocket and pushed the handbill she had earlier placed there a bit deeper. Turning away from the sidewalk, she began to hurry toward the privacy of her home, anxious now to read the flyer that had caused so much commotion.

Having already been warned by Ben that there was a house-to-house search in Yorktown, Alisha was anxiously waiting in the parlor when the knock sounded on her front door.

Alisha reached her front door and drew a deep breath to steady her nerves. There had been no way she and Amos could hide the printing press. It was far too large a piece of machinery to disassemble and remove from the Whitlaw house in daylight with so many British roaming about. The best she could hope for was to somehow try and keep the soldiers from the basement.

With a shaky hand, she opened the front door and stood face to face with Banastre Tarleton. A slow, consuming dread washed over her as she remembered their encounter the day before and she recalled her ill-concealed dislike for him.

"Good day, Miss Whitlaw." Tarleton's dark eyes roamed over her as familiarly as they had the day before and left Alisha feeling just as uncomfortable.

"And good day to you also, Colonel Tarleton. It's a

pleasure to see you again." Alisha forced herself to be polite knowing that her fate and that of those who depended upon her rested with this man.

Unable to keep from noticing the officer at Tarleton's side and several soldiers standing along the front walk of her house, she forced a warm smile as she inquired, "Surely, sir, you don't always pay a call upon a lady with so many soldiers in attendance?" She forced her voice to sound welcoming upon finding him outside her door, and hoped with a silent prayer he would not suspect that she knew the British were making a house-to-house search for the Vixen.

Banastre Tarleton took only a minute to recover from his surprise at her warm greeting. In his arrogant way he held little doubt of his prowess with the opposite sex; his initial surprise stemmed from the cool reception she had given him the previous day. He had believed she would be much more of a challenge, and would take more time to succumb to his charms.

"I assure you, Miss Whitlaw, I need no other in attendance when I pay a visit to a lady." Somehow her words had seemed to lay threat to his manhood and turning around, he spoke to the Lieutenant standing close to his side, telling him to take the troop on to the next house down the block. Since General Cornwallis had already told him the printing press had been stolen by vandals, there was little reason to search the Whitlaw house; and with her warm welcome, he quickly decided to take advantage of the situation by furthering their acquaintance.

Alisha was so relieved by his words dismissing the

officers that she flashed him a breathtakingly generous smile again. "Would you care to join me in the parlor, Colonel Tarleton? I was just about to have a cup of tea." She knew she could not easily leave him standing on the doorstep after he had come to pay her a visit. She would try to keep him distracted enough to forget about making a search of her house.

This woman was by far the loveliest he had seen in the whole of the colonies, Banastre thought as she smiled at him. "Tea would be more than welcome, Miss Whitlaw," he said genially and lightly played with the tantalizing idea of seducing her as she turned around and his dark gaze followed the gentle sway of her shapely hips as she led him into the parlor.

"Please make yourself comfortable, sir, while I tell my housekeeper to bring the tea tray." Alisha turned around after entering the room and was confronted by his lustful glare. Not waiting for him to take a seat as she would normally have done for a guest, she hurried from the room to find Mandy and catch her breath for the ordeal ahead.

Thank God it had been Banastre Tarleton who had brought the soldiers to her house, she thought as she entered the kitchen and told Mandy to hurry with the tea tray. Though the man was rather insufferable and he made Alisha very uncomfortable, at least she had been able to use his interest in her to persuade him to send his soldiers away. Now she would just have to bear his presence for a little longer and her household would be safe.

The ordeal of entertaining Banastre Tarleton in her parlor was not one that Alisha anticipated with any enjoyment. The man was far too bold and had an arrogant air around women that had not been lost upon Alisha the first night she had met him at the general's house. Entering the parlor she found him sitting at his ease in a comfortable wing chair.

"Mandy will only be a moment with the tea, Colonel." She nervously sat down upon the settee.

With slow enjoyment Banastre watched Alisha as she settled her pale yellow, muslin skirts. "I must confess, Miss Whitlaw, I had not expected to make such a pleasant call today." He had thought over the situation while she had been gone and decided it was best to try and win her over with light, bantering games of courtship. It would take some time to bend her to his will, he had reasoned. She was unlike the women he usually associated with since his arrival in the colonies. Her manners and her incredible beauty bespoke of a need for gentle wooing; believing he had all the time in the world now that she had greeted him so warmly, he set out to entrap her with his masculine charm.

Alisha forced herself to appear surprised at his statement, but all the time her heart was racing in her breast. "Whatever do you mean, Colonel Tarleton?" she said, feigning ignorance of any other reason he might have to be paying her an unannounced call.

Believing her as innocent as she pretended to be, Banastre Tarleton found himself thoroughly enjoying this refreshing encounter. "The truth is, Miss Whitlaw, my men and I were conducting a search of all the houses in Yorktown for your father's printing press."

Alisha reacted with wide-eyed surprise. "Why, I

never for a moment imagined that General Cornwallis would take such swift measures to retrieve my father's property from the vandals who broke into his newspaper office. I am indeed very appreciative of the general's thoughtfulness."

Tarleton was rather irritated by the fact that Cornwallis was receiving her gratitude. With the hope of garnering her regard himself, he boldly stated, "I can assure you I will not rest until I find those responsible for causing you such distress, my dear."

At that moment Mandy brought the tea tray into the parlor and halted further conversation as she placed the fine bone china, tea pot and cups upon a small table before the settee.

"Thank you, Mandy. That will be all for now," Alisha said softly, knowing that the housekeeper would be adverse to leaving her alone with the British officer even though she had assured her that all was well when she had gone to the kitchen.

For a moment or two, the large black woman hung back near the settee. "If ya be needing me, ya just got's to call, Miss Alisha." Mandy cast a cool glare in the direction of the officer one last time before turning toward the parlor door.

Tarleton noted the hostile look the black woman directed at him, but such actions by these colonists and their servants had ceased to bother him long ago. As Alisha began to pour tea into the gold-trimmed tea cups, he relaxed in the comfortable chair, his long legs comfortably stretched out and his helmet placed upon the foot stool to the side. He rather enjoyed this peaceful setting in a charmingly fashionable parlor and having such a beautiful woman tend to the little amenities.

"As I was saying, Miss Whitlaw, I shall find these vandals. I know you have been put through much since your arrival, but I will personally see that you are caused no more upsets." He intentionally did not make mention of the flyers and that this new blight upon British authority was the initial reason for a house-to-house search. If she believed that he and his men were taking such great trouble for her sake alone, it could only further his hope of obtaining this woman for his own greedy purposes.

Handing him a cup and saucer, Alisha lowered her long, thick lashes somewhat over her crystal-gray eyes, sweetly stating, "Thank you so much, Colonel Tarleton, for taking such an interest in my circumstances." Alisha was no fool even though she appeared grateful to this man. She knew without a doubt that his reason for avoiding mention of the flyers was to make his visit seem due to concern for her.

"It is certainly my pleasure to assist you in this time of grief over your father's untimely death, Miss Whitlaw." Tarleton took the cup from her delicate hand and could not help thinking of the payment he would one day extract as the price of his concern. Her unique beauty awakened all of his raging desires and he was hard pressed to keep a grip on his seething emotions as he sat in her parlor and bantered over tea.

Making no further comment, Alisha kept her eyes lowered and sipped her sweetened tea. His constant, heated perusal of her body made her flesh crawl with revulsion.

Noticing the slight flush on her cheeks and her sudden quiet, Tarleton grinned inwardly at his own abilities in the art of seduction. "I had hopes that you would consider an invitation for a carriage ride or a picnic sometime soon, Alisha." For the first time he used her given name in his bold pursuit.

Not wishing to make any kind of promises to such an invitation, but fearing to anger him and have her house searched along with the others, Alisha nervously raised her eyes and softly replied, "Perhaps sometime soon, Colonel Tarleton."

This was more than enough for Banastre Tarleton. He took her answer to be a promise for a future date. Setting his tea cup upon the small table, he reached for his helmet and rose to his feet. "I am afraid that I can spare no more time away from my duty, even in the presence of such beautiful company. My men await me."

Alisha sighed inwardly with relief and putting her cup aside, she smiled up at him. "I do understand, Colonel. I would certainly not wish to keep you from your duty."

Having used her given name, he now seemed prone to do so. "Make no mistake, Alisha, I would much prefer to spend the rest of this day in your charming company, but such pleasures will have to wait for another time." He boldly reached out and took the delicate hand he had admired earlier as she handed him his tea and placed a lingering kiss upon it, his dark eyes holding hers with a depth of promise.

The touch of his lips upon her flesh sent a chill of repugnance through Alisha, but for the moment her smile was frozen.

The moment the front door closed behind his tall form, Alisha leaned against the portal and in a weak voice called for Mandy to heat water for a bath. Every part of her felt invaded and unclean from the touch of his lips and the raking of his dark eyes over her body. She may well have saved herself and her household from the hangman's noose, but the price had been dear indeed.

Over the course of the next two weeks there was much speculation over the identity of the Vixen. Three more flyers had been circulated around Yorktown and secretly the townspeople awaited the next one eagerly. At last all the wrongs the colonists had been suffering at the hands of the British were being brought to public notice, even if by an unknown voice. The men were heard grumbling in the inns and taverns about the sour taste of British injustice. Heretofore, if a red-coated officer or soldier passed a townswoman on the street, she would keep her eyes lowered and hurry by; now they were met with utter contempt in the lady's eyes as she pulled her skirts back as they passed.

The British on the other hand were desperate to discover who this Vixen was and put a halt to the traitorous handbills. Though no more of the flyers had appeared upon Cornwallis's doorstep, he took the actions of the Vixen as a personal affront. Each morning after the report that more flyers had been tacked about town, he sent out soldiers to gather them and bring them to British headquarters.

Few of the flyers made their way to the general,

since the townspeople were fully aware of the risk if they were caught with one. Nevertheless, upon awaking and finding a flyer outside their door, they would quickly hide it until they could find a moment to read the content. As Cornwallis became suspicious of such actions, he grew more determined in his pursuit of the outlaw known as the Vixen!

Chapter Thirteen

The ball General Cornwallis had planned for well over a month was, in his mind, for the purpose of bringing some much needed culture to the colonist village of Yorktown. Beautifully gowned women, elegantly dressed gentlemen and regally bedecked officers mingled in the imposing ballroom which was alight with crystal chandeliers and glass-embossed sconces.

Musicians played for the general's guests in a small alcove designed specifically for that purpose. Long banquet tables were set up with a lavish display of food and drink for all who wished to partake.

Within the splendor of such grandiosity, Alisha was encircled by a gathering of young men vying to escort her to the dance floor. She truly felt in her element in such glamorous surroundings. She had attended many such functions in France and on Martinique. The young men, British officers and the sons of prominent loyalist gentlemen in Yorktown, complimented and pampered her. They hurried off to fetch her a plate of tempting delicacies from the banquet table or beg the honor of refilling her glass with sparkling champagne. Laughing and flirting as the gentlemen plied her with humorous anecdotes, Alisha thrived on being the center of so much male attention.

It was early in the evening when Charles Cornwallis approached her with a request for the next dance. As most of the young men made way for the high-ranking officer, Alisha graciously smiled and held her hand out toward him.

"I thought I would take this moment to steal you from all your admirers, my dear. Later I may well not be able to get through the throng." The General's eyes looked warmly into her lovely face and seeing the flush of her excitement, he was more than pleased that she was having such a pleasant time. Alisha Whitlaw had captured his heart, but he was no longer ruled by the brashness of youth. He didn't want to frighten her off by seeming jealous. What harm was there if she enjoyed herself while under his watchful eye and beneath his own roof, he had asked himself earlier as the flock of young men gathered around her.

"Everything is wonderful, Charles." He had insisted the night she had taken dinner with him at the inn that she call him Charles and with the pleasure she was having this evening it was an easy enough request to grant.

Feeling ever indulgent in her presence, Charles Cornwallis thought that if it took only the trappings of a ball to please her, he would certainly hold another in the near future. "You are by far the most beautiful woman here tonight, Alisha," he murmured, as many in the ballroom watched as the distinguished looking, bewigged general in his red uniform and the striking beauty dressed in shimmering silver danced across the floor. "I hope that before the evening ends we can steal away for a few moments and share a walk through the gardens." There had been much pressure upon Cornwallis the past two weeks, trying to find out who the Vixen was and then learning that Washington and his troops were heading Southward instead of directing their attention upon Clinton in New York. And only yesterday he found out that he might have a spy in his own camp. With all of that the general felt he had been remiss in his courtship of Alisha and wished for some time with her to let her know of his intentions. As soon as this war in the colonies was finished he would return home to England and he had already made plans in his mind for this lovely young woman to arrive on the shores of his homeland at his side and as his wife.

Feeling sure that she could easily put the general off if he made any unwelcome overtures, Alisha felt no threat in accepting the general's invitation. "A walk in the gardens later in the evening will be much appreciated, I am sure, Charles." She smiled and for an instant she felt the arm about her waist tighten.

Feeling almost able to forget the worries that his command forced upon him, Charles Cornwallis finished the turn about the dance floor with Alisha and then with some pride escorted her back to her group.

"Until later then, my dear." He brushed his lips on

the back of her wrist before releasing her to the eager young men begging for the honor of the next dance.

Laughing with delight, Alisha held out her hand to a young officer with sandy brown hair and twinkling blue eyes. He seemed to be enjoying the ball and the fun-loving atmosphere as much as she.

As the young man led her onto the dance floor, Alisha glimpsed Banastre Tarleton entering the ballroom with an elegantly gowned, attractive, young woman clinging to the arm of his jacket. Instantly realizing that the woman was not the same one he had escorted to the general's dinner party, Alisha was even more sure he was a womanizer. He had returned upon two different occasions to her home after the morning the British had conducted the search for the Vixen, but both times he had been turned away by Mandy with regrets that her mistress was ill and resting. That had been Alisha's request if he came back to her door, but here at the general's ball she knew if he approached her, she would have no excuse to avoid him.

"I have a sister back home, Miss Whitlaw, that you remind me of." The young man turning Alisha about on the dance floor drew her attention away from Tarleton just as his dark, piercing eyes found hers. "Last year was my sister's coming-out party and I've been receiving letters that lead me to believe she's the toast of London this year."

Trying to ignore the shiver that shot through her from the caress of those ebony eyes, Alisha tried to put all her attention upon her dancing partner. "I'm sure your sister is having a delightful time, Mr. Scott. I can say from my own experience that this is the most exciting time of a young girl's life." Alisha smiled with the memory of her own coming-out party given by her aunt in France.

Gregory Scott could well imagine that Alisha Whitlaw had left a trail of broken hearts before coming to the colonies. By the finish of their dance he was more than willing to admit that he also could be added to her list. There was little chance of his ever really drawing her interest, he knew. With men like General Cornwallis paying her attendance, his chances were slim indeed. It was enough though that she had chosen him to dance with and had been such charming company.

As the couple made their way across the ballroom Alisha's attention was drawn to a small group of ladies who kept glancing toward the entrance way, simpering excitedly.

"Have you ever seen such a gorgeous man in your entire life, Sybil?"

None of the group appeared too timid, as they spoke loudly enough for all to hear. The one called Sybil responded to her friend's words, "Why, he's so tall and look at those wide shoulders! I hear he only arrived in Yorktown a week ago."

"Look at those tight-fitting breeches," another murmured behind her black lace fan.

With her attention thoroughly caught up in the women's chatter, Alisha turned and looked to see who they were speaking so favorably about.

"Oh, that's Andrew Wentford," Gregory Scott supplied. He also had heard the ladies and saw Alisha look in the direction that held the other women's attention. "If you would like, I can make an introduction. He's a pleasant enough sort, I guess."

Alisha could certainly see why the women were in such a dither over the handsome officer. He appeared every inch worthy of all the praise from the small group that kept staring. However, Alisha desired no introductions. She was allowing herself some well deserved pleasure. Tomorrow she would once again face reality and take up the cause for vengeance against the British. She needed no more complications in her life, especially not those made by men. Her dreams of her sea captain lover still assaulted her each time she shut her eyes at night and with Cornwallis ever at hand and Tarleton paying unexpected calls, she had enough problems. "No thank you, Mr. Scott. We should leave some of the gentlemen for the other ladies, don't you think?" She smiled up at him and received an appreciative grin in return as he continued to lead her to the group of men waiting impatiently.

Standing head and shoulders above most of the people in the ballroom, Justin Martel's golden gaze slowly roamed over the couples on the dance floor and then in turn over those standing about the banquet table and in small groups about the room. A lazy smile came over his handsome features as he watched the copper-haired woman in the shimmering silver gown.

"She's a beauty, I'll grant you that, but I warn you now you'll have to stand at the end of a long line for her favors." Banastre Tarleton came up behind his fellow officer to warn him off.

"I admit that I myself have designs on Miss Whitlaw, but tonight she is the personal guest of

General Cornwallis." Tarleton desired no more competition in his pursuit of Alisha and having seen the knowing glances that women directed toward this newly arrived officer, he thought it only fair to set him straight from the start.

From his very first meeting with Banastre Tarleton, Justin had an uncanny dislike for the man and now as he listened to him talk about Alisha that dislike increased by slow degrees. Shrugging his shoulders as though only mildly interested in the woman across the ballroom, he replied easily, "It would appear that there are plenty of women in Yorktown to satisfy a man's appetite." And as though his only intention in life were to master this pursuit he spoke of so easily, he left Tarleton standing there in the entranceway of the ballroom and boldly approached the ladies who had been looking so greedily in his direction. After introducing himself as Andrew Wentford with a courtly bow that left two of the women giggling behind their fans, he asked a slim, willowy blond with a sprinkling of freckles across the bridge of her upturned nose for a turn on the dance floor.

Sybil Lancaster was hardly able to speak as she nodded her head and stared up into his warm, topaz eyes. She was swept across the dance floor in the strongest pair of arms she had ever felt.

Just as Alisha glimpsed the girl she had heard called Sybil being led onto the dance floor by the handsome officer, she smiled at the girl's success in capturing the man for a dance. She then felt a slight pressure on her forearm.

"I believe this is our dance, Miss Whitlaw."

Alisha's first reaction was to pull away, but

recognizing the voice as that of Banastre Tarleton and not wishing to make a scene, she forced a warm smile and slowly nodded.

"Of course, Colonel Tarleton. Gentlemen, you must excuse me this one dance for indeed it is already promised." She heard grumbles coming from the men around her and did not wish any arguments to break out. She would give Tarleton his one dance and then be finished with him for the evening.

Tarleton's arms held Alisha a bit tighter than necessary as he led her through the steps of the dance. "You look as beautiful as ever, Miss Whitlaw," he said with a note of hardness.

"Why, thank you, Colonel."

"I have twice paid a visit to your house only to be turned away by your housekeeper." His words were a statement but Alisha knew he expected an explanation.

"I'm afraid I've been a bit under the weather lately. You will have to forgive me, sir," she said, attempting to make light of the matter.

Feeling his strong arms tighten, Alisha felt Banastre's dark eyes probing her face as though for answers. "I would take it amiss if I believed you wished to avoid me, Alisha. The General may be put off but I will not!"

Alisha felt her anger beginning to surface over his highhanded manner toward her, but she forced herself to stay calm. It would not do to make this man her enemy. "Why, Colonel Tarleton, I have no idea what you're talking about. Putting you off indeed."

With the finish of the dance, Banastre held tight to Alisha's waist for an added moment. "I'll be paying another call upon you soon, sweet Alisha, so do not disappoint me this time. You owe me a carriage ride and I am not a man who easily forgets a promise." With this he led her back to her group and without another word started across the ballroom to his lady friend.

Alisha was inwardly seething. Who did the brute think he was? She had made no promise to go for a carriage ride with him! She had merely put him off that day in her parlor. She had no intention of ever going anyplace with him!

Having little time to dwell upon her anger or Banastre Tarleton, Alisha was soon swept back to the dance floor by a young man to whom she had earlier promised a dance.

"I wonder if I might call upon you during this week, Miss Whitlaw?" the young man questioned as soon as the dance began.

Alisha looked at him more intently and found him to be a much thinner version of the man to whom she had been introduced earlier in the evening. The father was overweight, the son far too skinny, but both had the same ruddy complexion and hawk-like nose. "Why, I'm not sure this week will be a good time, Mr. Smithers." She hated to disappoint him but she certainly did not wish to offer any encouragement.

"That's quite alright, Miss Whitlaw. Perhaps another time would be more appropriate." Hope still lingered in the young man's eyes and Alisha was powerless to do anything but nod as she went through the steps of the dance in his arms.

As she was led off the floor the music instantly

started up again, and a touch upon her arm drew her attention.

"I wonder if I might have this dance?" It was the handsome officer and before Alisha even looked up into his face, she felt the heated glare of Sybil Lancaster.

Smiling becomingly at the silly girl, Alisha held out her hand. "Of course, sir," she intoned sweetly and was soon pulled back upon the dance floor despite the wounded looks of both Sybil and Joel Smithers.

"I am afraid, sir, that you have quite upset your dancing partner," Alisha stated in some humor as she was encircled by powerful arms and swept across the ballroom floor.

"That's all right. You were the one I wanted to dance with from the first moment I stepped into the ballroom." His husky voice caused chills of delight to course through her entire body.

As Alisha went through the motions of the dance she began to feel a familiar stirring within her depths that she had only known while in the arms of Justin Martel. With a slow comprehension, she pulled away and for the first time looked at his face. She saw pale strands of sun-streaked hair, trimmed about his collar, his handsome face clean-shaven with a firm, square-cut jaw; his lips full and sensual; the nose had an aquiline tilt that lent him an air of daring and recklessness. The glimmer of a diamond stud earring caught her eye and as she slowly looked upward and was held by the power of gold-flecked eyes beneath arched brows, slowly her own features paled. It couldn't be, she told herself as her steps faltered and an inner trembling began. It was not possible! It could not be Justin Martel here at the General's ball!

Justin was well aware of her recognition and drawing her back into the tightness of his embrace, he whispered against her ear, "Did you think I could so easily stay away from you after our time aboard the *Vixen*? Have you not thought of me upon occasion, Alisha?" Though Justin had determined that once he saw her again, he would be able to banish her from his mind for good, he now realized from the very first moment he had glimpsed her across the ballroom in the company of other men, that this was not to be. From that first look he had desired her as he never had another woman.

Overwhelmed and confused, Alisha could not answer as she felt his warm breath on her ear and along her neck. This could not be happening, she repeatedly told herself. How could he be here? He was a ship's captain, not a British officer! But feeling the strength of his embrace and the sound of that all too familiar voice that seemed to plague her nights without mercy, she knew she was not dreaming. Justin Martel was here in Yorktown and he was now her enemy. He was no longer a ship's captain, but instead a British officer by the name of Andrew Wentford. She felt herself all but swooning in a mass of confusion, and as the music ended and he took her back to her group of admirers, she could barely go through the motions.

"We shall see each other later this evening, Alisha," he murmured softly for her ears alone before leaving.

She would have screamed that it was not likely she would give him the chance to get anywhere near her, this evening or any other! With her many admirers circling her she was unable to vent her fury as she would have liked. She could only stand miserably by and watch his retreating back as he once again approached the group of ladies and drew Sybil Lancaster with her pixieish features back onto the dance floor.

Those standing around Alisha were for the moment forgotten as she watched the simpering Sybil place her hand upon Justin's shoulder. The way he glanced down at the fair-haired blond with a more than interested look sent Alisha's temper skyrocketing. He was no more than the rutting stag she had believed him to be aboard the *Vixen!* And to think that over the past weeks, with the belief that she would never see him again, her feelings toward him had softened somewhat. She knew this to have come about because of the dreams she could not banish, but this moment as she watched him swinging Sybil Lancaster around on the dance floor, all of the anger she had held aboard his ship came back in a heated rush. Looking about the ballroom she desired only to find a way to disappear, to put as much distance as possible between them.

It was General Cornwallis who came to Alisha's rescue. Without a word he took her by the arm and led her from the group around her. For a moment it appeared he was leading her out onto the dance floor, but turning toward the open French double doors, he silently escorted her out onto the marble patio.

"I thought it was time for that walk in the gardens,

226

my dear." The hour was growing late and Charles Cornwallis had taken this opportunity after he had watched her being led back to her group by the new officer, Andrew Wentford.

"Indeed, General, I mean, Charles. A walk in the gardens would be wonderful. I fear the ballroom was growing rather warm." She hoped the fresh night air would revive her senses and help her to dispel her anger. Her carefree mood had totally vanished with the arrival of Justin Martel.

Tucking her hand gently in the crook of his arm, the general walked her down a stone path off the patio and into the bountiful display of sweet scented flowers.

"You know, Alisha, not until your arrival in Yorktown have I felt so attracted to a woman since the death of my wife." He had not meant to rush her, but watching the bevy of young men fawning about her all evening had brought home the need for him to make his intentions clear.

Alisha was far too wrapped up in her own thoughts to pay much heed to what the general was saying. How could it be possible that Justin Martel was here in Yorktown? And what of his ship, the *Vixen*, and his crew? How could he be a ship's captain one minute and a British officer the next?

Taking her silence for maidenly virtuousness over the fact that she was alone in the moonlight with a man, the general led her to a marble bench and softly smiled as she sat down.

"I do not know how much longer this war with the colonies will last, Alisha, but I hope the finish will be seen shortly." And with his belief that Hood and

Graves would wipe the French fleet from the seas and that Clinton would soon supply him with more men to scatter Washington's forces, this was not an impossibility to Cornwallis. "I hope that you and I will be able to grow closer in the time that is left to us. At the conclusion of the war, I will be returning to England, and I would . . ."

"Yes, of course, Charles, your company has been most pleasant," Alisha interrupted, only partly paying attention. Now that she had cooled down somewhat due to the pleasant night breeze, she kept remembering the manner in which Sybil Lancaster had wound her arms about Justin's shoulders and he had looked down into her face with such an agreeable look of pleasure. She could not remember a time when he had looked so at her.

Charles Cornwallis had almost come right out and asked her to consider returning to England with him as his wife before she interrupted him, but now as he looked upon her and knew her to be the most beautiful woman he had ever seen, fear of her rejection took a terror-filled grip upon his heart. He thought better of such a proposal at this time. Alisha Whitlaw was far to rare a treasure to be rushed, he sternly warned himself now that his fear of her refusal brought his reasoning under some control. There was still plenty of time. She had admitted that she enjoyed his company—was this not a good sign? Were not the best marriages based in the beginning on friendship?

"Alisha, I hope that you and I can be good friends. I want you to feel free to come to me at any time, no matter what the need."

"Why, Charles, I consider us friends already. You have helped me immeasurably since I arrived in Yorktown." Most of the information she had obtained for her flyers she had received while in the general's company. She now tried to give him all of her attention as she wondered at his seriousness.

Her answer only reinforced his beliefs that she was truly an innocent. He seemed hopelessly drawn to her, his head bent toward her with the desire to taste those tempting, pink lips.

Alisha quickly turned her head to offset his target. "Charles, I believe we should go back into the ballroom," she stammered softly as though beset with maidenly embarrassment.

Charles Cornwallis was delighted with her chaste reaction, if indeed a little disappointed and frustrated. "Perhaps you're right, my dear." He fondly patted her hands which were folded in her lap, before rising to his feet. He felt confident he had made his intentions clear enough without scaring her and over the course of the next few weeks he would break through this barrier.

Within the circle of ladies that coquettishly flirted and vied for his attention, Justin's gaze kept lingering upon the French double doors that led out into the gardens. He had watched Alisha leave through them with the General and it had taken all of his will power not to follow the couple out into the dark night. Feeling his insides tighten with every moment that passed, Justin forced himself to endure the company of the ladies around him. It was only a short time later that he watched Alisha step back into the ballroom with her hand tucked familiarly within the General's arm. Watching the General looking down at her and she in return smiling so sweetly up at him, an angry glint flashed from his topaz eyes.

Returning to her own group, Alisha found herself time and again looking over toward Justin and her anger increased with each glance. Her enjoyment of the evening had totally vanished and the more so now as she was witness to Justin Martel in the company of the clinging, love-struck women posturing so foolishly before him. If only they knew what manner of scamp he was, she fumed, as she noticed the fairhaired Sybil batting her lashes and preening before him in her low-cut gown.

No longer interested in dancing or the many men that flocked around her, Alisha made her excuses. She hurriedly left the ballroom to retrieve her cloak and make her way to the carriage that the General had sent earlier in the evening to pick her up.

From the corner of his eye, Justin watched Alisha's every move as she made her way out of the ballroom. He allowed only a few moments to pass before he also extricated himself from the ladies and left the ballroom. Glimpsing the flash of silver cloak going through the front door, a calculating smile settled over his lips. With a light step to his walk it was not long before he also left General Cornwallis's house.

Chapter Fourteen

Upon his arrival in Yorktown, Justin had made a point of finding the Whitlaw house and after the carriage ride from General Cornwallis's house, he stood on the front walk looking up at the lighted second-story window. The downstairs portion of the house was in dark silence and he imagined that any other occupants of the house were abed at this late hour.

Catching the outline of a shapely woman behind the sheer curtains of the lighted room, he smiled as he watched the double doors leading onto an iron grill-work balcony thrown wide to let the fresh night air into the chamber.

He reiterated to himself, as he had when he left the General's ball, that his reason for following Alisha to her home was to safeguard his new identity. She was the only one in Yorktown who knew him as Justin Martel and he could not have her mentioning this fact to General Cornwallis or Banastre Tarleton. He wanted no suspicions aroused, and with this thought he quietly began to climb the branches of the large shade tree that reached up toward the second-story balcony.

If he had believed Alisha to be as faithless and scheming as all other women, tonight that belief had been reaffirmed as he watched her dancing and flirting with man after man. He had also seen her step out into the gardens with General Cornwallis and return with a flush upon her cheeks. As Tarleton's words about having to wait in a long line for a chance with the lovely Alisha Whitlaw echoed in his mind, raw anger sparked anew.

With seeming ease for a man of his size, Justin pulled himself over the iron-grill siding of the balcony and took light steps across the tile flooring. He stood near the open double doors, his tawny eyes scanning the room and focusing on Alisha as she sat before the dressing table brushing her long copper curls.

Alisha had been in a state of panic since seeing Justin Martel and leaving the General's house. Was she never to be free from that roguish pirate? Along with her nightly dreams driving her to distraction, must she now contend with the man himself here in Yorktown? She had somehow been able to cope with the passionate nocturnal interludes with the handsome sea captain. At times during the past days, his image stole into her thoughts and she felt the warm ache of something shared and lost. But seeing him tonight, once again feeling his powerful, flesh and blood presence, she was beset with reminders of what they had shared aboard the *Vixen* and she could not calm her heart or quell her expectant exhilaration.

Dreamily, she looked at her reflection in the mirror. He had never been more handsome than he was tonight. With his gold-streaked hair trimmed and his tanned, handsome face cleanly shaven, he had easily been the most dashing man at the ball. He was so at ease in such a social gathering and his uniform set him apart from all the other British officers. *He is no more than a lying cad!* she swore to herself as she remembered the attention he had showered upon Sybil Lancaster and her group of ladies. Why, he had not even told her his true name when she had been aboard his ship! One minute she believed him to be the captain of a ship called the *Vixen* and the next minute she learned he was a British officer! "The deceitful scoundrel!" she muttered aloud.

"I hope that was not directed at me." Justin stepped into the room and for a fraction of a second saw a soft look cross her features as she stared at him in the mirror. Then her expression quickly turned to something more akin to the words she had mumbled.

Hearing his husky voice and seeing him stand there in the reflection of the mirror filled Alisha with a warmth that saturated her entire being. But she swung around at her intruder.

"You! What do you think you're doing here in my chambers?" Her hand rose instinctively to pull her robe over her breasts, but she had forgotten to put her robe on over the satin night gown. The movement of her hand covering the delicate lace bodice now only seemed to draw Justin's attention.

An easy smile hovered about his sensual lips as Justin's large frame leaned against the double doors as if he thought it the most usual thing to be standing in a lady's chamber at this late hour.

"We have some things to discuss." His gaze roamed freely over her thinly clad body, his topaz eyes sparkling with a consuming warmth that seemed to sear her flesh. It was no wonder men were drawn to her as bees to honey, he thought. There was something about this woman that drove men beyond normal reason.

Alisha felt the heat of his gaze from across the room. "We have nothing to discuss and if you do not leave my room this minute, I will scream for my servants!" Alisha was bluffing, knowing well that Mandy slept in a room off the kitchen and would never hear her cries.

Her threats had little effect on Justin. He left the balcony entrance and took long strides across the room toward her.

To Alisha's awestruck eyes he looked for all the world like a hungry panther advancing on his next meal. "Stay away from me!" She shouted and jumped to her feet as he came closer to her. She held her hairbrush tightly in her fist as though she would not hesitate to use it to defend herself. "We are no longer aboard your ship, sir, and I will not be forced to abide your presence ever again!"

Keeping his distance but knowing he could easily bend her to his will, Justin was fully aware of her magnificence as the lantern light turned her copper curls to gold and her wide, silver-blue eyes shimmered with a fierce passion. As his gaze was drawn lower he glimpsed the full peaks of her breasts and the slender curve of her body under the satin gown.

"Is this the way you receive all your male guests, Alisha? Do you tempt them with your beauty and then hold them at arm's length? Or is it just me, madam, you would threaten with a hairbrush?" He lashed out at her as the anger he had held back all evening washed over him anew. As he watched her at the General's ball, he had realized she had never laughed and flirted and enjoyed his company as she had done with the men surrounding her all evening, nor had she ever willingly taken his arm for a stroll in the moonlight.

Alisha was aghast at his accusations. "How dare you? You who cared naught of the effects on my life from what took place aboard your ship! You easily cast me from your life and now you appear with a different name and shower me with insults!"

In a single step Justin reached her and as she pulled back the brush to ward him off, he grabbed her wrists and pulled her body tightly against his own. "What is Cornwallis to you?" he demanded in a cold, hard tone. No longer did he remember the reason he had given himself for coming to her house tonight; his only thought was the raging turmoil deep inside as he imagined other men touching her.

His powerful strength was consuming and she could not break free. Looking into his golden eyes and feeling the strength of his embrace she began to feel heated excitement kindle throughout her body.

"He is nothing to me!" she shouted and tried once again to gain her freedom. She desperately wanted to pull away, to stand her distance and deny the power that his touch held over her.

Reading the desperation upon her features as she tried to draw away, Justin held her tightly and bent to touch the sweet, tempting lips that seemed to invite his attention even as she cried out against him.

Twisting her head to pull away from his lips, Alisha found herself crushed against his broad chest. One of his hands left her arm and held her head firmly, leaving her powerless to escape his kiss.

The taste of his lips, the heat generated from his body, and the way he curved her back toward the hand that held her head as the other hand captured a full, ripe breast brought a powerful reaction from Alisha. She was tired of fighting off these feelings. She no longer had the strength to deny that her body and yes, her very soul, craved the flame of passion that raged out of control each time he touched her.

The powerful dislike they seemed to have for one another was nothing compared to the need that filled her at his slightest touch. For the past few weeks she had been plagued by desire for this man and she knew now that the struggle was far too difficult to keep up. Wrapping her slim arms about his neck and pressing her body closer, for the first time she fully allowed herself to accept the truth of her own feelings for this man.

Ravishing her mouth then nuzzling the soft flesh of her jaw and the slim column of her throat, Justin was fully aware of the tempting curves pressing fully against him, but not able to fight off thoughts of another man holding her. His words were sharply cutting. "Is it Tarleton who kisses these lips and caresses your beautiful body? Do you cry aloud with passion for him as you did for me aboard the *Vixen*?"

He could not stop the vitriolic words even knowing she was at last submitting to him.

As though cold water had been dashed upon her, Alisha recoiled and tried to pull away; but he kept her pressed against his chest, his lips wandering along her cheek and near the soft indent beneath her ear.

His attack was painful for him as well; but Justin could not force himself to relent. "Does he kiss the tender flesh beneath your breasts? Or has he not as yet had the pleasure of hearing you moan aloud with the contact of his mouth in that most delectable area?"

Alisha could bear no more. "No . . . no . . . I have never allowed . . ."

Justin did not let her finish as he pulled her to the bed in the center of the chamber. "Is it here that he comes to you, Alisha?" His tone was no longer hard and demanding, but worse it held a touch of bitter anguish that was not lost upon her.

"No!" she cried, unable to break free of his grip. She tried to place her hands over her ears to stop his verbal attack.

Justin's distrust of women was deeply rooted, and the torment of what he imagined she had done drove him onward. "Tarleton, Cornwallis, what other loyal British officer have you enticed with your beauty?"

"I hate them . . . I hate them all!" She wished only to be free of his hate-filled glare and his accusations. She was tired of fighting him off and tired of the game she was forced to play with the British. She wanted only to be left alone.

For a moment Justin stopped as he looked down into her distraught face and heard her heated denouncement of the British. He almost believed her, desperately wanted to grasp at the slim chance that she was not the faithless woman he had imagined; but as quickly, images of her and the spell she seemed to cast over the very men she now swore to hate, filled his mind. "There was little hate in your smiles for the British this night, madam!" As though believing her to be a deceiving seductress, his arms dropped to his sides and he took a step away seemingly repelled.

With his arms no longer holding her upright, Alisha slumped to the side of the bed when she felt the chill of his gaze. At that moment she knew for certain that he was more than willing to give her what she had sworn from their first meeting she had wanted above all from him: her freedom. Her blue-gray eyes misted over with tears. The look on his face at that moment brought Alisha such weariness and loneliness she felt like giving in to the utter desolation that settled over her. She was weary unto death, she thought grimly, but could not look away from his condemning gaze. She was fed up with this pretense before the British in order to avenge her father's death, and weary too of being strong and brave in front of Mandy and Amos who depended upon her. Above all, she realized she was weary of fighting her desire for this man who now despised her.

"They killed my father!" she cried with an anguished sob as she looked into his face. All her unshed tears began to flow uncontrollably.

Hearing the utter despair in her voice, Justin's anger disappeared. He gathered her in his arms and sat down on the bed. Pulling her tightly against his chest, his large hands softly pushed titian strands from her damp cheeks as he whispered words of comfort.

Once the tears were unleashed, Alisha was unable to stop them. She wept for the loss of her father; for the storm at sea and being washed overboard; for all she had been forced to face alone since arriving in Yorktown and for all the times she had wanted to cry out and had not permitted it. Tears rained down her cheeks and dampened the front of Justin's white shirt front, her deep sobs setting her atremble in his strong arms.

Feeling his heart twist at her abject misery, Justin softly crooned, "Hush, hush my sweet. I'm here now, and I'll let no more harm befall you." She said the British had killed her father, but in truth he did not understand. Her actions at the general's ball did not reveal any such hate toward those she claimed to be killers. But nonetheless, he knew that the pain she was feeling at this moment was real and it tore at his emotions as though it were his own. His lips slowly began to make feather-like kisses over her cheeks, tasting the salty moisture and furthering his desire to console her.

At last giving vent to the powerful emotions that had been building up, Alisha reached out for the comfort now being offered. As Justin's lips lightly touched her mouth, she held back none of her turbulent feelings. Her lips opened, her arms reaching up and holding him as though he were her lifeline in this crazy, tilting world. Her mind and body craved the forgetfulness she knew only within this man's arms.

With this kiss all of the fierce emotion they had tried to push aside over the past weeks of separation came surging to the surface. For the first time Justin knew that Alisha wanted him. It was not that she was submitting because her mind and body were at odds and her body had won. Justin knew that this time there was more. She was at last accepting her need of him.

Tasting the salty tang of her own tears as Justin's tongue plunged into her warm depths, Alisha's tongue circled and deliciously dueled with his.

There seemed no hurry to their love. It was as though the lovers were discovering each other for the first time. The kiss lengthened as Justin drew Alisha's tongue into his mouth and gently suckled the tender sweetness as though it contained the most flavorful ambrosia. His hands stroked her glorious curls and roamed over the curve of her graceful throat, where her pulsebeat fluttered erratically beneath his palm.

Alisha gave herself no time to wonder at her own actions. All she knew was that she wanted this man desperately. No matter that she had believed him to belong to another or that she did not know his real name or if he were a sea captain or British officer. The only thing she cared about was that he was here with her now. He was holding her in his strong embrace and she was safe. For this moment she no longer had to pretend she could face whatever came her way alone, or hide the fact that she desired him with every fiber of her being. Her tears had set free not only the hurt and fear she had been feeling but also the shield she had built up around herself and her body's desires.

As Justin released the satin binding that held the bodice of her gown and her breasts were left bare, she caught her breath even as his mouth was covering hers, as his thumb lightly rubbed a ripened peak.

Justin's mouth left Alisha's, his achingly gentle kisses drawing a path downward along her jaw and throat; his tongue savored the fullness of her breasts and made delicious patterns around one engorged, rose-tipped nipple and then the other, his love-play sending Alisha into spasms of unbearable longing.

Clasping his shoulders, her body pressed more fully against his. Justin tossed aside the nightgown that separated him from tasting the nectar of her woman's body. His hot mouth and tongue roamed farther down, across her abdomen, over a rounded, shapely hip and then at last settling upon the triangle of her womanhood. In the grip of sheer, blinding ecstasy he plundered her very core until she lay writhing beneath him in the throes of pulsating, white-hot passion.

Sending her ever higher into a spiral of blissful rapture, his mouth and fingers played incredibly upon her body. From the very center of her being, her essence began to simmer and melt, leaving her trembling with the exquisite pleasure of release.

As Justin at last rose and looked into her beautiful, passion-filled face and his own body throbbed with desire, he marveled inwardly at his tender feelings for this woman. She had broken through all the barriers he had built to keep from being hurt. As she looked up at him and their eyes met, he softly asked, "Have you any regrets, Alisha?"

Alisha felt herself surrounded by tenderness as she looked into his warm lion's eyes. "Nay, no regrets," she replied gently as her hand caressed his face.

Justin's heart sang. He had wanted so desperately to see the welcoming warmth he now saw in her eyes. Within seconds he had removed his shirt and breeches.

Alisha tingled with anticipation as she felt the heat of Justin's body and his mouth on her own. She was afire with her growing need to be joined with this man; she no longer cared why. As her hand roamed over the crisp, short hairs on his chest, she could no longer fight with her own emotions. She wanted him!

Justin gasped and moaned as Alisha's hands slowly began to run the length of his body. Her silken fingers roamed at will over his chest, along the corded muscles of his arms and neck and feathered across the flatness of his stomach and the smooth hardness of his tapered hips. As her hand lowered and her fingers wrapped around the pulsing hardness of his enlarged maleness she slowly began to ease up and down against its length and Justin feared for a moment he would come undone.

The feel of her soft, velvet hand and the knowledge that she was willing to give all of herself to him threatened Justin's control. "My heart, I can take little more of this," he raggedly whispered as he took her lips and his body burned with a consuming desire to make her his. Rising above her, he gently spread her creamy thighs and as they gazed into each other's eyes, he plunged within her softly yielding, moist depths.

Gentle words of love filled her ears as he placed melting kisses on her ears, across her cheeks and above her eyelids. Justin stroked within her depths with a sensuous rhythm, her legs about his waist. He drove deeper and deeper, binding them together with a burning intensity.

Clutching his back as she rode out the tempest of their powerful love play, Alisha felt an unquenchable desire spread within the pit of her being. Her body pulsated in exquisite pleasure with each stroke of his fiery lance. She strained upward, feeling droplets of his perspiration mixing with the sheen of her own. As a brilliant spark took hold and raged within the foundation of her being and erupted into a culmination of glorious pleasure, she cried aloud the name of her lover.

For a moment Justin partook of her body's wondrous giving as he gloried in the fact that she had tasted the ultimate fulfillment of their bodies coming together. Soon, he too was swept into the eddy of sweet, consuming pleasure and he lost all reason upon the tide of total rapture.

Ever so slowly his body stilled atop her as he fought to regain his normal breath; but still he seemed not to be able to get enough of her taste and the feel of her soft body. His lips plied her with kisses and lightly settled over her sweet, passion-swollen lips; his hands entwined in her wealth of silken curls as he inhaled deeply of her scent and traced the smoothness of her upper arms and slim back.

"Ah, my heart, you are all that any man could ever dream of," he sighed against her cheek. He had known her to be a passionate woman from those nights aboard the *Vixen*, but he could never have imagined that once she accepted her own sensuality

243

she would be even more passionate and giving.

Tightly held against him, Alisha no longer chastised herself for wanting him. For the first time she acknowledged her desire and now as she relaxed in his arms, fulfilled and sated, she found a peaceful contentedness. As his words reached her ears she fleetingly wondered about the other woman she imagined who shared his life and if he held any great love for her, be she wife or mistress. Not able to stop the words, she softly questioned as he stretched out beside her and held her closely, "Is your wife not all that you should be dreaming of?"

As his chest rumbled with laughter, Alisha felt the movement against her cheek. He was thinking of the dreams he had had of her over the past few weeks. "There is no wife in my life to torment my dreams, Alisha. There is only you."

Although she wasn't sure she should believe him, Alisha felt comforted by his words. Not knowing what a relationship like theirs would ever bring, at least she knew that another woman did not claim him as husband. There were many questions that Alisha would have liked to ask him but at the moment she was far too content lying in his arms. The answers to her questions could wait for another time, she thought with the sleepy assurance that there would be a next time for them.

Justin also had questions that needed answers but as he looked into her eyes and her cheek rested against his chest, he told himself he would wait until tomorrow to find out her reasons for entertaining the men she claimed had killed her father.

Chapter Fifteen

Alisha awoke early the following morning to find herself alone in her bed. Glancing around the chamber she noticed Justin's clothes were gone and the doors leading out onto the balcony were closed. With a smile of blissful contentment, she snuggled deeper into the down mattress. Last night had not been a wild fantasy conjured up from the depths of her mind. Justin had been there with her and after their first coming together in blinding passion, his heated kisses had awakened her twice during the night and they had discovered new delights. Alisha's dreams of Justin Martel were nothing compared to the man himself!

She would have wished him to stay by her side until morning, but he vanished before she awoke as he always had aboard the *Vixen*. But unlike those mornings aboard his ship, she now had no anger or confusion over her body's lack of control. Last night had been right. She had at last given in to her desires and accepted the fact that Justin Martel was the man who could set her soul aflame. She would take this chance even if only for a short time. She would not allow herself to dwell on the full magnitude of what she had allowed to take place here in her chambers last night; nor would she think about the day when Justin would again step out of her life. She felt at peace for the first time in so long that she would allow nothing to destroy this wonderful feeling.

Paying special attention to her toilet this morning, Alisha held the hope that Justin would pay a call at the Whitlaw house and the two of them could share more time together. After dressing in a pale peach gown she arranged her lustrous hair atop her head in soft ringlets, with feather-light curls at her temples and brushing her shoulders and neck.

She thought of all the questions she had failed to ask Justin. Though she now knew him to be a British officer, she contented herself with the fact that he could not have had a hand in her father's death, because he had not been in Yorktown when the murder had taken place. She wondered about the name Justin Martel; why had he told her this was his name and why had he claimed to be the captain of the *Vixen*? Surely there had been nothing in the ship's cabin to reveal him as anyone other than the captain he claimed to be. Remembering Justin's tenderness the night before, she reasoned that all of her questions would soon enough have answers. As easily as she pushed to the back of her mind her need for answers, she also pushed away thoughts of her feelings toward this man; it was enough for now that she no longer fought a battle with her own emotions where he was concerned.

After breakfast as Alisha was making her way toward the parlor, a knock upon the front portal announced the presence of a visitor. Believing it to be Justin, Alisha instantly felt the heavy hammering of her heart. Her slippered feet flew across the glistening pine floors and taking hold of the door knob, she drew in a deep breath as she attempted to restrain her excitement.

Her happiness was short lived! As she opened the door wide, Banastre Tarleton stood upon her front stoop. Taking a step backwards, Alisha forced herself to appear calm even as the dark gaze raked over her from head to toe.

"Colonel Tarleton, what a surprise."

"Indeed, madam, it would appear that I have managed at last to pay a visit and find you well and about." His words, which were to be taken in jest, held a hardness about them that was not lost upon Alisha.

There was little to do except invite him in. She could not afford to make an enemy out of this man. He was far too dangerous an adversary and much depended upon her good will from the British.

"Would you care to have a cup of tea, Colonel? I'm sure Mandy has a pot brewing and perhaps there are also some of her delicious lemon cookies."

As Tarleton was about to accept her invitation, a carriage drew up in front of the Whitlaw house and with bold, panther-like strides the officer now known as Andrew Wentford made his way up the front walk and approached the pair.

Banastre Tarleton held the other man in a brooding stare, as much as to say, *I thought I warned you last night to stay away from Alisha Whitlaw!*

Justin in return wore his most charming smile as he looked toward Alisha and greeted her in a huskily seductive voice. Then he turned to Tarleton. "Why, Colonel, what a surprise to find you here. I heard this morning you were going to Gloucester Point to fortify our defenses across the river."

"I leave this evening," Tarleton supplied sourly. He had planned on spending some time with Alisha today before leaving for Gloucester Point, and it did his mood little good to find Andrew Wentford at her door.

Alisha was more than relieved that Justin had made an appearance. Perhaps now Tarleton would not linger at her house but go on about his business. "I was just asking Colonel Tarleton into the parlor for tea. Would you care to join us, Lieutenant?"

Tarleton scowled at her invitation to his rival but ignoring the dark look directed at him, Justin quickly responded. "It would be my pleasure, madam." Stepping before Tarleton, Justin took hold of Alisha's arm and said pleasantly, "Lead the way, Miss Whitlaw."

Following closely behind the couple, Banastre Tarleton simmered with barely controlled hostility.

"Make yourselves comfortable, gentlemen. I'll be gone only a moment to let Mandy know we're in the parlor." Alisha fled, glad for the moment's respite to pull her jumbled nerves together. She also knew her need for haste, having left such an unlikely pair together in her parlor. She was gone only a short time before she reentered the parlor and found the two men sitting in opposite chairs facing each other darkly.

With Alisha's presence the men restrained their hostile impulses. Tarleton was determined he would not be put off any longer where his feelings for Alisha Whitlaw was concerned, and he set out to entertain her with a charming story from his past.

Justin calmly sat back in the comfortable chair and with a bored smile, he also listened to Tarleton. Justin still had questions about this relationship between Alisha and Tarleton, so he quietly listened and watched.

Alisha tried to appear interested in the story Tarleton was telling of court life before he left England, but with Justin in the same room, it was hard for her not to let her eyes stray. He was so incredibly handsome in his uniform and his large body so at ease he was a sweet, potent drug to her senses. As Tarleton droned on and on Alisha imagined what it would feel like for Justin's sensual lips to take her own as they had the night before. Feeling a flush come over her as she looked at him, she quickly lowered her head and kept her eyes on her hands folded in her lap.

Justin was aware of her silvery gaze traveling over him and then holding for an instant on his face. He also saw the light flush on her creamy cheeks, and he smiled warmly.

Entering the parlor none too quietly, Mandy interrupted Tarleton's story as she set the tea tray down before the settee. She directed a dark stare at both men before turning to Alisha. "Ye be wanting me to stay and pour fur ye, Miss Alisha?" It had been bad enough that Alisha had entertained this Colonel Tarleton one other time here in the parlor, but now there were two British officers and Mandy was loath to leave the young woman alone with them.

"No, thank you, Mandy. Everything is quite all right. You can go about your work." Alisha smiled at the elder woman with reassurance, but knew she would not be put at ease until both men left the Whitlaw house.

"So, Lieutenant Wentford, I find it rather odd that the General has not kept you busy and you have the time to pay visits to young women so soon after your arrival here in Yorktown." Tarleton spoke up as Mandy left the room and Alisha began to pour the tea.

"There was little for me to do today around the garrison, and the General himself gave me leave to amuse myself."

"Well, I am afraid you will have to entertain yourself somewhere else for the rest of the afternoon." Tarleton glared at the other man as he felt his temper stirring. "I plan to occupy Miss Whitlaw with a carriage ride, if she will consent." His chest appeared to swell and his eyes shifted from Justin to Alisha as though awaiting her agreement.

Alisha glanced from Justin and then back to Tarleton, feeling trapped. She stuttered, "I . . . I . . ."

"I am afraid you are a little late, my good fellow," Justin boldly stated and as Alisha's eyes widened he added, "Miss Whitlaw agreed only last evening at the General's ball to accompany me this afternoon for a carriage ride in the country." He had easily read

Alisha's distress at the other man's invitation.

"Yes, yes, of course I have already agreed to a carriage ride with Lieutenant Wentford." Alisha looked from the settee to where Tarleton sat and easily glimpsed his anger. "Perhaps another time, Colonel," she added before sipping her tea.

"Then perhaps I am the intruder." Tarleton stood to his full height and set his cup and saucer upon the table before the settee.

Alisha dared not openly make an enemy of this man, but not wishing to prolong his visit either, she also rose. "I will see you to the door, Colonel." She smiled warmly at him. Now that he was leaving, she felt she could afford to treat him graciously.

Justin finished his tea and wondered at Alisha's actions. It was obvious that she did not care for Tarleton, but why was she entertaining him and General Cornwallis? If she had spoken the truth and they were responsible for her father's death, this whole affair made little sense.

The few moments Alisha spent at the front door seeing Banastre Tarleton on his way were not pleasant. He was angry and did little to hide his feelings. She had tried to pacify him with a promise for another day, and though he had nodded his head stiffly, she could sense that he was not used to being put off by a woman.

Reentering the parlor, she found Justin standing before the double doors that led out into the gardens. For a moment she allowed her eyes to devour the sight of him, feeling rather shy over the fact that she was now a willing recipient of his attentions and no longer denied the attraction she felt.

"Thank you for saving me from a most unpleasant afternoon."

"Well, madam, I certainly don't wish to go for a carriage ride alone." He smiled, content for the time to be with her. Once again he told himself there would be time for the answers to his questions.

"Oh, I would love to go for a carriage ride with you. I thought you had only invited me in order to give me an excuse to avoid Colonel Tarleton."

"That too, madam, but I have my carriage waiting. I hoped we could go on a picnic together," Justin said with such boyish endearment she was powerless to resist.

A picnic in a quiet setting with just the two of them—the thought filled her with heady anticipation. She was instantly caught up in his enthusiasm and smiled in return, all thoughts of Tarleton banished from her mind. "I'll have Mandy prepare a basket for us."

"I've already taken care of that, my sweet. I but need you to make the afternoon complete." Justin stood before her and bending he softly kissed her smiling lips. "Now hurry off and fetch your shawl or what other womanly things you'll need." He took his arms from her and she hurried off to tell Mandy of her plans and to get a light wrap from her chamber.

Justin had rented a handsome, two-horse buggy from the blacksmith earlier and after making Alisha comfortable on the seat beside him, he directed the horses toward the Virginia coastline.

The day was gloriously warm as they left York-town and reached the peacefulness of the countryside. Alisha felt overwhelmingly atuned to the man sitting next to her. She watched his large, sun-browned hands as he expertly held the reins and she remembered the feeling of those same hands as they had so gently caressed her the night before. From the corner of her eye, she looked at him. He was so commanding and powerful. A warm flush touched her cheeks. The women at the General's ball had certainly been correct in their assessment of him when they had proclaimed him the most handsome man in all of Yorktown. For a moment her thoughts filled with images of Banastre Tarleton and she knew there was no comparison between the two men.

In a little less than an hour Justin slowed the vehicle and guided it down a little-used path toward the same small, secluded cove into which he had sailed the *Vixen* the night Will took Alisha to Yorktown.

She had been far too involved with her own thoughts that night, so Alisha did not recognize the area. "It's perfect for a picnic!" she exclaimed in an excited breath as she took in the picturesque setting. Lush green grass sloped down to the water's edge and a small wooden dock reaching into the calm depths of crystal water. Off in the distance, at the sea entrance of the cove, the ocean could be seen—a majestic, shimmering splendor as the afternoon sun glittered on the blue-green surface.

Coming around to her side and reaching up, Justin held her for a long moment against his body as he replied in that husky tremor that had the power to set Alisha's heart to fluttering, "I hoped you would like the quiet scenery."

After soundly kissing her, as the temptation was

253

far too much as she pressed against him, Justin released her reluctantly and reached into the back and drew out a large wicker picnic hamper. "Watch your step," he cautioned as he noticed her delicate slippers and began to lead her toward the water's edge where he spread out the blanket.

Placing the hamper down beside the blanket, Justin looked at Alisha with a warm grin. "Shall we eat first or take a swim?"

Alisha was not prepared for his question and began to stammer. "I . . . I . . . didn't bring anything to wear for swimming!"

Bending toward her, Justin took her in his arms and playfully swung her about in carefree abandon. "Clothes, my lady? We need no such hindrance to cover your fair beauty."

Alisha was giggling by the time he set her back on her feet. "You, sire, are indeed the rake I swore you to be aboard the *Vixen!*"

"Perhaps you're right, my heart." And for a second he appeared contrite over his suggestion, but as quickly the devilishly handsome grin was back on his face. "But can you imagine a better way to spend such a glorious afternoon? The cove is secluded from the outside world. There is just you and I, and I for one would very much like to take a swim!"

Alisha could not resist him. It had been far too long since she had been able to shed all restraints and enjoy herself to the fullest. She loved to swim in the nude and let the sun kiss her body, and with those warm, golden eyes looking down upon her with a twinkling gleam of mischief in their sparkling depths, she slowly nodded her head in agreement.

Justin was not a man to linger once his invitation had been accepted. His hands quickly unbuttoned the tiny row of buttons down the back of her gown. Then she pulled off the dress and her underclothing and the silky stockings with little lacy garters as well. He in turn hastily set about removing his own clothing.

Still feeling somewhat hesitant about being naked in his presence and particularly in broad daylight, Alisha moved quickly toward the water.

For a second Justin stopped and watched her delicately curved body until she disappeared into the water's depths. His heart racing, he hurriedly finished undressing and followed.

As Justin stood on the bank, Alisha surfaced and her sulfur-blue eyes marveled at the sight of his sun-bronzed body. The brilliant afternoon sun played on his massive form and his golden hair shimmered to his shoulders. His entire body seemed to surge with rippling muscles, his manhood rising proud and large. He looked like a sun god of Pagan lore, Alisha thought, feeling her body tremble as though afire even in the depths of the cool water.

She glimpsed his manly image for only a few seconds before he dove into the clear aqua depths. Standing in shoulder-deep water, Alisha watched the rippling surface for him and as long seconds drew on, she began to feel a moment's panic. With a gasp of strangled surprise, her arms flayed about widly as she felt her ankle being encircled by a tight grip and she was pulled under the water.

Gasping and sputtering, Alisha kicked out and made contact with a broad expanse of chest. As she pushed, her slim arms propelled her over the crystal surface of the lagoon and put a few yards between them to ward off his playful antics.

Justin grinned broadly as he saw her retreat, his golden eyes watching the outline of her trim backside as the soft flesh of her shapely buttocks was revealed tantalizingly as her movements brought her to the surface. "You cannot flee me, my winsome beauty." He laughed aloud with a self-assured tone and Alisha turned around and looked back in his direction. Too late—he was already gaining on her!

In the seconds left to her Alisha prepared for his attack and with a gleam of playful revenge twinkling in her eyes she took him unaware as she measured her distance and at the exact moment that Justin was at arm's length, she rose out of the water and with all the strength she could muster, she pushed against his chest, knocking him off balance and backwards beneath the water.

She did not await his recovery but hurriedly swam toward the other side of the water's edge; a tinkling round of feminine laughter filled the air as she delighted in dunking him thoroughly.

Justin was fast to recover and in good-natured fun he gave chase. His powerful body skimmed across the water and as he closed the gap between them once again he dove beneath the surface.

Rising from the blue-green water, Justin held Alisha tightly against his body. The silken feel of the liquid surrounding them cast an erotic spell about the pair.

As her hands wound around his expansive shoulders, Justin lifted her legs and cradled her against him; his mouth hovered above hers and slowly lowered until he stole Alisha's very breath. Feeling her body going limp in his arms, Justin suddenly released her.

Splashing down toward the bottom of the cove, Alisha shot back up with a mouth full of salt water and a fiery look in her eyes. "Why you . . . you!" She took off after him as he swam away and his laughter filled her ears.

The afternoon was given over to frolicking fun and when at last Alisha was exhausted from her play in the cool water, Justin carried her to the lush, grassy slope at the cove's edge.

Tenderly he placed her golden body in the splendor of the sweet-smelling emerald grasses; as his golden eyes locked with those of the most sparkling amethyst, he lowered his body to her.

Swept away with the total pleasure of the afternoon and knowing that they both wanted this moment to last forever they gloried in a wild, tempestuous passion with no bonds or restraints.

The smell and feel of the sweet grass and soft, moist earth beneath her as well as the sun's warmth and the taste of salt water all served as heady inducement to the surging rapture that stormed through Alisha's body. She gasped aloud as Justin's swollen shaft filled her. Wrapping her sleek legs about his waist she rose upwards to accept all of him. Her body moved in rhythm with his as she clutched his shoulders and the flame of his ardor carried them toward glorious fulfillment.

With his heart pulsating against her breasts and his mouth plundering hers, Justin held back nothing as he thought only of pleasing this woman who had somehow stolen through the icy shield he forged around his heart. Her soft, yielding body was like a temple of love, quenching his thirst with its heady liquid and setting his very soul afire with its passion. Never had he felt such earth-shattering pleasure in the arms of a woman!

Alisha was aflame in a world of bittersweet passion as Justin huskily whispered words of endearment. At this moment it mattered not at all about the tomorrows to come. Only Justin mattered! Only the sensations that he evoked held any meaning. Caught within the raging power of such ecstasy, a spark quickened throughout her body and sent her mindlessly over the brink of rapturous fulfillment.

At the same moment she found this all-consuming climax, Justin's lion's eyes gazed down into Alisha's passion-filled face and something in her expression as she clung to his shoulders and called out his name touched off a flame deep within him. He had sworn never to care for another woman; he had believed himself incapable of bearing the pressures that caring for a woman forced upon a man; but as he looked down at her he knew there was something between them that he could not deny. And though he pushed aside these thoughts with fear of their true meaning, he knew that one day he would have to face this call from his inner heart. His large hand tenderly caressed the creamy skin over her cheekbone, his lips once more seeking out the sweet-honey taste of hers and his body moving with harder thrusts as he too was soon brought to blinding peaks of pleasure.

Neither spoke as they clung together in the bower

of the tall, sweet-smelling grass. Both marveled at the feelings that had so recklessly overtaken them. It was a warm, heady euphoria that settled over them and had them gazing in wonder into each other's eyes.

At last with a laugh Justin broke the spell. He rose and pulling Alisha into his arms he carried her to the embankment at the water's edge and with the tenderest care he rinsed her body. Leaning with her arms on the bank, Alisha held her head back and enjoyed the warm kiss of the sun caressing her naked flesh as Justin cupped the cool liquid in both hands and allowed the moisture to cascade over her neck and breasts.

"This has been a wonderful day," Alisha said dreamily as she shut her eyes and felt the titillating seduction of the sun's rays drying the droplets of water he was showering over her.

"You say this only because you have suddenly realized you enjoy running about without benefit of clothing." Justin smiled as his golden eyes took in the full magnitude of her naked splendor as he leaned over her.

Soft, tinkling laughter filled his ears as Alisha languidly stretched before him and eased a portion of her lower body into the silky-cool water that lapped along the embankment. "I don't wish to disappoint you, but I usually swim without attire. My cousin Estelle's husband's property ran along the beach on Martinique, and in privacy Estelle and I spent many afternoons as we are now."

"Not quite as we have." Justin grinned at her with a devilish glint in his eyes as he remembered the last couple of hours. "Come, Alisha, I'm starving. You can tell me about your family as we eat." He had hoped to find out more about her this afternoon and with lighthearted grace, he pulled her to her feet and for a moment held her in his embrace.

Carrying her to the picnic blanket Justin playfully kissed and nipped at the tender flesh of her throat and the creamy tops of her breasts before placing her on her feet.

Flushed and light-headed, Alisha felt rather awkward standing before him naked so she hastily pulled on her peach satin chemise. As soon as her body and hair dried she would put on her gown, but until then at least she had something to cover herself.

As Alisha sat on the edge of the blanket, Justin thought her the most desirable creature he had ever seen with her flushed cheeks and the skimpy, peach-colored bit of material she had put on. Silently he slipped into his breeches and then began to lay out the food and the bottle of wine that were in the wicker hamper.

Feeling totally relaxed in his presence, Alisha bit off a chunk of the tangy cheese he had placed on the plate and watched with admiration as his muscled upper torso flexed and curved with every movement. "China and crystal," she murmured lightly. "'Tis a fitting tribute to such a glorious afternoon."

Justin stretched out on his side and leaning on an elbow, sampled the tasty variety of cold meat, fruit and cheese as he sipped at his wine. "I'm pleased you've enjoyed our day together, Alisha." He could well remember a time when he would never have believed that the two of them could share such an intimate interlude.

Alisha's thoughts were running in the same direction and as she took a bite of the fragrant dark bread, she broached the subject that had been on her mind since last night. "You have not told me what I should call you, Justin or Andrew."

Justin sighed softly, knowing that sooner or later he would be forced to answer some of her questions. "Andrew Wentford will do for now." He tried to sound cheerful as he refilled his wine glass and hoped he could discourage her from prying too deeply into his affairs. He was still unsure of how far he could trust her and how much depended on safeguarding his identity.

Seeing tht he was not at all willing to open up and tell her all, Alisha sat up a bit straighter and her silvery eyes searched his face. "But why did you tell me your name was Justin Martel and allow me to believe you were a ship's captain?" She was still as confused as she had been at the General's ball. She had thought that after what had taken place last evening in her chamber and here today, he would willingly confide in her.

"When the *Vixen* rescued you at sea, I was on my way to the colonies to honor my oath to the cause I believe in and at the time I gave you the name I believed most appropriate." He did not tell her that the cause he spoke of was the patriot's own, nor did he fully explain that instead of the name Justin Martel he could have given her the one most of the populace of the Caribbean called him, Captain Fox.

Alisha listened attentively, but still had the feeling he was not revealing everything; but before she could question him further, he set aside his plate and leaned closer.

He slowly ran his fingers through her damp russet curls and with his warm, gold-flecked eyes riveted on her, he had the power to make her forget all the curiosity and distrust she was feeling.

"Now tell me something about yourself, Alisha. You said last night that the British were responsible for your father's death. Is this the reason you came back to Yorktown?" He would have said more about her friendly manner toward those she claimed to be guilty of murder and the fact that Banastre Tarleton seemed to hold more than a passing interest in her, but he did not want to break the trusting mood of the afternoon. He had tried all morning to find out about her father and had been told only that Charles Whitlaw was a newspaperman who had been killed by unknown assailants a few months past.

Alisha had her own distrust of sharing confidences too easily. Now that she knew him as a British officer named Andrew Wentford, she warned herself to be very careful. Revealing too much could threaten not only her but also Mandy, Amos and Ben. Looking into his eyes, though, she felt herself wanting to trust him, wanting to share all that she had been through in the past months and wanting to believe he would understand. Taking a sip from her wine glass, she said softly "The British did kill my father. They have denied their part in the affair, declaring that the patriots were at fault, but there was a witness they did not know about who watched a British troop leave my father's office the night he was killed." She would not tell even him that her witness was Amos

McKenzie. "When I received the news of my father's death I was on the Island of Martinique and hurried to book passage on the next ship heading for the colonies. You know the rest after I was washed overboard."

"Yes indeed, my sweet. I was the lucky man who fetched you from the sea." He bent and lightly tasted her wine-sweetened lips for a few moments before questioning her further. "I still don't understand why you would wish to be in the presence of those who have brought about such tragedy in your life— nor do I understand why you would entertain Banastre Tarleton in your parlor." Justin had little doubt that the British were responsible for her father's death. After all, Charles Whitlaw was a newspaperman and if he were reporting the facts, the British would surely find him a thorn in their side. He was surprised, however, at her claim of having a witness. It was well for the sake of this witness that she did not reveal his name. Remembering the smitten look on General Cornwallis's face at the ball and the way Tarleton watched her with greedy fire in his dark eyes, Justin was positive that if either man knew of any who had witnessed the foul deed, which surely would have been carried out by their orders, the General or the Colonel would not hesitate to add her witness's name to the list of mysterious deaths in Yorktown.

"How else can I find out the truth and the names of those who went to my father's office that night?" Alisha asked, not daring to divulge that she also gained the much-needed information for her flyers by entertaining the British.

Justin digested her words slowly. "Then this is your only reason for being in the company of men such as Cornwallis and Tarleton? To find out who the men were who killed your father?" There was some niggling doubt in the back of Justin's mind as he wondered if there was something she was not telling him. Perhaps they were both too fully atuned to each other, or perhaps it was the fact that their earlier relationship kept them so wary of each other; they both were suspicious.

Alisha slowly nodded. "What more could there be?"

What more indeed, Justin wondered as that small blade of jealousy twisted in his heart once again remembering her in the company of other men at the General's ball—and the image of Banastre Tarleton's dark features stole into his mind.

Finishing her food and wine Alisha rose to her feet. "I believe I'm dry now and able to put on my gown." She could accept the fact that Justin was a British officer if she had to, and she would go over the answers he had given her about his name and the ship called the *Vixen*. She knew with certainty that there was something he was holding back, but she knew also she would get no more answers today.

Lyng on the blanket with his hands behind his head, Justin quietly watched as she bent and pulled up the sheer stockings over her delicately slim legs and fastened them above the knee with the lacy peach garters trimmed with tiny rosettes on the outer border. Settling the abundance of pale peach petticoats about her hips, she wavered for a moment before putting on the gown as she pulled her thick,

264

unruly hair back at the nape of her neck. "I have no brush with me. What will Mandy and Amos think when I return to the house?"

A brow arched over a golden eye as Justin said in a possessive tone at her mention of another man, "And who pray tell, madam, is this Amos you are worried about seeing?"

"Why, Amos McKenzie is a dear friend of my family. He worked for my father for years and lives in the carriage house on my property." Alisha barely paid attention to his tone of voice as she worried over her own predicament.

Remembering the vague report given to him by Will when he had returned back to the *Vixen* after taking Alisha to Yorktown, he remembered that Will had made mention of an old man greeting her at her father's house. He felt rather foolish over his jealous reaction. Reaching a hand toward her with a warm, generous smile, he huskily offered, "The solution is a simple one, my sweet. We shall remain here for a while longer and when the sun goes down I will take you home. Perhaps with any luck you'll be able to steal into your home without being noticed."

Considering his solution to her problem, Alisha was more than willing to stay a while longer in this delightful setting, alone with this man. She felt her heart beat with pure pleasure as she bent toward him and his hands pulled her down against his side.

"It's a shame you wasted time on all that dressing," Justin murmured throatily before his lips lowered to take hers while his hands unlaced the satin strings of her petticoats.

Her soft moan of agreement reached his ears as her

265

hands roamed over his broad chest and took hold of the fastenings of his breeches. "I have forgotten to thank you for the chest of clothes and the purse of gold coins," she said in a silken undertone.

"You can thank me later." Justin's lips fastened over hers as he pressed the length of his manhood against the softness of her passion's jewel and within the breath of a spellbinding kiss, they were joined.

As is the way of young lovers, the rest of the afternoon was spent in the magical discovery of the full elixir of passion's sweet pleasures. They were swept beyond thought of duty, honor and vengeance; their sole purpose was the age-old union of man and woman. Soft, whispered love words, tender caresses and moans of utter fulfillment settled around the peaceful seclusion of the cove as the bright orange sun slowly set over the ocean.

Chapter Sixteen

Wearing a dress of soft, pale blue muslin with tiny sprigs of flowers which had been hand stitched over the full skirt and puffed sleeves, Alisha made her way through the Yorktown streets toward British headquarters. She had made plans earlier in the week to have tea this afternoon with General Cornwallis.

With time for her own thoughts as she made her way, her inner reflections once again turned to Justin Martel. It had been just as well that he had claimed to have had business to attend to last evening after returning her home. She had barely made it up the stairs and to her chambers and brushed out her hair when she had heard Mandy's heavy footsteps outside her door, reporting that Amos was awaiting her downstairs.

While she had passed a glorious afternoon with her lover at the cove, Amos had printed another batch of flyers to be distributed throughout Yorktown that very night.

She was quickly learning how taxing this double

life as a crusader against the British and a woman involved with a man could be. And the man was a British officer himself!

She had to make sure that the person she now believed to be Andrew Wentford learned nothing of her activities on behalf of the patriots. She realized that if he had accepted her invitation to come to her house later in the evening or if he suddenly had arrived unannounced just as she and Amos were preparing to leave with the flyers, he could easily have the opportunity to denounce her as a traitor and see that she pay for her crimes against England. She was unsure how deeply he honored his pledge to uphold the Crown's dictates, but believing from the little she knew of him that he was indeed an honorable man, she knew she could take few chances were he was concerned.

One more proof that this job as the Vixen was wearing thin was, in truth, that she was exhausted. She and Amos had not returned home until the early hours and now here she was with her lacy parasol and copper curls appearing as fresh as a spring day. She entered the dark corridors at British headquarters, all the while desiring no more than to be home in her soft, warm bed.

But the price had to be paid, she reminded herself as she approached the young officer sitting outside the General's door. To get her revenge she had to put out her flyers and to keep up her actions as the Vixen, she needed the General's help.

The young man sitting outside the General's office door no longer detained Alisha out in the hall, but now flashed her a welcoming smile. "I will inform the General that you have arrived, Miss." He quickly left his desk and hurried through the General's door. Gone only a few seconds, he returned with the assurance that General Cornwallis would indeed see her now. There was no denying that the General was quite taken with her, the young man thought as his eyes followed her with some longing as she disappeared through the open doorway.

"My dear Alisha." Charles Cornwallis stepped around his large desk and hurried to take her hand. "You look breathtakingly beautiful as ever." His dark eyes traveled over her from head to foot as he led her toward the settee in the corner of his office.

"And you, Charles, are as gallant as ever." Alisha forced a smile, still finding it hard to call him by his first name and to appear to welcome his advances when inwardly she cringed each time he touched her.

"Make yourself comfortable. Our tea should arrive shortly." The General sat down upon the settee next to her, and Alisha stiffened. "Now tell me all you've been doing since I saw you last." He noticed none of her negative reactions. He was too busy watching her with eager anticipation as he desired to win her confidence. His one hope was that she would realize that she depended upon him.

"It seems there is very little to tell since I saw you last at the ball, Charles. I rested most of yesterday." The lie brought a light flush over her cheeks as she recalled the manner in which she had spent the previous day. "I intend to do a little shopping this afternoon," she added as she saw him watching her intently.

Charles noticed her flushed features, but never

269

could have imagined the reason for it. He thought her far too delicate, and hoped she had indeed gotten enough rest; now that he looked a bit closer he noticed that she did appear fatigued.

"Ah, shopping is a lady's true calling." He reached out and lightly patted her slim hand which rested on her lap. "You must watch you do not overdo though, my dear." The thought of something happening to her now that he had found her filled him with a terrible dread.

His solicitous manner annoyed Alisha, but she didn't show it. "Now tell me, Charles, what has been keeping you busy lately?" She was desperately hoping he would inadvertently supply her with more information for her flyers. Her feelings for these British had to be put aside, for many depended solely upon her to bolster them in this time of English rule here in Yorktown. She had noticed that Amos had a lighter step these days and Mandy sang more often as she went about her work and always had a ready smile. Even Ben seemed to hold his head higher and his shoulders straighter; all this was due to the effort they were making to strike a telling blow against their oppressors. She could not let them down—or the townspeople, who awaited the flyers as their only hope of hearing about the war raging all around them.

"I'm sure you don't wish to spend our time together listening to the problems that beset the Crown at this time, my dear. We should speak of lighter, more interesting things."

"But Charles, I truly am interested in everything you do. Do you find me the type of woman to whom

270

you can only speak of frivolous matters?" Her tone sounded hurt as she hoped to sway him into opening up to her.

In the past Charles Cornwallis had shared a very agreeable marriage with a woman who had appeared to hold his best interest at heart. He had often confided in her about his work, the good and the bad, and oftentimes he had felt easier after the telling. Perhaps that was one of the things he had mourned the most after her passing—being able to share everything with a woman who truly cared. Looking at Alisha now and hearing the upset in her voice as though she felt he was rejecting her, his heart soared with the thought that this woman and he were fated to be together. "Of course you are right, my dear. I only thought not to bore you with any problems that may be on my mind."

"Why, I'm never bored with anything you might have to say, Charles. You're the most interesting man I have ever met."

In the past Charles had mentioned some of his minor problems here in Yorktown and he remembered how intently she had appeared to listen to his every word. Believing her to have a young woman's infatuation toward a man with his authority, he was not about to shatter any of her youthful illusions.

"I do admit, my dear, that the last few weeks have indeed been a bit trying. Being a man with such high power in service to the Crown is not an easy undertaking." He was more than willing, if it would help his cause to win the lovely Alisha Whitlaw, to further her high regard of him with mention of his great responsibilities.

"I quite understand, Charles. I know it cannot be easy on you, what with so many under your command, and your being responsible for keeping order here in the southern colonies." Alisha boosted his male ego more than a little with her words. "Now tell me, I have heard little about this Vixen lately. Have you perhaps put a stop to those dreadful flyers?" She knew from his comments in the past that the Vixen was indeed a sour subject with him.

"Nay, the identity of this Vixen has not been found out as yet. There was another of those traitorous handbills plastered around town this very morning!"

"Oh, how dreadful," Alisha replied, but before more could be said the young officer brought in the tea tray. *What timing!* Alisha thought to herself. *Just when the general was beginning to loosen up somewhat!*

After the tray was placed upon the small table before the settee and Alisha had poured two cups, she looked at him with a generous smile hoping he had not lost his train of thought with the disturbance. "Now where were we, Charles? You were telling me about this rebel known as the Vixen."

"Yes, yes, the Vixen." Cornwallis took a sip of the tea and lowering the cup in his hand, he sighed deeply. "And if these troublesome flyers are not enough to keep my men busy searching over Yorktown for his identity, this morning I discovered that several important papers have been stolen from a locked drawer in my desk. I can only assume it is the work of this spy who goes by the name of the Fox."

"I do hope the papers were not too important?" Alisha would have given her eye teeth to take a look

272

at those papers, but she forced her tone to sound concerned for him.

"They were mostly correspondence with Clinton. Now that we know Washington is heading southward it is imperative that we get reinforcements here in Yorktown. Henry Clinton, in his usual indecisive manner, is acting slowly in that regard. Promises are all I have so far!"

"And what about the rumor of the French fleet?"

"We have heard little more. The French troops here in the colonies have joined with Washington. I received news that they put on a colorful spectacle in Philadelphia with a complete band and dressed to the hilt before an audience of twenty thousand. That's about all those damn French are good for, pomp and ceremony!"

Alisha heard the scorn in the General's voice, but she secretly envied those who had had the wonderful good fortune to watch as the French and American colonial troops marched through the streets of Philadelphia to the cheers of their supporters. "What will happen if they reach Yorktown before Clinton's help arrives?" Alisha pretended concern for the General's benefit, but inwardly her heart raced with the anticipation of the patriots at last taking such a grand step to liberate the colonies from the British for once and for all.

"Do not worry, my dear," Cornwallis was quick to assure as he glimpsed the brightness of her blue-gray eyes and read it as fear. "Clinton's troops will arrive in time but if not, there are enough ready men right here under my command to send the French and American rabble scrambling back to where they have come from!'' Cornwallis did have great faith in his own abilities as a leader and the strength of his command, but he knew his worries over holding this strategic position in the southern colonies would be better allied with the reinforcements that Clinton kept promising. Perhaps any day now the men would arrive, he thought, trying to ease his mind.

"So, Charles, tell me more about this spy known as the Fox.'' Alisha changed the subject, hoping to keep Cornwallis talking for she sensed that he worried over her delicate sensibilities.

"There is very little I can tell. Whoever he is, I believe he's in my command. He's as sly as his name implies; garnishing information for the enemy about our base here in Yorktown and seemingly right beneath our very noses, he has stolen documents and military maps along with valuable correspondence.''

"My, he does sound rather wily!'' Alisha's curiosity was more than a little piqued as she wondered who this spy called the Fox could be and what information he had thus far gathered.

"Be sure, he will make a mistake sooner or later and when he does we will be ready!'' Not wishing Alisha to worry over any of these affairs and wanting her to believe him fully in charge of every situation, he smiled broadly. "I do believe our tea is getting cool with all this talk of defenses and intrigue.''

Alisha saw that he was becoming quite anxious about talking about his problems here in Yorktown. Not wishing to arouse his suspicions unduly, she told herself she had learned much for one day. With a smile in return she sipped the now tempered tea.

*   *   *

Leaving Cornwallis's office, Alisha spent the rest of the afternoon at her writing desk in her bedchamber, laboring over the contents of the next flyer. She made mention of a new ally to the cause known as the Fox and entreated the populace to take heart for the French and American militia forces would soon overthrow the tyrants. Her main desire was to give the colonists hope of a brighter day ahead. She wanted to get word to them that their suffering would not last forever, and in doing this she also was able to strike a blow against the wrongs that had been done to her own family.

Alisha had been disappointed that she had not seen Andrew at the British garrison nor had she heard from him throughout the rest of the day. Their secret moments yesterday were the most romantic she had ever known.

Inwardly Alisha pondered these new feelings she harbored for this man she knew so little about. No longer did she feel the overwhelming hurt and anger toward him that she had aboard the *Vixen*. These new feelings that filled her heart every time she looked at him, or as today when she could think of little else but him, left her with an aching need.

There had been no talk between them of the future. She had already made her own plans to return to her cousin on Martinique when this war with England was finished, and these plans certainly did not include Andrew Wentford. But still it crossed her mind to wonder what it would be like to have such a man for her own. To hear that husky voice each morning and go to sleep each night in those powerful arms with that masculine body pressed tightly against her.

She was being silly. What she and Andrew had discovered between them was far too new to analyze, or to believe there was enough to warrant a lifetime together. Perhaps being intimate with any man could bring about these strange inner feelings she was experiencing. But upon reflection, she knew there was no other she had met in Yorktown since her arrival, nor any man from her past who was capable of making her pulse beat so recklessly.

By the time dinner time came Alisha appeared more animated and carefree than either Mandy or Amos had seen her since her arrival in Yorktown. As she enthusiastically told them of her meeting with General Cornwallis and all the information she had gotten while taking tea with him, Amos wondered if her mood had been brought about by the man he had seen her with the day before.

He had been watching from the carriage house window when the buggy brought her home after dark yesterday evening. Silently he made his way to the side of the Whitlaw house when he recognized the gentleman at her side as a British officer. His only thought had been for her safety when he had been witness to the tender kiss shared between the two outside her front door.

Silently Amos had stayed in the shadows of the house and with concern he had watched Alisha go into the house and the tall British officer climb back into the buggy and drive off. He had not seen the man until that evening, but this morning he had made several inquiries and had found out that he was only recently arrived in Yorktown. Amos had debated with himself all day about cautioning Alisha over

276

becoming too close to one of the same group she had sworn her vengence upon, but as he noticed the special attention she had paid her toilet this evening and her cheerful mood, he had not the heart to dampen her spirits. There would be time enough to watch and find out more about this officer called Andrew Wentford.

"You need to try and find out who this Fox is, Amos."

Jolted from his thoughts Amos shook his head, unsure that he had heard her correctly. "What was that you said, lass?"

"We should find out who the Fox is. Perhaps we can help him, or he may be willing to help us get information for the flyers." Alisha had thought about this all day and now her eyes sparkled with the hope of setting such a plan into action. If they could find out who the Fox was, perhaps he would give them some of the information he had gathered from British headquarters. She would dearly love to know what the letters from Clinton contained.

"But, lass, what makes you think we can find out who this Fox is? The British have been looking for him over the past two weeks and have not turned up a clue. Why do you think we could do any more?"

"The British think they can strong-arm information from people," Alisha said in disgust. "You on the other hand, can watch and take notice of what they do not see. I have every faith in your abilities." Alisha gave the older man a wink as she took a bite of Mandy's savory beef stew.

"Why now, that be a fact fur sure, Miss Alisha. Old Amos here, he knows more of what takes place in this town than anyone else." Mandy voiced her support of Alisha's intent to set Amos on the trail of the Fox. "If'in anybody can find this Fox it surely be Amos!"

Amos was pleased at their confidence, but he was not sure how he was to go about discovering the identity of this spy. "I'll see what I can find out, lass." There was no way out for him but to agree given the expectant attitude of the two women.

As dinner was finished there was a knock on the front door and Alisha dashed out of the kitchen before either Mandy or Amos could step away from their chairs. It had to be Andrew, she told herself, and felt her heart beating with fevered anticipation at seeing him once again.

Disappointment was written on Alisha's features when she opened the door to find a youthful, sandy-haired soldier standing on her front step. After her initial surprise receded, she softly questioned the young man. "Is there something I can help you with?"

He stood nervously before Alisha clutching a long, narrow, beautifully wrapped box. At the General's ball he had watched her from afar, too bashful to approach. As he stood before her, the young man felt his face flush as he held out the box. "I . . . I was instructed to deliver this to you, miss."

"Why, thank you." Alisha took the foil-wrapped box from him, imagining it a present from Andrew and anxious now to see the contents.

For a moment longer the young soldier stared at her admiringly before turning away.

Closing the door, Alisha went into the parlor and hurriedly took the lid from the box. Beautiful red roses and a tiny card on top! How thoughtful of Andrew, she told herself as she set the box upon a table and began to open the card.

Disappointment once again overcame her as she read the message and signature of Banastre Tarleton. Would the man never give up, she asked herself in irritation. She stared at the small card, the beauty of the roses having faded considerably since she had first seen them.

Amos entered the parlor and glimpsing her annoyance, did not ask her about the box of flowers. "Have you finished with the material for the next flyer, lass? I thought I would run them off tomorrow and we would get them out tomorrow night." He sat down in one of the wingback chairs with the intention of spending a few minutes in her company before making his way to the carriage house for the rest of the evening.

Wishing to push aside all thoughts of Banastre Tarleton, Alisha took the chair opposite Amos. "I worked on the draft for the flyer all afternoon. I have it now on my desk. I put in much of what I told you and Mandy. I only wish we could find out more information about this French fleet. If it is to meet with Washington and the French troops heading southward, it could make a vast difference in the outcome of the conflict here in the south when they come up against Cornwallis's forces."

"It could well be just a rumor, lass, or if there is a French naval fleet coming to the colonies it could well be on its way to New York to attack Clinton."

"I wish there was more we could do to help fight against these arrogant British intruders." The part they were playing in this struggle for freedom seemed very insignificant to Alisha.

"You're giving the people hope, girl. That's more than they have had since Cornwallis took over Yorktown." Amos noticed her mood and hoped to cheer her.

"Yes, I guess we are able to do at least that much, and the Vixen has become a rough thorn in the side of the British." She smiled with remembrance as she recalled General Cornwallis's words today about the Vixen.

"Aye, lass, and every setback in the way of the British is a help to the cause for freedom."

Alisha knew that Amos was right. Her spirits were low because the hour was growing late and she had not heard a word from Andrew Wentford. Receiving roses from Tarleton only made her feel more vulnerable with this new relationship she had with the handsome sea captain—or British officer. "Of course you're right, Amos. I guess I just feel a little down tonight. I think I'll go to my chamber and have a long, hot bath." She had given up all hope that Andrew would come for a visit as the hour drew late.

"I'll carry up the water, lass, before I go to the carriage house." Amos smiled warmly and as he started toward the kitchen he knew instinctively that her mood swing from high to low was somehow because of this new man in her life. Well, perhaps a good hot bath would soothe her somehow, he thought and hurriedly went about heating the water.

Resting her head against the rim of the brass tub,

Alisha luxuriated in the soothing warmth of the rose-scented water surrounding her. Closing her eyes she was immediately caught up in a dream-sleep as the liquid left her limbs feeling weightless.

Alisha's mind was far from the confines of her bedchamber as she relaxed in the tub. Her dreams took her to the day before when she and her dream-lover had spent the afternoon at the secluded cove. She saw him as he had stood along the bank with the sun shining on his naked form. There was no doubt in Alisha's mind—he was truly the most magnificent man she had ever known. His suntanned features and golden eyes seemed to melt her senses as she was caught up in the splendor of her dream vision.

Thus it was that she did not hear the opening of the French double doors leading from the balcony, nor did she hear the footsteps of the man who strode with panther-like grace across the chamber and now stood looking down at her.

Suddenly she felt a splash of water hit her face as the man reached down and stirred the water, and with some surprise her blue-gray eyes flew open. Surprise instantly turned to pleasure as she saw the same golden-eyed features that had consumed her dreams.

"Ah, my sweet, you look so enticing with your eyes shut and your beautiful face looking so contented. Tell me what you were dreaming about, my heart?" Justin spoke as softly as a lover's caress as he bent to the rim of the tub and his eyes took in the full measure of her beauty through the crystal clear water.

Alisha shook her titian curls, too embarrassed with thoughts she could not possibly share with him.

"You're mistaken, Andrew. I was but resting. The warmth of the water made me drowsy." She felt herself blushing and thought to turn the subject to him. "Do you make a habit of sneaking into a lady's chamber and startling her?"

"So you're trying to change the subject, are you?" A husky light laugh escaped him. "You think to refuse my questions, but I will not hear of it. Tell me of your dreams, my lady; were they perhaps of a lover? And did he do this?" His lips stole over hers in possessive tenderness.

Caught up in the joy of the moment, Alisha's breathing grew ragged, and the tops of her breasts, peeking out of the water, rose and fell as his lips heatedly devoured her own.

When he released her, Alisha quickly brought her hands up against those same rose-tipped breasts, trying to shield them from those golden eyes.

With another small, husky laugh Justin reached out and took her hands away from the object of his penetrating gaze. "You surprise me, my sweet. After all we have shared, you still blush and seem demure as an untouched maiden." He thought of the day before when they had spent the afternoon together without the hindrance of clothing. That had been one day he knew he would not easily forget. Standing to his full height, he turned away from the tub.

Believing he was allowing her the time to finish her bath, Alisha was surprised as he purposefully made his way to the chamber door and turned the lock with a little click. "What are you doing?" her eyes grew large and desire sparkled in their depths as he made his way back toward the tub.

"Why, sweet Alisha, I'm going to share your bath." He casually began to pull off his boots, his shirt and his pants.

"But there is little room in the tub," Alisha weakly protested as she gazed upon him in all his naked, virile splendor and felt herself begin to tremble from the sheer visible force of his masculine beauty.

Justin's strong arms reached out and gently lifted her back down upon his lap. "Nay, my sweet, there is plenty of room. Perhaps now we can partake of more of the dreams you wish to keep secret. Only this time we shall discover these dreams together." His head bent to her lips in a heady blending of their senses.

Facing him as she sat upon his lap with the water flowing to the top of the rim of the tub, Alisha could harldy breathe as Justin took up the soap and lathered a cloth, then so very slowly began to wash the upper part of her body. Every touch caused shivers of desire to course over her body. The cloth roamed over her slim throat, across the fullness of her breasts and intoxicatingly over her shoulders and down her arms. She could but hold her eyes tightly shut as her breath escaped in short, ragged gasps.

Discerning her sensual pleasure, Justin was hard pressed to go slowly as he watched Alisha's features and felt his blood pound hotly in his loins. The very beat of his heart cried out for a swift end to this lust-filled agony that had beset him. With far greater determination than quickly slaking his own needs, he endured the torturous ache of his own cravings to lose himself within the sweet folds of her trembling body.

With the finish of his washing, Justin rinsed away

the sweet smelling soap and instantly his lips began to blaze a scorching path upon the same avenue the washcloth had earlier ventured.

Squirming upon his lap with delicious tremors of passion licking through every portion of her body, Alisha came into contact with his large pulsing maleness, and caring only for the consuming fulfillment his powerful manhood could bring, she pushed her lower body closer.

With the last bit of control Justin had, he resisted the temptation of a hasty joining. He felt her soft, tempting bottom pressing against him but still his lips roamed over her neck and shoulders; his tongue devoured the sweetness of her tender flesh as he licked and kissed the tops of her breasts and as his mouth captured a rose-crested-peak he heard her cry, "No more, please! Take me now!" Her anguished plea was far too great an invitation to resist.

With a thrust of tormented longing they came together. Her hands clutched his neck and her hair, free from the pins which had held it atop her head, flowed freely over her back and his upper body. Alisha rode the pulsing fire of his love. Her body moved up and down, undulated, and shuddered as wave after wave of intense rapture filled every part of her body.

The moment was much too erotic to last forever; the warmth of the water flowing around them, the delicate rose scent filling the air and the feel of Alisha's body moving atop his brought Justin's desire to the boiling point. Clutching her hips he brought her down more fully against him and with her cry of delighted fulfillment, his mouth covered hers as he felt the fiery explosion of an earth-shattering climax.

Alisha lay weak and gasping against Justin's broad chest as the heat of their joining finally cooled. As she felt his hands gently caress the length of her back and his lips kiss her forehead tenderly, she fleetingly wondered once again what a lifetime would be like in this man's arms. She felt such a tender ache deep within as she heard the beating of his heart and silently asked herself if this could be the love that great poets wrote about. Had she truly allowed herself to fall in love with this man?

"I fear, my sweet, that we have made a great mess of your chamber." Justin spoke a bit raggedly as he glanced over the rim of the tub and noticed the dampness from the large amounts of water that had gone over the side and onto the carpet.

"I care not about any mess," Alisha breathed against the side of his neck as she savored the feelings she had for him.

Justin smiled down on the top of her head, loving the feeling of her so close against him. Rising to his feet he cradled her against him and carried her to the side of the bed. Standing her on her feet, he tenderly dried the satin curves of her body and the dampened strands of her hair with the fleecy towel he had brought from the side of the tub.

Alisha's mood was mellow, her heart filled with tenderness for this man as she lay upon the bed and watched by the lantern light as he dried himself and with a naked grace went across the room to extinguish the lantern's glow.

As he lay beside her, Alisha would have asked him

then his plans for the future, but she forced herself to still the words as she feared his answer. Instead she said, "Will I see you tomorrow?" Her heart already beat with anticipation for the day ahead.

"Nay, sweet. My duties shall keep me away tomorrow." Justin felt his loss at the thought of a day's passing without seeing this woman, but late tomorrow evening he had a meeting with a patriot courier. He had gathered together some important documents and letters and had to get them to Lafayette as quickly as possible.

Hearing Alisha's soft sigh of disappointment, Justin leaned over and before taking possession of her soft lips, he whispered against the side of her mouth, "We still have the rest of this night, Alisha. Let us not waste a moment of our time together with regrets about tomorrow."

Powerless to resist as his lips captured hers, Alisha wondered if this was all she would ever have of this man. But as the magical spell of his body overtook even these thoughts, she lost all reason under the onslaught of his wonderful lovemaking.

Some time later in the early hours of the morning Justin stood beside the bed fully clothed and looked down at the sleeping Alisha Whitlaw. He also was beset with strange, new feelings that this woman had caused to stir within his heart.

By a sliver of moonlight that stole through the double doors of the chamber he could see the iridescent beauty of her heart-shaped face. A tenderness filled him with such a fierce desire never to leave

286

her side—it almost blinded him to everything else in his life.

No one, not even Chelsea, had had this effect on him. He wanted to protect her from every hurt, to see joy shining in those beautiful silvery eyes and to be close to her day and night.

He knew well what these feelings meant, but there was little he could do about them for the time being. He had nothing to offer her, no home and no country, until this war with England was finished. Bending down he lightly rubbed a curling strand of soft hair between his fingers and then gently brushed a kiss upon her soft cheek.

In her sleep, she sighed as though welcoming the caress of a lover and with a warm feeling in his chest, Justin left the chamber through the balcony window.

Chapter Seventeen

It was just as well that Justin did not arrive at the Whitlaw house the following day. Alisha and Amos painstakingly printed their flyers and then as nightfall settled over Yorktown they began the risky task of distributing the handbills throughout the main section of Yorktown.

This job of tacking the flyers around town was becoming increasingly dangerous and time-consuming. Several times during the night she and Amos had to step back into the shadows of buildings or trees to hide from a group of patrolling British soldiers. With each new batch of flyers, Cornwallis appeared to increase his security.

This night Alisha had barely escaped detection after she had slipped a flyer beneath a citizen's door. She started to step back to the sidewalk when her attention was caught by the sound of clumping boot heels.

In a panic, Alisha looked about for an avenue of escape as she heard the sounds draw closer. She could not run for surely such movement would draw notice and the troop would give chase; but she certainly could not remain here on the sidewalk, she told herself. If she were noticed and questioned, and then tomorrow it was discovered that more flyers had been distributed, surely it would be her downfall and more than likely the downfall of those in her household.

Slipping back into the shadows of the doorway, she drew the cowl of her cloak closer about her head and face. Pressing her slim form tightly between the cool brick of the building and a potted plant, she did not dare to breathe as she awaited her fate.

There were at least a dozen soldiers in this troop and as the last one filed past the doorway where Alisha was hiding, she all but slumped to her knees with relief as they went on their way.

Waiting only long enough to be sure that the troop had moved far enough down the sidewalk and could not make out her shape, she stayed in the shadows as she made her way back to where she was to meet Amos.

Relief filled her as she rounded a corner and Amos caught up with her. "Lass, there are too many British out this night. We had best not separate again." He spoke in low, guarded tones that did not carry, as his eyes sought out every movement in the darkness that surrounded them.

Alisha was in full agreement, feeling infinitely safer with Amos at her side and nodding her head with the fear that her own voice would carry upon the night breeze. They finished tacking the rest of the flyers, twice more having to hide from British soldiers before safely reaching the security of the Whitlaw house.

This latest batch brought even greater outrage from the British. The information in the handbills gave public knowledge now of the spy called the Fox and also reported that Washington and the French troops were making their way southward. General Cornwallis demanded action on the part of his officers to find out who this Vixen was and the officers in turn incited the soldiers beneath them, which brought an even heavier toll upon the populace of Yorktown.

Several people were arrested, suspected of harboring knowledge of the identity of the Vixen. The number of British soldiers were increased on the streets, thus bringing more discomfort to shop owners and inn and tavern keepers, as they were harassed daily and threatened for not revealing any information about the notorious Vixen.

The British harshly intimidated and threatened, but the people kept a burning hope of freedom and silently cheered this unknown hero known as the Vixen! Many of those who were arrested and later released confessed to family and friends that even if they had known the identity of the Vixen, they would never have admitted such to the British. Shop owners and inn and tavern keepers also smugly savored the fact that the British were being outwitted.

*　　　*　　　*

Over the course of the next few days Justin often found himself seeking out Alisha's company, spending an afternoon in the Whitlaw parlor over tea just relaxing with the assurance that she was so near. Or they took an afternoon carriage ride through town and along the coast and as he felt her warm eyes upon him he stole a kiss which many times led to much more if they found a secluded spot.

Alisha spent most of her time thinking about Justin if she were not in his presence. Her feelings seemed to grow stronger with each passing day. She had little time to gather information for her flyers as she awaited him. She would never know, day or night, when he would arrive and she dared not leave her house in case he might pay her a visit.

She did remind Amos about searching out the identity of the spy known as the Fox. She knew that soon she would have to make up another flyer for much depended upon her getting word to the populace of Yorktown, no matter the danger to herself. She could not remain in this smitten state. She was the only voice in Yorktown standing up against British injustice.

Amos was more than relieved as one day passed and then another and Alisha made only slight reference to the flyers or her need to visit Cornwallis to gather information. The atmosphere in Yorktown seemed charged. The British appeared on edge and on the slightest whim they would lash out at the citizens of Yorktown. There were troops roaming about day and night in search of any malefactors, and Amos knew that the danger of being found distributing the flyers was much greater than it had been only a week ago.

Amos did not delude himself into thinking that Alisha had suddenly listened to him about the danger they were in. He wisely knew that her attentions had been temporarily diverted by this Andrew Wentford.

There was no hiding the fact that Alisha was quite taken with the handsome young man, Amos thought. He could see it in her eyes when the gentleman paid a call at the Whitlaw house and before Amos could excuse himself he caught the glow of her smile as she led the young man into the parlor.

Amos did not fault Alisha in her choice. Andrew Wentford seemed a nice enough sort for a British officer, but still there was something about him that did not quite set right with the older man. Of all the British officers who had tried to catch Alisha's attention, why had it been this one who had broken through her defenses and her oath of revenge against his kind? He also pondered the fact that Alisha had been ensnared so quickly. Seeing them together one would believe they had known each other much longer than the few short weeks he had been in town.

There was much that needed checking into besides the identity of this spy called the Fox, he told himself. Alisha's happiness and safety meant much to him, no matter that she believed herself to be in love.

Aye, he thought, the lass is in love with the golden-eyed-stranger. He would have been happy for her if not for the feelings he had in his gut about this Andrew Wentford. Lifting his mug of rich, dark ale, he drank deeply as he nodded to an old friend who had glimpsed him from the bar that ran the length of one side of the large common room of the tavern.

Desiring little company this night, Amos hoped the man did not decide to approach him. It had been some time since he had enjoyed an evening alone with a mug of ale and his thoughts his only companion.

Swanson's Tavern was on the outskirts of Yorktown and usually was not as busy as those in the center of town; for this reason Amos had decided to come here tonight. Sitting alone at a corner table near the stairwell, he was more than a little relieved when the man he knew stepped away from the bar and approached a table in the center of the common room with two other men whom Amos did not recognize. The pair must be newly arrived in Yorktown, he reflected as he took another drink.

A few minutes later Amos was distracted once again as the tavern door swung open and a tall British officer with a dark cloak thrown about his shoulders entered.

The lighting in the front room was dim. Tallow candles burned at the tables that were occupied and the sparse light given off by a pair of lanterns glowed dimly at both ends of the bar. This did not keep Amos from recognizing the newcomer. Andrew Wentford's gaze circled the interior as he made his way to a small table near the front door. As his glance wandered to where Amos was sitting the elder man slumped down in his seat, lifting his mug up to his face. He lowered his head, hoping his wide-brimmed hat would help to hide his identity.

Not recognizing the bent form of the little man sitting at the corner table in the common room, Justin smiled with an easy warmth at the pretty, buxom tavern wench as she approached his table with swinging hips and a fair amount of bosom displayed over the top of her bodice.

Amos watched from beneath the brim of his hat and kept the mug before his lips. It struck him as odd that Andrew Wentford would arrive at Swanson's Tavern alone. Usually the British went about in small groups, but already finding this British officer different from his cohorts, he secretly studied the other man.

Could it be possible that his presence here at such a late hour was due to the tavern girl, Lucy? It did appear to be taking the young woman an inordinate amount of time to take his order and as Amos heard the girl's laughter, he felt a spark of anger as he thought that the man was somehow betraying Alisha. "The lass would surely be broken-hearted," he mumbled into his mug of ale.

"Just ale will do for now." Justin smiled at the young woman as she stood before his table and leaned over to display her bountiful charms.

"And how about later, me lord? Do ya be thinking ya might be needing something a bit stronger than ale?" Lucy's purring invitation was as plain as she could make it as she devoured the handsome officer with her wide, violet-blue eyes.

Justin was in no way lost to the tavern girl's charms; after all, he was a man and Lucy had certainly been amply endowed. But he felt no desire to take this young woman to his bed. The image of Alisha in his heart kept all thoughts of sexual pleasure with another woman at bay.

"Now what would you suggest. Whiskey, perhaps?" Justin grinned at her, having met many women just like this tavern wench and never being adverse to a little harmless joking.

Lucy's throaty laughter filled the common room as she sidled closer. "Now, me lord, ya can be having all the whiskey ya want, but Lucy here be offering ya something extra special this night." She boldly leaned over and whispered something in his ear as her overly abundant bosom rubbed against his forearm.

Another man might have dared to blush over Lucy's offer, but Justin only grinned the wider and as she straightened he gentled his tone. "I'm afraid you'll have to keep that promise of paradise for another night. I have time for only a mug of ale."

Lucy was indeed disappointed, but his manner softened the blow and gave her hope for another evening. With a last beaming smile, she made her way toward the bar for the desired mug of ale, stopping by the table with the three men and taking their order for refills in the same flirting manner that she had taken Justin's.

Watching Lucy and Justin with a wary eye, Amos was not lost to the intimate manner in which she pressed herself against the young man. Amos dreaded the prospect, but he knew Alisha would have to be warned of her suitor's roving ways. Perhaps all along this is what had made him uneasy about this Andrew Wentford. He must have somehow sensed that the young man was only playing with Alisha's feelings.

With an ever-watchful eye, Amos followed Lucy's movements as she returned with a mug of ale and lingered at Justin's table for a few moments before going on about her duties.

The younger man, whom Amos now believed to be a womanizing rascal, appeared to take his time drinking his ale. Now and then his gaze would travel about the common room as though he were watching for someone. As he took out his pocket watch, Amos wondered if he were waiting for Lucy to get off duty. Amos did not favor being witness to what he imagined was going on between them, especially because the outcome would affect Alisha. There was no help for it though, he told himself. It was too late now to leave the tavern. If the young man saw him, he would be sure to have a ready excuse to give Alisha about what Amos had witnessed here at the tavern.

Two more local patrons entered and as Amos watched the tavern wench go toward the table the pair took, he noticed from the corner of his eye that the officer he had been watching was making his way out the front door.

His actions surprised Amos as he had been sure that the young man's motives for being at the tavern in the first place involved Lucy. There was certainly something strange going on, he told himself as he placed a few coins on the table and silently made his way out of the tavern.

It was a dark night with but a crescent of moon. For a few lingering moments Amos stood outside the front door so his eyes could adjust before he started toward the back of the building to the stables. He would fetch his horse and watch and see if Andrew Wentford left the tavern or if he had just gone outside to relieve himself or get a breath of air while he waited for Lucy.

As he rounded the side of the tavern with quiet steps and approached the stables, a slight sound drew his attention to the side of the building. He was curious as to what Andrew Wentford could be about, for he had not seen him ride off and knew that the outbuildings were behind the tavern and away from the stables. Amos stealthily rounded the side of the stable and, remaining in the shadows, saw the tall frame of Andrew Wentford. Standing next to him was another man who held the reins of a horse.

Giving himself little time to think, Amos clutched the side of the stables in the hopes that the shrubbery and small trees around the yard would hide him as he slowly drew closer toward the two men as they spoke in low tones.

"Make sure this packet gets to Lafayette," Justin said as he handed the large envelope over to the courier.

"Aye, sir, that I will," the darkly-clad man replied as he tucked the packet in his saddle bag.

"Is there news of Washington?" Justin asked anxiously.

"All is going well. His troops and those of the French should arrive in Williamsburg within the next few days and if DeGrasse is on time we'll have these British licked and running for cover!" The courier was a young man in his early twenties, and plainly revelling in his zeal for the cause.

"Tell Lafayette that my ship will be arriving in the cove below Yorktown at any time and my men and I will be ready when the time comes." Justin felt a rush of excitement in his blood with the young man's news about Washington. It would not be much longer before the American Continentals and the French troops would meet the British here in Yorktown, and he was more than ready for such a confrontation.

The two men shook hands as the courier assured Justin that he would tell Lafayette his exact words.

Amos was stunned with disbelief as he listened to their conversation. Andrew Wentford was a spy! He would never have suspected! As he watched, the two shook hands and the courier mounted his horse. Amos slowly drew himself back along the side of the stable wall. Later he would go over what he had been witness to, but for now he did not wish to let his presence be known to either man.

As the courier disappeared through the woods behind the stables, Justin turned back to retrieve his horse. Perhaps he would go by the Whitlaw house and pay Alisha a visit; the thought hurried his steps. He knew well that the hour was late, but his desire was hard to resist.

Just as Amos rounded the front of the stables, Justin's sharp gaze spotted a figure hurrying away just up ahead. Afraid that someone had witnessed what had taken place and that his cover could easily be broken if his actions were reported, he silently drew the pistol he had tucked in his breeches and in a matter of seconds was gaining upon the intruder.

Reaching out and grabbing Amos by his shirt collar, Justin held the barrel of his pistol against the little man's chest. "Who the hell are you, and what are you doing out here all alone and prowling around?" Justin demanded in a low voice. He had to know how much if anything this man had overheard before he decided what he was going to do with him.

Amos was all but lifted off his feet, the front of his shirt drawn up so tightly against his windpipe he could barely breathe. Feeling the hard steel of a pistol against his heart, he dared not attempt to fight off Justin's attack. "I'm Amos McKenzie," he managed to say with a strangled breath he feared would be his last.

His answer caught Justin unaware. He had grabbed hold of the little man from behind and had not as yet seen his facial features. "What are you doing out here near the stables? Were you following me for some reason?" he still distrusted the smaller man, but his hold upon him eased up somewhat as he realized that this was Alisha's man.

With the pressure off his throat, Amos was able to breathe once again and taking a deep breath, he slowly nodded. "I saw you in the tavern and followed you outside." Amos answered with the truth, knowing that his very life depended upon saying the right thing. This was no callow youth playing at this game of spying, but a very cold-blooded and dangerous man.

Justin was confused by the man's confession. "I did not see you in the tavern. Why would you follow me?" His grip upon Amos's collar clenched and unclenched with his agitation.

Amos felt rather foolish now about the earlier thoughts he had of this man, but having already confessed as much as he had, he admitted, "I saw you with the tavern wench, Lucy, and thought she was your reason for being here at the tavern at such a late hour. When you left the common room, I wanted to see for myself if my suspicions were wrong."

Justin admired the little man's loyalty to Alisha, but still there was the matter of Amos having watched him hand over the packet of British papers to the patriot courier. And he more than likely had listened to much of their conversation. "Your worry over my faithfulness to Alisha is wasted, Amos."

Hearing such an admission, Amos was forced to believe he had terribly misjudged the man. Before he could broach the subject of what he had witnessed, Amos had to be sure of this man's true feelings for Alisha. "You do care about the lass, then?"

"With all of my heart, I care about Alisha," Justin admitted, still holding firmly to Amos and now not quite sure what he should do with him. "Listen, Amos, I'm not sure what you think you saw out there behind the stables." Justin at last released him, and thought to try and bluff his way out of this one. He did not wish to hurt Alisha's man, for he knew now that Amos's main concern was for her.

Pulling his shirt into some kind of order, Amos did not reply for a full moment. Perhaps he had not given this man enough credit in the past, he told himself, and knew instantly the truth of that thought. Knowing now that he cared deeply about Alisha and appeared to hold little loyalty to the uniform he wore, he ventured, "You are the spy known as the Fox?"

It was a simple question, but it implied much. Justin stared down at the man with a hard glint in his eyes. It mattered little now if he admitted the truth. Amos knew him to be a spy and must have witnessed the entire exchange between him and the courier.

Slowly Justin nodded. "Aye, I have been known by that name upon occasion." He would listen to what the old man had to say and then he would deal with him as he thought best. Knowing that he could not possibly allow him to go to the British with the information he had, Justin was prepared to take Amos's life. Too much depended upon the information he was gathering from the British and in only a few days the outcome of the efforts put forth by many brave men would tell the story.

Amos sighed softly as he answered. "You can trust me with your secret," he said as he remembered that Alisha had wanted him to find out who the Fox was and he had definitely done just that, even if it would now cost him his life. He smiled at the irony of the situation.

Justin heard his laughter and with it his suspicions grew. "How can I be sure you will not turn me in now that you know who I am? You say I can trust you, but how can I be sure?"

"You can trust me because we're both on the side of the right cause. I am in league with the Vixen!" Amos looked fully into his face and tried to see the effect of his words.

"You know who this Vixen is?" Justin was taken aback by the old man's admission.

"Aye, I know the Vixen well enough." Now sure of Justin's true feelings for Alisha, Amos hit upon the idea that perhaps this man could be the only one to curb Alisha's obsessive revenge against the British. Perhaps he could talk some sense to her where Amos had been unable to sway her thus far. "I tell you this only because of my fear for the Vixen's safety. It is a dangerous game she plays against the British."

"She?" Justin questioned in a low voice fearing he knew already.

Nodding slowly, Amos had revealed far too much to stop now. "You swear you will not betray this confidence?" Amos waited a moment for Justin's agreement before continuing. "Alisha is the Vixen. She is set upon this course to extract vengeance for the death of her father."

"Then this is the reason she indulges the presence of those arrogant, red-coated swains? To gather information for her damn flyers?" Justin felt his anger stir even though at the same time he felt a great relief knowing Alisha was not entertaining these men for any other reason.

"I have warned her time and again about the danger, and now with so many troops roaming about Yorktown with the express purpose of catching the Vixen, I truly fear for her. Alisha is too strong-willed for her own good and won't listen to reason when it comes to the British. Knowing how the lass feels about you, perhaps you are the only one who can save her."

Justin fully knew how strong-willed Alisha Whitlaw could be. Listening to Amos now, an even greater admiration for her filled his heart for her determination in the face of such great danger. "How is it you think I can help to stop her?" Justin was anxious to hear him out and if possible protect Alisha.

"The lass thinks to find out who the Fox is and enlist his help to gain information. Perhaps as the Fox you could warn her about the danger she is in."

Justin was not yet willing to reveal himself to

Alisha. Their relationship was far too fragile for him to take a chance that anything could come between them. Also the fact that she had not trusted him enough to tell him that she was the Vixen forced him to accept the hard truth: her feelings may not be the same as his own. "Tomorrow go to the newspaper office that belonged to her father and beneath the door will be a letter to the Vixen from the Fox. Perhaps I will be able to presuade her to listen to reason or at least to use caution right now while the British are so hot to put a stop to her."

Amos hoped that a letter would be effective enough, but knowing Alisha he was unsure. "I thank you for anything you can do." Amos reached out and shook the other man's hand.

With one final word of caution, Justin said, "Listen, Amos, if you heard everything that was said between the courier and myself then you know it is only a matter of days before the French fleet will sail up the Chesapeake and meet with Washington's forces. When this takes place everything will happen rather quickly. Cornwallis will be attacked with everything the patriots possess. I want to be assured that Alisha will be safe. Keep her in the house until I come for her." Justin wished there was some way he could get her out of Yorktown, but he knew that the only way to do it was to force her.

"You have my word, I will watch over her, Mr. Wentford." Amos was feeling more and more respect for this man who only a short time ago he thought was a scamp.

"The name is Justin Martel." Revealing as much as he had to Amos, Justin saw no reason to let him believe his name was Andrew Wentford.

The name rang a bell. "Isn't Martel the name of the sea captain who rescued Alisha when she was washed overboard?"

"So she told you about her rescue, did she?" Justin grinned with the remembrance of the beautiful sea goddess he had snatched from the sea. He would stake his life though that Alisha did not tell this old man everything about her rescue.

"I'm of the mind now that the lass told me very little." Amos reflected as he wondered how much more he had been left in the dark about Alisha's past. It was no wonder the pair was so familiar with each other.

"You're a good man, Amos, and I'm entrusting you with Alisha's safety." He really had little choice in the matter. "Now I believe we should be away from the stables before someone takes notice."

Justin did not go to the Whitlaw house as he had earlier planned but instead made his way back to his own quarters. He needed time to think about all he had learned tonight before he saw Alisha again. The news that she was the notorious Vixen had quite taken him by surprise. But as he rode his horse down the Yorktown streets toward the British barracks, his chest swelled with a feeling akin to pride. Alisha Whitlaw was indeed an unusual woman!

Chapter Eighteen

On August 30, all of Yorktown was taken by surprise as the rumble of cannon-fire was heard in the distance. DeGrasse and his French fleet of twenty-eight ships and three thousand troops arrived at Chesapeake Bay, anchoring in Lynnhaven Bay, off Cape Henry. There he awaited the British fleet. Graves arrived on September 5 at the foot of Cape Charles where the mouths of the York River and James River flow down past Yorktown and open into the Bay.

Cannon-fire erupted throughout the afternoon. Graves's fleet of British ships was damaged and dispersed, leaving DeGrasse in total command of the Bay.

The citizens of Yorktown, including Alisha, were taken totally by surprise at the resounding boom exploding like thunder. There was much speculation that the French fleet had arrived but had been soundly beaten, and there were others who claimed that the French flag now waved proudly in the Bay.

All roads leading to Yorktown were now being closely patrolled by the British, so there was no way Alisha could seek out information about what had taken place without going directly to British head-quarters. Even Andrew had not made an appearance at her house in the past few days, nor had any British officer whom she might have questioned.

Charles Cornwallis seemed a bit more distracted than usual when Alisha arrived at his office several days following the cannon-fire over Yorktown. However, the General did not act like a man who was beset by an enemy force as he sent a young officer to fetch them tea.

Fearing that some of the rumors circulating through town may indeed be true and the French fleet had been defeated, she came right to the point. "Can you tell me, Charles, what on earth was all that cannon-fire I heard in the Bay?" She watched his features intently to see if he was going to tell her the truth or try and spare her any unnecessary bad news about the condition of the military strength of the British.

His warm smile gave her more reason to worry for the patriot cause, but his words made her heart race with joy. "I'm sure everyone in Yorktown has heard that our ships fought with the French fleet. What is not being broadcast is the fact that Admiral Graves, considering his damaged ships and the enemy's superior numbers, decided he could not give effective succour to the garrison here at Yorktown and made the decision that his proper course of action was to take his fleet back to New York. There he will get repairs and refit them with necessary supplies for his return to Yorktown.''

Alisha was clearly amazed as she listened to Cornwallis speak so lightly of the British defeat. ''Are you not in the least concerned that you have sustained such a great loss?''

Tea was brought in before Cornwallis answered, and as the young officer left the office and Alisha poured, he spoke in a bantering tone to her. ''There is truly no reason to worry yourself, my dear. Everything is being taken care of. I have received lengthy letters from Clinton in New York, and he will send troops posthaste for our defense. I have a promise of at least four thousand additional men to reinforce our position here in Yorktown.'' He leaned back on the settee with his tea cup in hand and paid homage to her beauty with his warm, thorough regard.

Alisha was unsure if the General was addled in his lack of apparent concern over such dramatic events, or if in fact his confidence was well founded. ''But what if the attack on Yorktown comes before reinforcements arrive?'' Surely, she reasoned, he had already thought of this.

''No fear of that, my dear, no fear. The French fleet will sit in the bay like so many targets for our good British war ships. They will not make a bold move until they are joined by that riff-raff that calls itself an army, led by George Washington, and by that time Clinton will have the necessary troops landed here in Yorktown. We will not only defend our enterprises, but we will run the French and the colonist rabble out of the area once and for all. We will show them they are not above British authority!" This latter part of the General's statement brought a flush to his sagging jowls as his tone rose a bit higher with the fervor of his belief.

Alisha was not as confident as the General that Henry Clinton would send the promised troops and ships in time to be of use to the British. Clinton had a history of indecision. She had heard weeks ago of this same promise and thus far not much had occurred! She could only hope that Washington and his troops would act with as much haste as possible. If they could somehow arrive before the British, much good might come from their efforts.

Charles Cornwallis noticed her frown and took it as a telling sign of her worry. "There is truly no need for you to give this whole affair a second thought, my dear. Our troops will arrive in plenty of time and then perhaps we will see an end to this war." As Alisha forced herself to nod in agreement, the General reached out and captured one of her hands. "There is much that remains unsaid between us, Alisha. I know that now is not the right time to approach you about the future, but I would have you know that you are ever in my thoughts. My hope is that with the conclusion of this war we will be able to come to an amicable agreement about these unspoken feelings that we share for one another." Of course, he believed she was as taken with him as he was with her, and he could not wait for the day when he could request the honor of her hand and return to his homeland with her at his side.

Feeling trapped as he held her hand and watched her every expression, Alisha endeavored to keep her voice steady. "Why, Charles, I do believe that most of Yorktown is in agreement with you." He looked at her, not understanding her answer to his supposed declaration of love and devotion, and she added quickly, "We all desire a hasty conclusion to this dreadful war."

Not wishing to push her too fast and remembering that she was still mourning the loss of her father, Charles Cornwallis gently placed her hand back in her lap. "Yes, of course, a hasty conclusion I can almost assure you." He was not totally disheartened. The fact that she had not rejected him or claimed disinterest carried him through the moment. Perhaps she was also waiting for the end of the war before voicing her feelings.

Alisha did not linger over tea after the General had given her intimate knowledge of his feelings toward her. Declaring herself late for an appointment with her seamstress she begged her leave with the promise of a future dinner date.

It was shortly after her arrival home that Andrew Wentford paid a call and Alisha happily allowed her handsome officer to monopolize the rest of her afternoon.

Over the next few days Alisha found little time to call her own and settle down at her desk to pen out her next flyer. When at last she had an afternoon free, she debated with herself over how much of what she had learned from General Cornwallis should be put into the handbill. She knew that the British read every word and she had no desire to scorn their inactivity or lackluster efforts. She certainly did not wish to tempt them into taking any kind of hasty

311

action. As far as she was concerned they could sit back and await the help that Clinton had promised, for with any luck, Washington and his troops would arrive at Yorktown first.

With the hope ever in mind that the French and colonial forces would achieve victory over the British, Alisha filled the paper before her with words of inspiration for the day when the British would no longer be able to hold sway over the patriots and all of the colonies would know freedom.

As she labored over the parchment, her thoughts kept returning again and again to Andrew. The attraction between them seemed to grow stronger each time they were together and she worried less and less over his making a return visit. Her only fear now centered on these strong feelings she harbored in her heart for him. There had been no mention of a future together and at times Alisha caught herself wondering what her feelings would be if suddenly he announced that he was leaving Yorktown. How would she cope now with a life without him? Would the void grow and grow until she was entirely consumed? With a deep sigh, she boldly signed the signature of the Vixen at the bottom of the paper.

A knock sounded on her bedchamber door and when she called for entry, Amos stepped inside. "Oh, Amos," Alisha greeted him warmly, surprised that he was paying a call. "I just finished the outline for our next flyer."

"You had best take a look at this, lass." He made no mention of the paper in her hand, but held out a sealed envelope. He pulled out his cotton handkerchief as a sneeze and then another caught him by surprise.

Before taking the envelope, Alisha looked at Amos with some concern. "Your cold sounds as though it has taken a turn for the worst, Amos." His voice sounded scratchy today and she noticed that his eyes were red and puffy.

"Aye, lass, I guess it's not getting any better, but don't you fret none. I'll be fit again in no time at all." He did not wish her to worry over him and his bothersome cold.

"You will only recover when you listen to reason and do as Mandy and I have been telling you for the last week. You need to rest more and let someone else take care of you for awhile." She knew that her words would do little good. The stubborn little man had been sick for well over a week and now he appeared to have regressed even further.

At last she seemed to remember the reason for his visit. "What is this, Amos?" She took the envelope as he was struck with a coughing seizure. Looking down at the writing on the plain white envelope, she was surprised to see the name of the Vixen written in a bold, neat script. "Where did you get this?" She questioned after Amos had recovered.

"I went by your father's office after lunch this afternoon to get some more ink for the printing press and I found this envelope had been pushed beneath the door." This was all Amos would say as he felt uncomfortable with his part in this deceit. The truth was he had been holding this letter since the morning after he found out that Andrew Wentford was the

Fox. Since that night Alisha had made no mention of printing another handbill and he had feared that if he had given her the letter from the Fox, it might provoke her into action. Today though, when she mentioned over lunch that she was going to outline the next flyer this afternoon, he took the chance that this letter would somehow quell her need to outsmart the British once again.

"Why would someone put a note to the Vixen beneath my father's office door?" She looked at Amos and then back to the envelope. "Do you think it's from the British?" Quickly her eyes went back to Amos and in their blue-gray depths there was a trace of fear mingled with excitement.

Amos was quick to reject her question. "Nay, lass, why would the British write a letter to the Vixen? If they had any suspicions that the Vixen could find such a note at your father's newspaper office, you can be sure that they would have already approached your father's household."

That made sense, Alisha thought, as she slowly began to break the plain wax seal on the back of the envelope. As her eyes scanned the contents, she said breathlessly, "It's from the Fox!"

Amos forced himself to react with surprise, knowing that this letter might be the only way to reason with Alisha. "The Fox you say, lass? Now what would the Fox be doing sending the Vixen a letter? Is there any information you can be using?" He knew there would not be, but he wanted to sound convincing.

Alisha allowed her gaze to roam over the few short lines once again before answering. "He only warns

314

that it is dangerous to put out any more flyers. He warns that the British are growing more and more restless because of the French fleet in the Bay and the approach of Washington's troops. He claims that even more soldiers have been ordered to patrol Yorktown at night. It would seem according to the Fox, Amos, that Cornwallis is set upon catching the Vixen *and* the Fox!"

Amos nodded as though he were in full agreement with this mysterious Fox. "You should heed his advice, lass. The Fox should be knowing what he is talking about since he is claimed to be within the British camp." Amos hoped that his agreement with the Fox would encourage Alisha to think twice before tacking another batch of flyers around town, but as he watched her slowly turn her head as her eyes began to sparkle with some inward mischief, he knew his words would have to be more persuasive.

"Perhaps this Fox just wants all the glory and wants to brag that he's the only one who could best the British here in Yorktown. It could even be that he fears that the Vixen will find out more information than he can and he wants us out of the way." Even to Alisha her words made little sense, but there had to be a reason for the Fox to send her such a letter. If they were both on the same side and fighting for the same cause as she had first supposed, one would think the Fox would secretly applaud her efforts and be well pleased with the biting sting that her flyers were causing the British. She did not believe for a moment that the Fox's only intention was to caution her for her own safety.

"I don't be thinking that the Fox is the kind to send

315

a letter just to be getting you out of the way for his own purposes, lass." Amos ventured to bring some common sense to bear.

"Have you found out who this Fox is yet, Amos?" Alisha's question came so quickly that it took Amos off guard. "Would I not have come directly to you with such information?" he countered her question with one of his own, and felt only a small amount of relief at not having to lie to her. If she would not think about her own safety, others would have to do the job for her, he told himself.

"Of course you would have told me," Alisha murmured aloud and felt guilty over her question put to this faithful friend. Tossing the letter on her desk, she picked up the outlined flyer. "Well, there's certainly no telling what this spy known as the Fox has in mind, but you can be sure I will not cast aside my role as the Vixen now! The price I'm forcing these British to pay for the murder of my father is slim indeed, but still it's some measure of revenge. Without the Vixen, I would be like thousands of others here in the colonies. Just another name on the long list of family members who desire satisfaction for the death of a relative but have no way to extract an ounce of justice from the Crown!"

In truth Amos had not believed a letter from the Fox would affect Alisha's actions as the Vixen. He would have to contact Justin Martel and try to sway the young man to confront Alisha with the fact that he knows that she is the Vixen and try to reason with her. "I'll go down to the basement and run off the flyers for you, lass." Amos wiped at his nose and covered his mouth as another seizure of coughing overtook him.

"When you're finished, Amos, you had best go to the carriage house and rest. I'll have Mandy bring you some of her delicious chicken soup."

"Aye, lass, I'll do that." His voice sounded tired as he smiled for her benefit before leaving the chamber.

Alisha was not one to worry over simple matters and to her the letter from the Fox was simply that: a simple matter. She did not understand his reasons for the use of such extreme caution. Now was the time to strike hard against the British, while they were being harassed by the French and patriot troops.

Searching out Mandy in the kitchen Alisha mentioned Amos's worsening health and the need for a pot of chicken soup. "Has Ben been by to see you today, Mandy?" she asked as she sat down at the small work table and nibbled at one of the sugar cookies Mandy had baked earlier and left to cool.

"He ain't been by yet, Miss Alisha, but I be specting him later this afternoon."

"When he arrives, will you please tell him I need just a moment of his time?"

"Yes, mam, I sure will do that." Mandy nodded as she set a big pot of water to boil to cook the chicken for her soup.

"I'll be in the parlor." Alisha grabbed up a handful of cookies before leaving the kitchen. Her plan was simple: she and Ben would deliver the flyers tomorrow night. Amos did not need to be told, she decided, as she settled in a comfortable chair in the parlor and took up the book she had started some

317

time ago. Once she and Ben had posted the flyers she would then tell Amos all about their adventure.

Ben arrived after dark at the Whitlaw house and Alisha handed him a handful of flyers. "If you'll be able to take the portion of town nearest the docks, I think I'll be able to take the flyers around the shop district by myself, Ben."

"Yes, mam, I's glad to be of help," Ben agreed aloud though he questioned her plan in his mind. He would have spoken his thoughts about her placing herself in such danger by going unprotected through the streets of Yorktown at night, but he had learned long ago that it did little good for a black man to argue with a white man or woman. Taking the flyers in his large hand, he cautioned, as he was leaving through the back door, "Now, miss Alisha, ye be careful fur yerself. Jest tack ye a few of them handbills on some of the houses in the area and a few of the shops. That be enough this time. The townspeople pass them around anyway." This was as much warning as he would dare give.

Alisha smiled fondly at the black man. "You just be seeing to yourself, Ben. I'll meet you right back here when we finish." As Ben left the house, Alisha slipped on her dark woolen cloak and pulled the cowl over her head before stepping through the front door. Earlier in the evening she had gone out to the carriage house and found Amos resting comfortably, so now she held little fear that the elder man would catch her as she was leaving.

318

A full moon rode high in the heavens as Alisha stepped away from the stone steps that led up to the front stoop. Just then a dark cloud covered the moon and sent myriad shadows among the trees and shrubbery along the sidewalks. She had only herself to depend on and with her thoughts consumed by her need for caution, Alisha clutched the flyers tightly as she approached the portion of town where she was to distribute them, and she prayed silently that the moon would reappear to light her way.

It was due to this fearful abstraction of the shadows around her and her need for caution that Alisha did not notice the tall form of a man who stepped quickly back into concealment as Alisha left the front door of her house.

Earlier in the day Banastre Tarleton had been at Gloucester Point across the bay, but with little activity among his men he had decided to leave his post at first dusk and come into Yorktown. All afternoon his thoughts had been upon the lovely Alisha, so without checking in at the British garrison, he made his way toward the Whitlaw house with the hopes of paying her an uninterrupted visit. He had halted in his tracks as he watched the slim form step out of the door and onto the stoop. The light projected from the small lantern outside the house revealed the glitter of copper curls as the woman pulled the hood of her dark cloak over her head. A frown settled over Banastre's face as his dark eyes sparkled with jealousy as he instantly assumed that Alisha was on her way to a secret interlude of a romantic nature.

His anger increased as he remembered the numerous times he had appeared at her home and in public with the intentions of furthering a relationship with the young woman. Watching her walk down the stone steps and noticing the way her head kept turning about as though fearing she might be noticed, Banastre stepped back into the shadows. He would follow her and find out for himself who this other man was who now held her interest. It certainly was not the General, he told himself as he carefully kept his distance while she entered the business section of town.

Perhaps her lover was the new officer, Andrew Wentford, he wondered, turning the name of his fellow officer over in his mind. Though he had been at Alisha's while Wentford was there and the couple had taken a carriage ride, Banastre had not truly considered the other man his competition. Now he thought better of the matter!

Unsure how he would react when he found the pair together, he kept up a steady pace behind her as she hurried down the sidewalk. As the dark form started up the walk of the first house she came to, Tarleton watched as her cloaked shape stood within the entranceway of the front door. What was she up to, he wondered, as he noticed that the house remained silent and dark.

Just as he thought she would enter the house, he watched her leave the entranceway and hurry down the sidewalk and up the steps leading to the next house.

Truly baffled as he watched her approach the front

door of this house and remain for a few seconds as she had at the first house, Tarleton silently stepped within the entranceway of the first house.

Ever watchful for a British troop, Alisha listened for any sound of heavy bootsteps. So it was that she hurried around tacking up her flyers without a clue that she was being silently stalked by one of the deadliest of her foe!

It was just as she rounded the corner at the end of a street that she inwardly sensed some unseen danger. For a moment she stood quietly there on the sidewalk and listened to the sounds of the night. She thought she had heard a footstep behind her, but now as she peered into the darkness she could make out nothing unusual in the shadows. Even with this slim assurance, she still had a keen sense of lurking disaster. The heels of her soft kid boots made a small clicking noise as she turned and hurried down the sidewalk. She would finish up this next street and then make her way back home. She tried to calm her thoughts and indeed felt some relief with the decision.

Slipping a flyer beneath the front door of the town's bakery, Alisha straightened and as she did her upper arm was clasped in a firm grip. Paralyzing dread swept over her in that moment as she turned around and stared into the hard glint of piercing, ebony eyes. "Let me go!" she cried aloud and tried to pull her arm from the clasp of the savage band that tightened as she struggled.

Banastre Tarleton was not one to easily oblige her demand for release. His grasp was like a steel vise encircling her tender flesh and as she struggled to pull away, he tightened his grip and shook her to maintain a forced control. Without saying a word, he pulled the few flyers she still held out of her hand. He had already read one he had taken from a house.

"You are the Vixen!" He did not question her but stated this with much confidence and allowed her no room to argue.

Chapter Nineteen

Caught in the act of treason against the Crown,
Alisha was powerless to defend herself against the
accusation. Banastre Tarleton was a brutal enemy
to come up against—no matter that she was a
woman! The fact that he had been paying court to
her only a few weeks past was given no consideration
at this moment. "Please let me go." Alisha's pleas for
release turned to sobs as she realized the jeopardy she
was in.

Hearing her beg, Banastre felt some hidden delight
at his mastery over her as he tucked the remaining
flyers in the breast pocket of his uniform jacket. This
woman had put him off time and again, but now he
had the upper hand. She was completely at his mercy
and he was entirely without charity at this moment.
All of the slights imagined and otherwise that she
had shown him over the past weeks came to mind and
as his lips drew back into a leering sneer, he spoke
with little kindness. "We will let General Cornwallis
handle this affair, my dear. He is still at British

headquarters working late. I'm sure he would enjoy a surprise visit from the Vixen!"

"No, please, you cannot take me to the general! You do not understand. Let me explain!" Alisha searched her mind for a passable excuse for her to be distributing the Vixen's flyers around town, but she could find none. She had been caught with the evidence of her crime right in her hand and there was no way to get around it.

Tarleton did not give her the courtesy of listening to her excuses for being on the Yorktown streets in the middle of the night with a handful of flyers with the Vixen's signature scrawled across the bottom. He felt a certain delight in her being brought low. He would even relish the look on the General's face, he told himself, when he presented Alisha Whitlaw before him as the infamous Vixen. Paying no heed to her outburst, he began to pull her along with him down one street and up another. His direction was the British headquarters, his purpose to reveal a criminal. He would exact the ultimate price from her for shunning him and at the same time he would also be witness to the surprise and betrayal that Cornwallis would feel with his announcement. He knew how much the General cared about her and he intentionally savored the power he held to destroy his superior's illusion.

Alisha stumbled as she was pulled along behind him without mercy. She could not break away from his arm and by the look on his stern features, she knew he would not easily be swayed from his purpose. She had to try, she told herself as they drew closer and closer to British headquarters; Alisha knew that once they stepped through those doors her fate would be sealed.

"Please, Banastre," she called breathlessly. "We can go to my house and talk this over. We can be comfortable there and when you give me the time to explain, you'll realize that this has all been a terrible mistake." She forced her tone to sound as inviting and warm as possible under the circumstances, and she prayed that he would read more into her words and not be able to refuse her. Once they arrived, she would then think of some way to free herself.

The only answer she received was a jerk on her arm. Banastre Tarleton had his own plans for Alisha Whitlaw. He would benefit all the way around by turning her in as a rebel and traitor to the Crown. While all of Yorktown was looking for the notorious Vixen, he would be the one to boast of capturing the outlaw; and once she was put into the guardhouse, he also would be the one to enjoy her charms without anyone interfering. After all, who would deny him access to a known criminal? And at that time, he promised himself, he would remember all the times she had cast him aside.

Alisha's fear intensified with his refusal to respond. She had never truly expected to be captured and was at a loss as to what she could do. She should have carried a gun, she thought belatedly, even a lesser weapon might have helped to stave him off. Seeing the lights of the British garrison a short way ahead, Alisha tried one last time to sway Tarleton. "I have some gold coins I can give you. You'll be a rich man if you'll only let me go!"

"You can make all the promises you wish later

tonight," he grunted down to her as he relentlessly pulled her along. "The cot in your cell in the guard house will not long stay cold and lonely, I promise you that, my little traitor."

His implied promise of what would await her as a prisoner of the Crown filled her with overwhelming dread—she had to escape! She had never known another man intimately and she could not imagine herself being touched by any one other than Andrew Wentford. With one last surge of panic, she pulled away from his tight grip. With the strength of her action, Alisha took him totally off guard and without looking back, she took to her heels.

It took Banastre Tarleton only a few seconds to react and follow the cloaked figure running down the sidewalk. Tarleton was a man of action. Fit and trim, he trained daily with his men and the excitement of the chase only added to his eagerness to have her alone later this evening.

Alisha's lungs burned as though afire as she ran without a backward glance. Her sides ached, her breath escaped in short, ragged gasps. Her only thought was to reach the safety of her home and flee the British and the threat of imprisonment.

Tarleton's blood rushed with exhilaration as he came within a few feet of Alisha. He longed for complete possession of her and could taste the sweet nectar of victory. He could feel, almost hear her heartbeat as his long arm grasped the back of her cloak and he pulled her off her feet and over his broad shoulder.

Alisha nearly fainted as she felt herself being

grabbed from behind and thrown upward. With a scream of unbridled terror, she knew her flight had been in vain.

"You will not flee me, Alisha Whitlaw! You're no different from any other rebel trash here in the colonies and before this night is over you will realize the mistake you made in placing your loyalties with the enemy!" Tarleton swung around with Alisha over his shoulder and started back toward the British garrison. He would not give her another chance to escape, he told himself. Though the chase had been exhilarating, there was always the slim chance that she would somehow elude him. The feel of her soft body assured him that the risk of losing her would be far too costly. He would take great delight in teaching her later this evening how great was her mistake of throwing her lot in with the patriots! This very night he would hear her cries of regret and he would also at last know a release of the ache in his loins that he felt whenever he was in her presence!

His chilling words washed over Alisha and created the threat he had intended. She could not let him take her to Cornwallis! If she was charged as a traitor, her father's house and everything else he had acquired throughout his lifetime would be confiscated. And what would become of Mandy and Amos? More than likely they would both be charged with crimes against the Crown and hanged alongside her! With this horrible thought she began to fight. Her legs kicked and flayed the air; her fists pounded on his back and over portions of his head. She attacked anyplace that she could as her body squirmed precariously on his shoulder. She would not let herself be taken to prison without a fight! "Release me at once, you British cur!" she cried out in anger and loathing.

Banastre Tarleton appeared little affected by Alisha's outburst. His large steps never faltered as he reached up a hand to subdue both her small fists as his other hand wrapped around her waist to prevent her from falling from his shoulder. Her temper tantrum reminded him that he knew very little about this woman. He had believed her mild of manner, and her beauty had clouded over all thoughts of disloyalty. Now he had seen for himself how very dangerous she could be. Her antics as the Vixen had disrupted and undermined much of the effort on the part of the British here in Yorktown.

Making his way through the front door of British headquarters, Tarleton strode boldly down the dimly lit corridors toward General Cornwallis's office. The cloaked woman was thrown upon his shoulder as though little more than worthless baggage, lashing out at him, sputtering abusive remarks and drawing the attention of anyone they passed.

Without waiting for permission, Tarleton burst into the General's office. The solid oak door slammed with a deafening roar that pulled Cornwallis to his feet behind his desk.

"What is the meaning of this disturbance?" he shouted as the battling pair stepped into the room. "I thought you were at Gloucester Point watching those damn French bastards!" Charles Cornwallis had just about had enough of Tarleton of late. This was the last time he was going to put up with his overbearing manner. It was not enough he had to worry over the French and those misbegotten rebel traitors who called themselves patriots; his own officers were now set upon driving him to distraction. He could not wait for the day when he would be able to retire to his home in England with Alisha Whitlaw. Before he could say anything further, he noticed a flash of copper curls from beneath the hood of the cloaked form on Tarleton's back. His curiosity tempered the harshness of his question as he wondered if the younger man had dared to bring one of his trollops into the British garrison. "What have you over your arm, Colonel Tarleton?"

The moment Alisha heard Charles Cornwallis's voice her efforts to dislodge herself stopped. She felt frozen to the tips of her toes as she knew that in a moment her captor would reveal her to the General as a spy and the sought-after traitor known as the Vixen.

Charles Cornwallis watched as the bundle on Tarleton's shoulder stilled and the dark gaze of his officer held him for an added moment before he reached up to release his burden. Cornwallis imagined that he caught a glimpse of some deep craftiness mixed with amusement in those dark depths, which forced him to look more keenly at the woman.

Charles Cornwallis was correct in his assumption that Banastre Tarleton was enjoying the moment. For the first time since he had started this southern campaign with the General, he felt he had the upper hand. It was as though he held the trump card to the General's heart and the taste of his victory would not be complete until he witnessed the look of hurt and betrayal that would momentarily possess the General's features. "Why, General, I am sure you'll be pleased to know I have captured the notorious Vixen!"

Alisha groaned, her body trembling as she heard Tarleton's words. Until the very last second, even as he carried her into the garrison, Alisha had hoped, had prayed that she would somehow be released before having to face Charles Cornwallis. As much as Tarleton longed to witness his general's hurt and betrayal, Alisha dreaded the moment when she would have to look into his eyes and see for herself the full extent of her deceit. There was little she could do but brace herself for the coming confrontation, she thought as she felt Tarleton's hands tighten. With seeming ease he swung her off his shoulders and to her feet. At that moment, as she stood before Charles Cornwallis, she knew her fate was sealed.

Charles Cornwallis stared into the pale features of the woman whom only he knew he was in love with. Gazing into her silver-blue eyes, at first he did not comprehend what was happening. His mind kept turning over and over the import of Tarleton's pronouncement that he had captured the criminal known as the Vixen. Why was Alisha standing here in his office at this late hour? And why had Tarleton been carrying her in such a fashion? His searching black eyes held the questions that could not come to his lips as he looked from her beautiful features to the gloating countenance of Banastre Tarleton.

With a push that was ruthlessly cruel, Tarleton nudged Alisha in the General's direction. "I believe you already know Mistress Whitlaw, General?" Reaching into his breast pocket, he pulled forth the remaining flyers that he had confiscated from Alisha. "To her friends and allies, the patriots, she is better known as the Vixen," he added and twisted the blade of deception all the harder into Cornwallis's heart.

For a full moment Charles Cornwallis could not react, his eyes held upon the blue-gray eyes staring steadily at him. Gradually Tarleton's words penetrated and his reaction was typical of a man who is told that the woman he loves has used and deceived him. He looked at Tarleton with total disbelief.

"What the blazes are you blabbering about the Vixen for, Colonel? And why were you carrying Miss Whitlaw in such an outrageous fashion? You had best have a good excuse, man!" He saw the fear upon Alisha's face and would have reached out to her except for the fact that Tarleton took a step between them, holding the flyer beneath Cornwallis's nose.

"Look for yourself and you will know the truth of my words," Tarleton sneered. "Alisha Whitlaw is the Vixen! I followed her myself through town while she was posting these treasonous handbills.!"

Snatching the flyers, Cornwallis still could not formulate his thoughts. Alisha Whitlaw would never do anything so criminal he thought. To him she was the very essence of what all womanhood should be. Graceful, beautiful, attentive and the fire that blazed in his heart. She could never be a traitor. Scanning the contents of the paper in his hands, he looked back to Tarleton and saw the leering smile playing about the thin, hard lips. Drawing his eyes at last to Alisha, he softly questioned, "Is what he says the truth? Are you this Vixen who has been so plaguing York-town?"

Alisha knew she could simply say Tarleton was lying and General Cornwallis would believe her. She read in his haggard features that he wanted her to deny the charges, wanted to believe her innocent and direct his rage toward his officer. It would have been so easy to say the words that would clear her and her household of the charge of treason; but looking into his features, she felt her face flush with hot anger. She could not forget what these British had done to her family, nor could she forget that Charles Cornwallis, no matter how kind and protective he had been toward her, was in charge here in Yorktown and the one directly responsible for her father's death. Perhaps she had pleaded with Tarleton for her release, but she would never plead with the man who had ordered her father's murder! Straightening her backbone, she stood tall and proud. Looking directly into Charles Cornwallis's face, she stated in a clear voice: "You killed my father!"

Charles Cornwallis was astonished as he confronted all the venom of her hatred of him and his kind. As she glared up at him, he took a backward step.

The die had been cast! Alisha could not back down now, nor did she want to. All of her hatred of the British welled up inside and demanded release. "You imperious British think you can so easily impose your will upon the colonies, ravage our land and imprison our people because of your laws and ordinances, and you think we will abide your dominance without a move in our own defense! You hope to enrich yourselves by the sweat of our labor and expect us to take your leavings! But I will tell you now, the time is at hand when we will not so easily be subjected to the will of a king who sits on his throne far across the sea! We shall fight you until our dying breath, as my father did!" She pulled her shoulders back defiantly. "Aye, I am the Vixen! I am proud of the small part I have done to uplift my fellow countrymen and to stand up for my belief in freedom!"

Cornwallis had heard enough! Each word she flung at him pierced his heart. All the feelings he had for this woman, the love and adoration, his desire to make her his wife, everything had been a lie, a terrible waste. She had used him, he realized now, to gain information. She had never cared for him at all, but had only wanted revenge for her father's death. Drawing back his hand, he swung at her with much of his strength, his hurt and fury in the slap as it struck her cheek and sent her reeling.

Alisha staggered from the shock of the blow and as she fell to the floor she braced herself with her hands and glared at Cornwallis and Tarleton with all the hate and loathing she could muster.

Both men looked down at her with a mixture of admiration and contempt. She was no whimpering mass of feminine flesh crying before the onslaught of abuse. She braved the assault, her cheek turning scarlet, but her pride and her hatred of the British intact.

"Get her out of my sight!" Cornwallis shouted at Tarleton, knowing that his own strength was not as great as hers and fearing that at any moment he could crumble from the anguish in his heart.

"It will be my pleasure, General." Unlike Cornwallis, Tarleton felt his loins swell with passion. He dismissed the burning rage that fired her eyes and the stubborn tilt of her chin as so much nonsense. The General might well draw back in the face of her hatred, but it only increased Tarleton's lust. By the time he finished with her, she would no longer have the strength to hold her head up and glare her hatred from those slate-blue eyes. "I will have her placed in the guardhouse," Tarleton stated as he grabbed Alisha's arm and dragged her to her feet.

General Cornwallis made his way back to the chair behind his desk with a heavy heart. Watching as Tarleton took hold of Alisha, he felt older than his years. The ache of loneliness that he had known since the death of his wife became acute with the loss of Alisha. Forcing himself to stem the disappointment searing his soul, he tried to make his voice sound normal. "As soon as you see her to the guardhouse, report back to me. I have reports that Washington met up with Lafayette and they are approaching Yorktown." With the closing of his office door Charles Cornwallis wondered if he would ever love again or if Alisha Whitlaw had stolen his heart before she shattered it.

Tarleton pulled Alisha from the General's office and with some disappointment that the rest of the evening was not his own, he ushered her down a long, dank corridor. Stepping out of the main entrance door with Alisha in tow, he made his way toward the side of the large compound where the British guardhouse was located.

After making sure Alisha was put in a cell near the back of the old stone building and that there was a guard awake in the outer office, Tarleton cursed his luck as he made his way back to the General's office. With any luck Cornwallis would not keep him very long and he could return to Alisha Whitlaw's cell and begin teaching her what she could expect as a prisoner of the Crown. He felt the blood rush through his veins as he envisioned her soft naked flesh held tightly against his own. He would not be so easy in his handling of Alisha Whitlaw as Cornwallis had been! He would tame her hostility in his own fashion and with the greatest pleasure!

Chapter Twenty

After posting the flyers Alisha had given him, Ben made his way back to the Whitlaw house. Usually when he helped to distribute the flyers around Yorktown he went back to his own small house near the wharf, but this evening he wanted to make sure that Alisha was well and had returned home safely. It was the first time she had gone out by herself and he knew he would never find peace of mind if he did not make sure she was safe.

Just as Ben started making his way through the business section of town, he caught a glimpse of a dark figure far up ahead. Using all the stealth possible for a man of Ben's large size, he hurried along the sidewalk in the direction of the figure, wondering if it were Alisha.

Drawing closer he soon noticed that there were two people out at this late hour and it was plain that the larger one was a man. He would also guess that he was a British officer by the paleness of his trousers and the sparkle of his jacket buttons and the insignias on his shoulders and sleeves.

As he drew a bit closer and quietly studied the couple it appeared that the smaller person had been running away from the man and was being caught. The officer slung his prisoner over his shoulder. Ben crept as close as possible without giving his presence away as he drew up against the buildings along the sidewalk.

With a firm will, he forced himself to smother a gasp of disbelief as he heard Alisha's cry for help. He could sense her fear and anger as he watched her hands and legs flay wildly as she fought for her release.

As the officer briskly started off in the direction of British headquarters with Alisha thrown over his shoulder, Ben drew himself further into the shadows. At first he debated whether he should try to overpower the officer and rescue Alisha or if he should silently follow and make sure of the officer's destination and then find help. The latter won out as Ben feared that the officer was carrying a pistol or other weapon. If he were wounded or killed while trying to rescue Alisha, there would be no one to help her.

Making sure that he was indeed taking Alisha to British headquarters, Ben did not linger long on the Yorktown streets. He hurried to the Whitlaw house to seek out Amos.

Without a second thought on the part of Banastre Tarleton or the soldier on watch at the guardhouse, Alisha was pushed into a tiny, dark cell. Looking about fearfully, she could make out a small pile of straw in a corner of the cell with a rag rug thrown over the lumpy stuff which she supposed was considered a bed. In the opposite corner of the dank, stone jail was a bucket which she hurriedly glanced away from for the time being. The smell of filth and human excrement was overpowering here in the back of the guardhouse and left her nauseated as she stood with her hands around the cell bars. She could hear the scampering of small living things behind her.

God help her, she thought in desperation. She could not be expected to remain in this horrible jail cell for any length of time! She would be driven mad by the stench and the rats! Stinging tears filled her eyes as the anger she had felt earlier now quickly slipped away.

She should have listened to Amos. She should have heeded the Fox's advice and for the time being allowed the Vixen to lie low. She should have; she should have; she thought of all the warnings she had not heeded. It was far too late now, she thought as she wiped at the tears flowing over her cheeks. She had listened only to her own inner need for revenge and now she was forced to pay the full price. As her tears dampened the front of her dress, she pulled her cloak tighter around her shoulders to stave off the dampness of the godforsaken place.

Minutes seemed like hours as Alisha stood near the cell bars, afraid to go any further into the cell and all her horrible imaginings. She was equally loath to accept the fact that this stockade would be her home until she was tried as a traitor and more than likely hanged for her crimes against the Crown.

Perhaps she could have endured more bravely if the conditions of her imprisonment were less harsh, and also if she could somehow banish from her mind Banastre Tarleton's parting words.

"As soon as I am free from the General, I will return and we shall begin your first lessons in curbing that willful temper." The touch of his hand, which had gone from her bruised cheek down the slim contours of her throat and had caressed the material of her cloak over her breasts had filled Alisha with horrible premonitions. She could face the punishment from the enemy if not for the cruelty of the retribution promised by Tarleton.

She could not even ease her mind with thoughts of Andrew Wentford. If anything, thoughts of the handsome officer filled her with trepidation. He would surely be just as horrified at the revelation of her crimes as had been General Cornwallis. Though they had shared such glorious moments of passion and his attentions toward her had been favorably received, she now had to face the fact that as a British officer, the man whom she loved beyond all reason would feel duty-bound to push her aside in the face of her disloyalty to the Crown.

An anguished sob rose from her throat and echoed within the stone walls of the guardhouse. She had already faced the fact that she was hopelessly in love with Andrew Wentford. Every time she was in his presence her heart skipped breathless beats and with just the sound of his husky voice she felt her body melting. His sun-bronzed, golden-haired handsomeness stayed in her thoughts day and night. But this evening's events had destroyed any hope she might have had for a lifetime at his side. She would go to her death remembering all they had shared, and knowing the loss of what could have been.

Alisha's thoughts were so taken with her own ill-fated thoughts she did not hear the front door swing wide or the conversation between the guard and the late night visitor.

And so it was during Alisha's anguished yearning for what could never be that Andrew Wentford appeared in the dimly lit corridor. At first Alisha imagined that she had conjured up the vision of her lover and with her heart aching she pressed her forehead against the cold steel of the bars, her eyes tightly shut against the brutal teasing of her own imagination.

The slight pressure of a hand squeezing her own forced Alisha's eyes to open and as her heart pounded within her breast she was forced to return to reality. Andrew stood before her and as his golden gaze locked with her own, Alisha knew the full meaning of sheer misery. He was as handsome as ever, standing tall and proud in his officer's uniform. Silently she drew her hands from the bars as though she feared that the touch of her hand would contaminate him. "Andrew . . . I . . I . . ." She tried to say something, to explain to him what had brought her to such a sorry state.

His frown silenced her. From deep in her soul she mustered all the self-will and determination she could as she wiped away her tears with the backs of her hands and forced herself to stare directly into his handsome face.

The anger that coursed over Justin's features was

not from disappointment in her as Alisha imagined, but rather the sight of the purplish-yellow bruise upon her cheek. Stepping away from the cell bars, he called loudly for the soldier on duty.

The soldier hurried to Andrew Wentford's side and as he commanded the younger man to open the locked door, Alisha wondered if Andrew had come to the guardhouse to inflict some new form of punishment upon her. Was the intention to allow her to taste a moment's freedom within her lover's arms and then be jailed once again?

"My orders, sir, are not to open this cell for anyone but Colonel Tarleton." The soldier stood at Justin's side and refused to obey his command. The Colonel had been explicit regarding this woman and Joel Newmore was not one to disobey an order from Banastre Tarleton.

"Hang your orders, man! I've just come from General Cornwallis and he wants this woman in his office in the next ten minutes!" Justin did not want to harm the young man; all he wanted was to get Alisha out of this hellhole as quickly and as quietly as possible.

"But, sir, Colonel Tarleton . . ."

The soldier never got to finish his statement. As he felt the push of a pistol barrel against his chest, he slipped the key to the cell from his belt and slowly unlocked the door.

For a moment Alisha stood in the open door and stared from Justin to the soldier who was being ordered about at gun point. It was not until Justin's husky voice directed Alisha to step to his side and ordered the young soldier into the jail cell that Alisha began to fully realize what was taking place.

Andrew Wentford was carrying out a jail break! He was rescuing her! As the soldier stepped around her and into the cell she ran through the open doorway and into the arms of the man she loved. With a strangled sob, she cried softly against his broad chest as he directed his pistol at the man taking her place in the cell.

"Close the door and relax until someone comes and finds you." Justin drew his arm around Alisha protectively but kept his gaze upon the soldier. "I'll also warn you that if you cry out for help, my accomplice outside the guardhouse will answer your call. He will not be as tolerant as I have been."

His warning was well taken. The young soldier silently nodded and stepped away from the bars as he watched the officer lead the woman toward the front of the guardhouse.

"You must believe me when I tell you I never believed my role as the Vixen would come to this." Alisha wept aloud, as she realized what her rescue was costing this man. He was a British officer and by taking such bold measures, he would also now be an enemy to the Crown.

Justin took a lingering moment to comfort her as they entered the guardhouse office. Knowing well that at any moment Tarleton or another British soldier or officer might appear, he soothed her anguish as he held her tightly. "Hush now, my love. I'm here and will let no more harm befall you." He softly touched her swollen cheek and had to fight the raging impulse to do bodily harm to the one who had dared to strike this woman.

Alisha welcomed this moment of protection. She had believed only a short time ago that she would never again feel the warm embrace of his arms, so she savored the moment as being that much more precious. It was the deep love that she had for him that forced her to allow him the chance to reconsider the bold step he was taking by rescuing her from her fate at the hands of the British. She knew she would never be free from her guilt if she did not offer him a change of mind. "I don't know how you found out that I had been arrested, Andrew, but you must reconsider what you're about to do. Perhaps it's not too late to release the soldier and put me back behind those bars. I would not have you known as a rebel to the Crown. You're a British officer, and you must consider what you're doing!" With this plea, she knew she would be content with the few moments she was allowed in his arms. She would return to her prison and await whatever punishment that would be meted out to her, for she now had the memory of his embrace to hold in her mind and cherish.

"To hell with the British, my sweet!" Justin swept her up into his arms as he started toward the front door of the guardhouse. "There's not a chance I would reconsider your rescue. I'm taking you away from this foul place and God help any man who tries to stop me!"

Stepping through the door and out into the cool night, he called in low tones toward the side of the guardhouse. "I have her. Let's get out of here before someone comes!"

Alisha was caught by surprise as Ben and Amos stepped out of the shadows. "Amos, why are you here? You're sick and should be in bed!" She knew how absurb this sounded but she was completely taken off guard.

Justin ignored her as he began to give orders to the two men. "Ben, you go to the Whitlaw house and get your mother to safety. The first place the British will search will be Alisha's house and I don't want them to find anyone there. Amos, you come with Alisha and me."

Both men quickly complied without question and Alisha leaned her head against Justin's chest with a soft sigh, glad for the moment to relinquish any authority and allow someone else to take charge. As Justin carried her to the carriage awaiting them, Amos opened the vehicle door and then climbed atop to take hold of the reins. Alisha asked, "Amos told you I had been captured and arrested as the Vixen? But why did he go to you, Andrew?" She was totally confused by the events that had taken place this evening.

Before placing her on the carriage seat, Justin pulled her tightly to him and placed his lips over hers in a brief kiss. "Who else would Amos carry the news of your arrest to but the Fox?" His golden eyes sparkled in the dim light of the moon as he slammed the vehicle door and within seconds Amos was whipping the horses into a fast run.

"The Fox?" Alisha questioned absently as she stared across the carriage to where Justin was sitting on the opposite seat. "But how can you be the Fox? You're Andrew Wentford, a British officer."

"The name is Justin Martel, sweet." Justin leaned across the interior and took hold of her hands. "Amos knew my identity and when Ben told him you had been arrested he sought me out.''

"Justin Martel, the Fox?''

"One and the same, my love, and if you had heeded my advice when I wrote you that letter and left it beneath your father's office door, you would not have found yourself in such an unfortunate position as you were in tonight,'' Justin scolded lightly.

"But how was I to know that you were the Fox? Why did you not tell me?'' Now that Alisha felt reasonably safe she began to feel some anger over his deceit.

"I can ask you the same question, Alisha! Why did you not tell me you were the Vixen? Why did Amos have to tell me because of fear over your safety?''

"I . . . I . . .'' She did not wish to confess that she had not been able to trust him, but now upon reflection, she realized that he had had the same distrust of her. "I guess we both lacked trust,'' she finally confessed and felt her cheeks grow flushed.

Husky laughter filled the interior of the carriage. "Now I would call that an understatement, my dear. Our distrust of each other was born of our very first meeting. But all that will now have a swift end. As soon as we reach the safety of my ship, we shall have time for a long, private talk.''

"We're going to your ship?'' Alisha asked in a soft, breathless tone as she remembered their days and nights aboard the *Vixen*.

"Aye, the *Vixen* is in the cove where not long ago we shared a glorious picnic lunch.''

Remembering that day with other fond memories,

Alisha asked anxiously, "But what of the British? Is it safe for your ship to be so near Yorktown?"

"I was told this afternoon by a patriot courier that Washington and Lafayette should arrive sometime tomorrow at the outskirts of Yorktown. The British will be far too busy with the approach of the French and American militia to be overly concerned with the *Vixen*. Besides, as soon as we reach the ship we shall be setting sail and meeting several other ships that have been running blockade since the start of this war." He hoped that John Paul Jones would be one of the captains of the ships he was to meet. He would love to introduce Alisha to his friend.

Alisha's eyes sparkled with anticipation as she listened. It seemed as though the colonists had been fighting this war against England forever and now in only a matter of days the culmination of all their efforts would be realized.

"Will you be leaving Yorktown after the war is over?" The question slipped unbidden from her lips. She had not meant to question him or to appear overly concerned with his plans for the future. After all, he had given her no sign that he cared for her any more than any other woman. But she could not still the longing that filled her voice.

Justin's hesitation was more from his instinctual distrust of females than from having to search out his answer. He had already made up his mind that he would never let this woman go, but years of skepticism gave him a few seconds' pause. "I thought I would stay here in the colonies. Lafayette mentioned that he would petition the Continental

Congress on my behalf for a ship in return for my help during the war. I've been playing with the idea of starting my own shipping line here in Yorktown."

Alisha's joy knew no bounds. He would not be leaving Yorktown for the sea as she had feared! But as quickly as her happiness had spiraled, she suddenly felt let down. He had not said a word about the two of them and any kind of future together. Perhaps his only reason for staying in the colonies was this new business opportunity.

Justin did not miss her look of sudden disappointment. "I do have another reason for staying in Yorktown, Alisha. In fact, my reason is more important than any plans I may have for a shipping line."

"What reason is that?" She waited for his answer with breathless anticipation, hoping it would have something to do with his feelings for her.

Sitting across from her and holding her hands in his own, Justin's golden eyes appraised her. "Of all my travels to different lands, I have found the most wonderful treasure right here in the colonies. A treasure that I find I cannot live without." Those same lion's eyes locked with hers of silvery blue as he laid his heart bare. "I had nothing to offer in the past. No home, no country, but fate has taken a hand in my affairs and changed all this. I now offer all that I own: my ship, my wealth, my heart and my life. Do not turn me away, Alisha. Agree to be mine, and I promise I will live only to see happiness in your beautiful eyes."

Alisha felt the sting of tears. "You mean you want

to stay in the colonies because of me?'' She could not believe her own ears and make full sense of all he was saying, so great was her joy at that moment. She loved this man will all of her heart and if he meant what he was saying and she had not misunderstood him, he felt the same way about her!

Justin chuckled deep in his chest as he eased his large frame into the seat next to her and still holding her hands within his own, placed them against his broad chest. "I mean exactly that, my sweet. I wish you to be my bride; to be my very own.''

Looking up into his handsome face, Alisha could not speak for a few seconds. She thought she was dreaming, but as his words began to permeate every portion of her mind and soul, she flung her arms around his neck and jumped into his lap without a second thought. "Oh Justin, you truly want to marry me? You really do?''

Justin could not resist the sweet temptation of her lips so close to his own and for a moment his mouth slanted over hers and drank fully of her sweetness. "Marry you? Aye, my sweet. I wish to wed you, claim you, and join your heart with my own! I love you beyond any reason. You are the rare sweetness in life that I've been missing. Your brilliant beauty guides my heart. I'm lost without you, Alisha!''

"Yes-yes-yes!'' she cried, covering his face with kisses.

Justin's heart swelled with happiness as he held her tightly and their mouths joined. At last he had found the peace he had been searching for. Here in Alisha's arms he would be content forever!

On Sept. 28 Washington arrived in Yorktown with all of his forces. The following day he began his siege against the British.

Charles Cornwallis drew back his defenses with the expectation of the promised help from Clinton.

On Oct. 9 the first American guns at Yorktown opened fire on the British defenses.

With the assault of the enemy fire against him and his casualties mounting and men falling sick with fever, Cornwallis decided upon a last effort to escape Yorktown. On Oct. 16, he attempted to send his troops over the York river to the Gloucester side and from there meet the relief ships that Clinton had promised or to somehow make it northward by land. It was the elements itself that defeated Cornwallis this night. A heavy storm at midnight and a cloudburst of pelting rain saturated the British and left them shivering and chilled as their boats were tossed against the rocky shore where it was impossible to make a landing. Before the light of the following morning, most of the British returned to their starting point under allied fire.

On Oct. 17, the allies opened fire on the British positions early in the morning, knocking out the British batteries which were still able to fire. With escape blocked, there was but one course of action open to Cornwallis!

Under the bombardment of allied forces against the British a small, red-coated drummer boy, standing on the parapet of the Hornwork, beat a rapid tattoo on his drum. A white flag of truce was waved in the air by an officer who delivered a note from

Cornwallis, which was quickly taken to George Washington.

The note read:

Sir,

I propose a cessation of hostilities for twenty-four hours and that two officers may be appointed by each side to meet at Mr. Moore's house to settle terms for the surrender of the posts at York and Gloucester.

I have the honour to be,
Cornwallis

Promptly, at 2 p.m. on Oct. 19, the British marched forth in surrender before the French and American forces to the tune of "The World Turned Upside Down."

The war was not over officially for another two years. A peace treaty was finally signed in 1783. There was no shot fired, nor one heard around the world to announce the fact that the colonies had won their freedom, but for every man and woman there was the knowledge that they had fought and won the right to claim themselves free people.

With the British occupation gone from Yorktown, Alisha and Amos reopened the Yorktown Press. Justin began his shipping line with the help of his crew and his bride. It was a bold new start in a land that welcomed all who were willing to work hard to make a difference.